GILLBERT

BY ART BALTAZAR

THE CURIOUS MYSTERIOUS

PAPERCUTZ

NEW YORK

Here's what you missed in 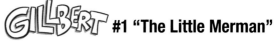 #1 "The Little Merman"

Underwater, Gillbert, the young prince of Atlanticus, discovers a message in a bottle with his turtle best friend Sherbet. Only problem? Gillbert can't read. He needs his mom to translate it. While waiting for the translation, Gillbert and Sherbet see a mysterious mermaid lurking around and follow her. She leads them through the current of communication bubbles deep down to the submarine party of Wewillrocktopolis. There, she reveals her name is Anne Phibian and introduces them to her partying fishy friends. Meanwhile, deep in space, a fiery asteroid is on a collision course with Earth along with some flaming space invaders named Pyrockians. It lands on the ocean floor. The asteroid is actually an egg and King Nauticus and the Queen Niadora raise it like their own child. They name her Matilda. But this baby grows and grows and grows out of control. Back at the party, Anne teaches Gillbert to communicate telepathically and takes him to meet the mysterious space creature, Teeq, in her crashed space shipwreck. Teeq shows Gillbert her communication control center where she makes contact with intelligence from beyond our galaxy. She is attempting to make contact with her long lost sister. After a busy night, Gillbert falls asleep and wakes up back at the palace. Things heat up when fiery Pyrockian invaders invade the ocean, increasing the ocean temperature. King Nauticus struggles to hold off the invasion. Matilda returns to send to a warm volcano to call their own. Teeq shows up to the kingdom letting the King and Queen know that Matilda is actually her sister. The queen recognizes Teeq as her old friend and a celebration is in order. Gillbert never did see that his message in a bottle said he was destined for greatness.

#2 "The Curious Mysterious"
By Art Baltazar
Production – Big Bird Zatryb
Managing Editor – Jeff Whitman
Jim Salicrup
Editor-in-Chief

Papercutz books may be purchased for business or promotional use. For information on bulk purchases please contact Macmillan Corporate and Premium Sales Department at (800) 221-795 x5442.

Hardcover ISBN: 978-1-5458-0348-6
Paperback ISBN: 978-1-5458-0349-3

Printed in Turkey
January 2020

Distributed by Macmillan
First Printing

SHERBERT   ANNE PHIBIAN   GILLBERT   KING NAUTICUS

AW, YEAH! PAPERCUTZ PRESENTS...

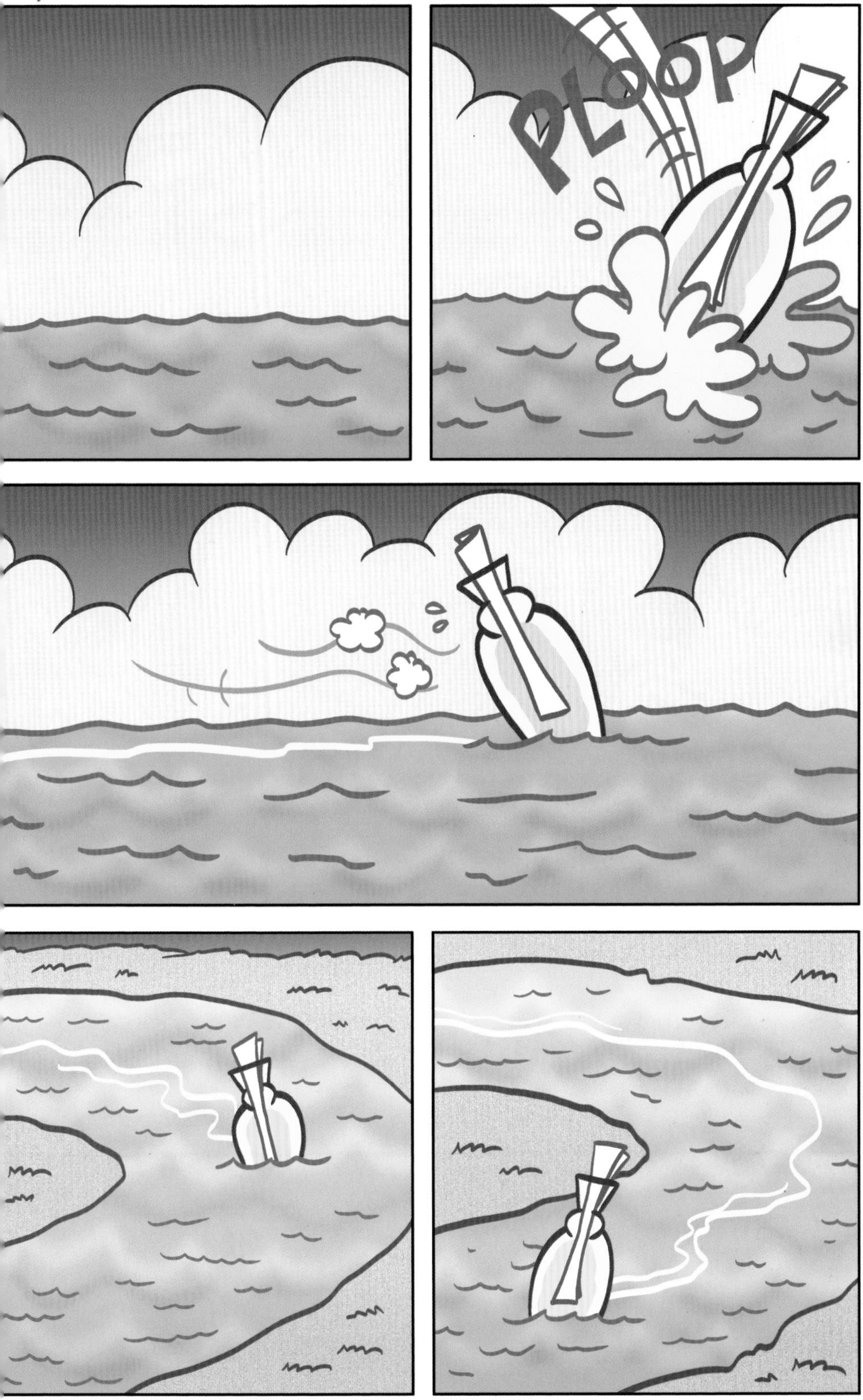
PLOOP

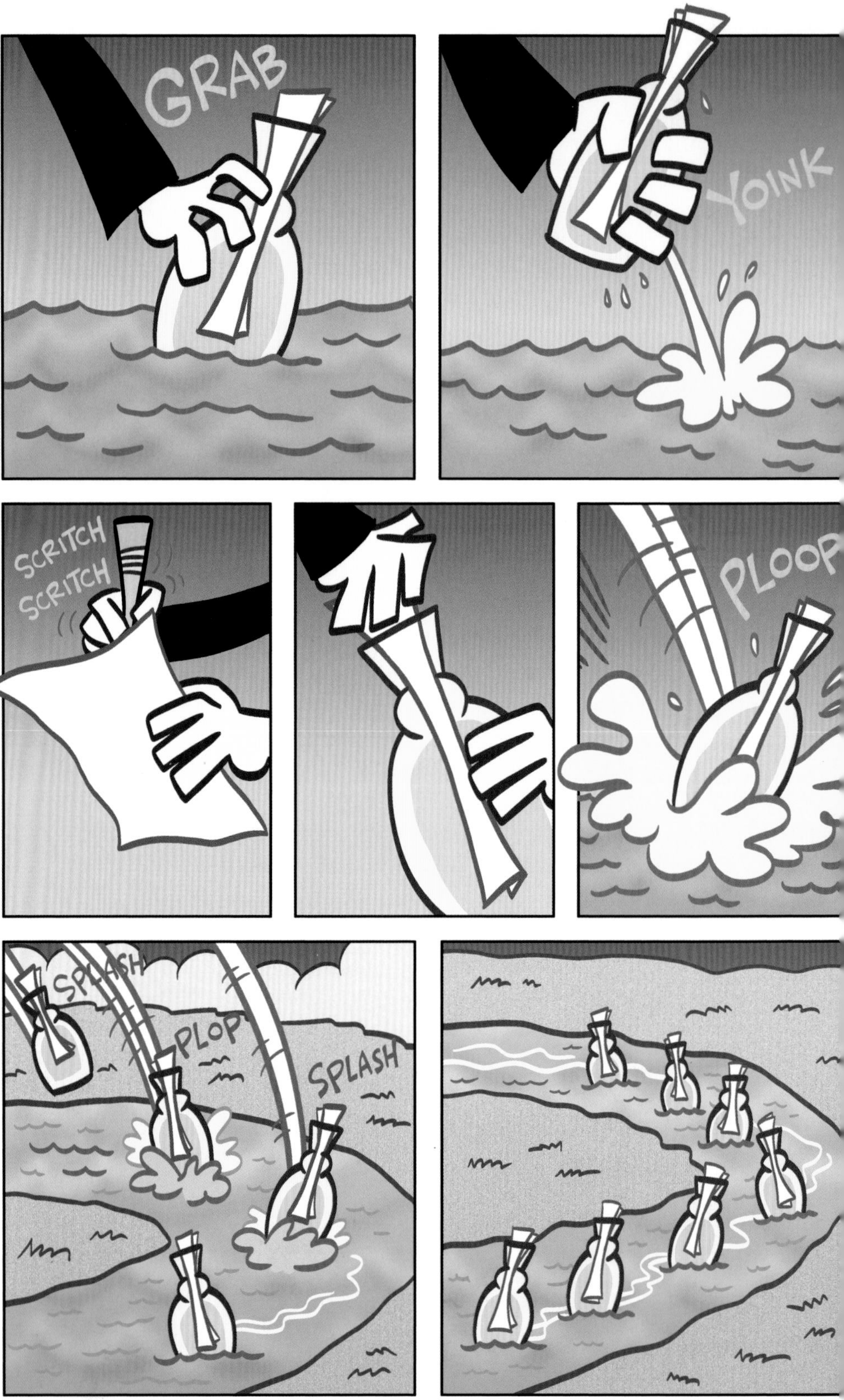
GRAB
YOINK
SCRITCH
SCRITCH
PLOOP
SPLASH
PLOP
SPLASH

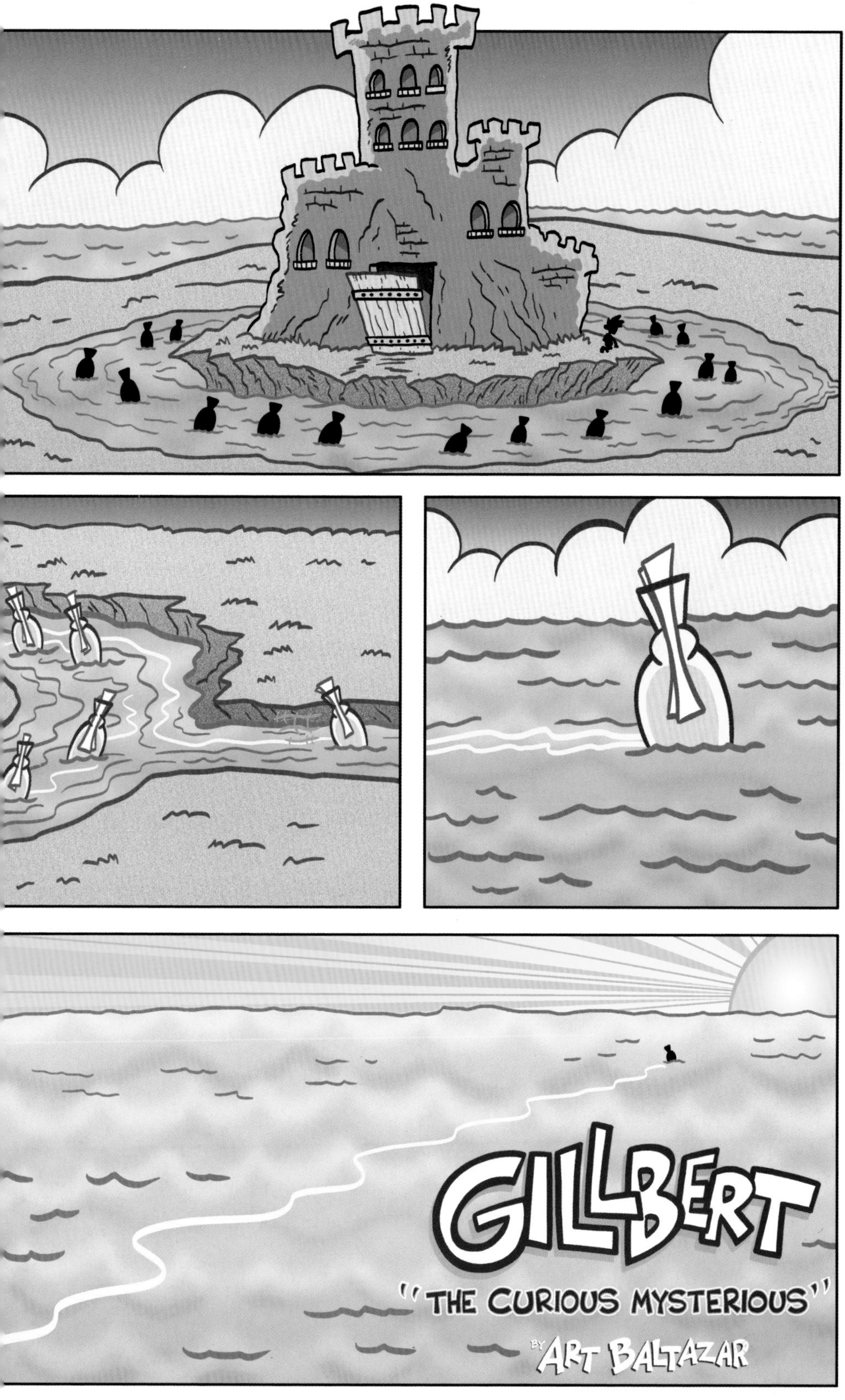
GILLBERT
"THE CURIOUS MYSTERIOUS"
BY ART BALTAZAR

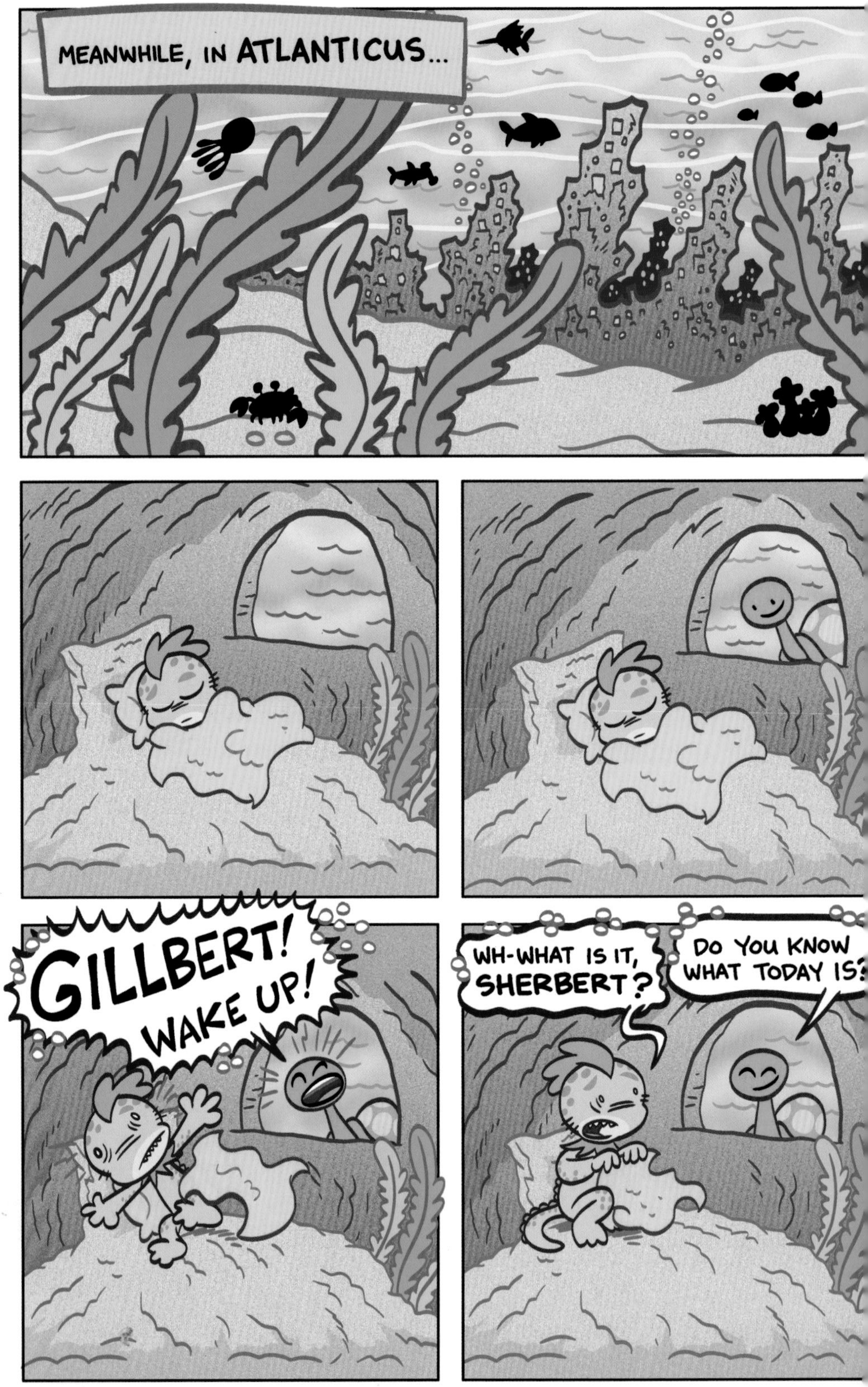
MEANWHILE, IN ATLANTICUS...
GILLBERT! WAKE UP!
WH-WHAT IS IT, SHERBERT?
DO YOU KNOW WHAT TODAY IS?

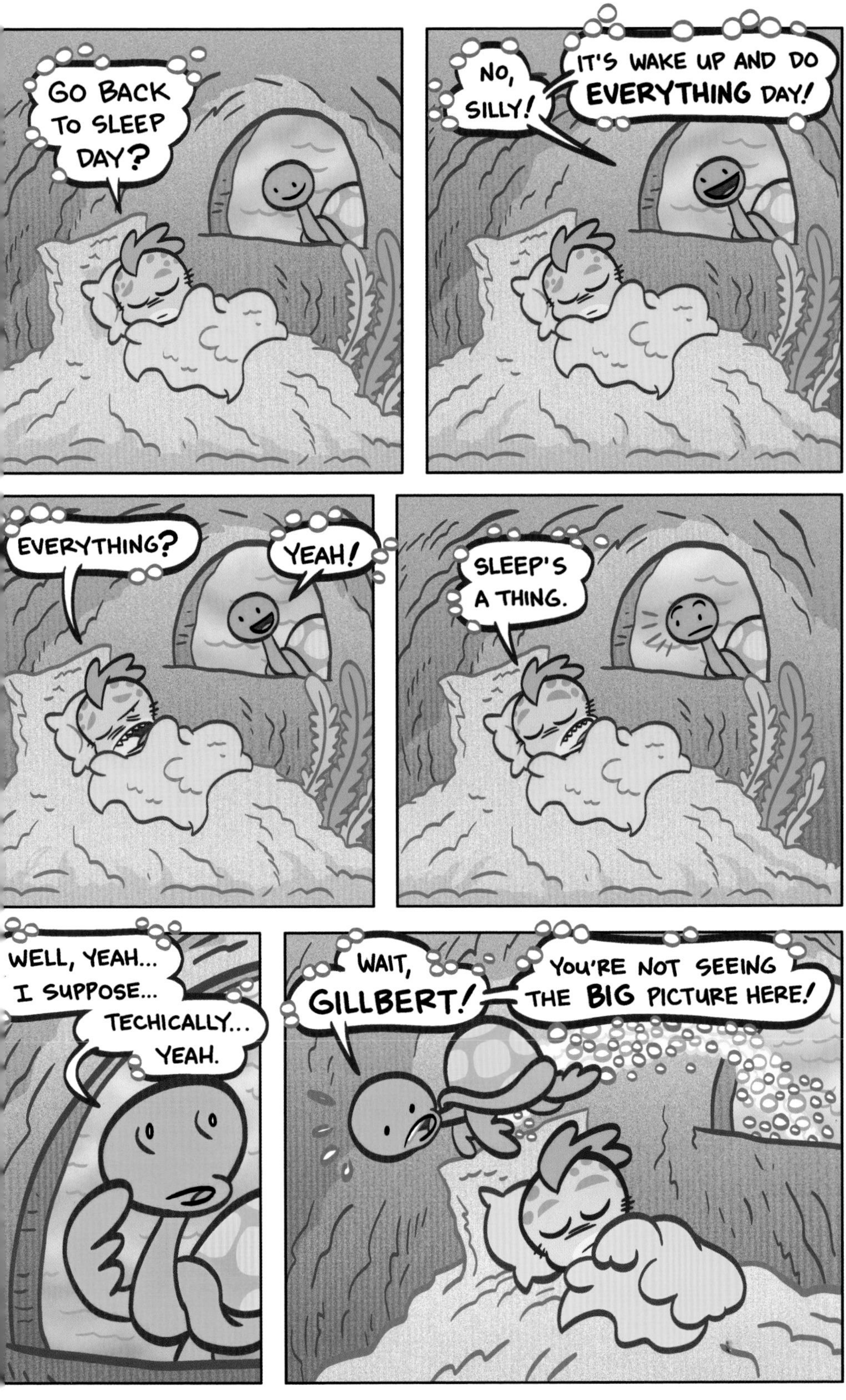
GO BACK TO SLEEP DAY?
NO, SILLY!
IT'S WAKE UP AND DO EVERYTHING DAY!
EVERYTHING?
YEAH!
SLEEP'S A THING.
WELL, YEAH... I SUPPOSE...
TECHICALLY... YEAH.
WAIT, GILLBERT!
YOU'RE NOT SEEING THE BIG PICTURE HERE!

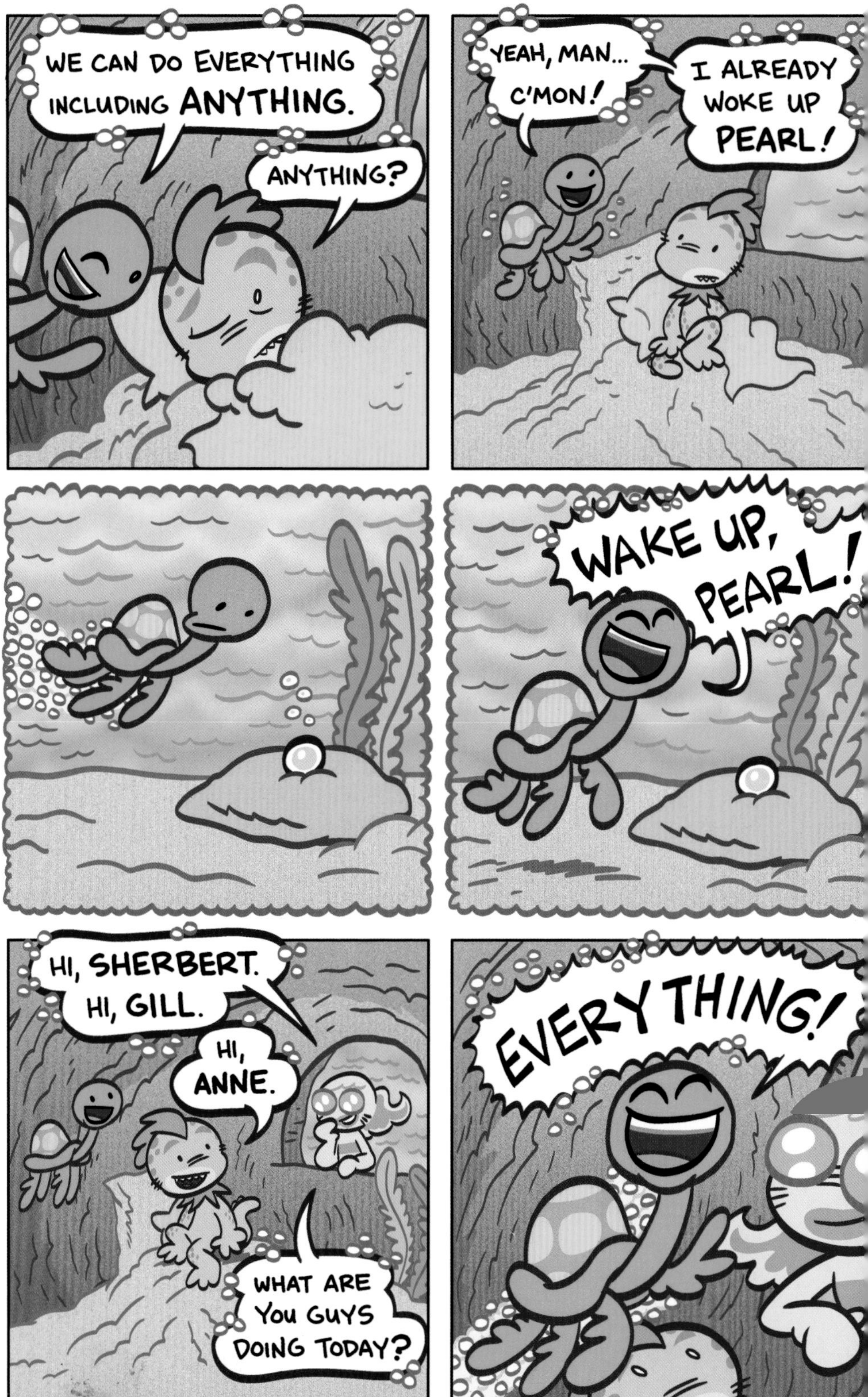
WE CAN DO EVERYTHING INCLUDING ANYTHING.
ANYTHING?
YEAH, MAN... C'MON!
I ALREADY WOKE UP PEARL!
WAKE UP, PEARL!
HI, SHERBERT. HI, GILL.
HI, ANNE.
WHAT ARE YOU GUYS DOING TODAY?
EVERYTHING!

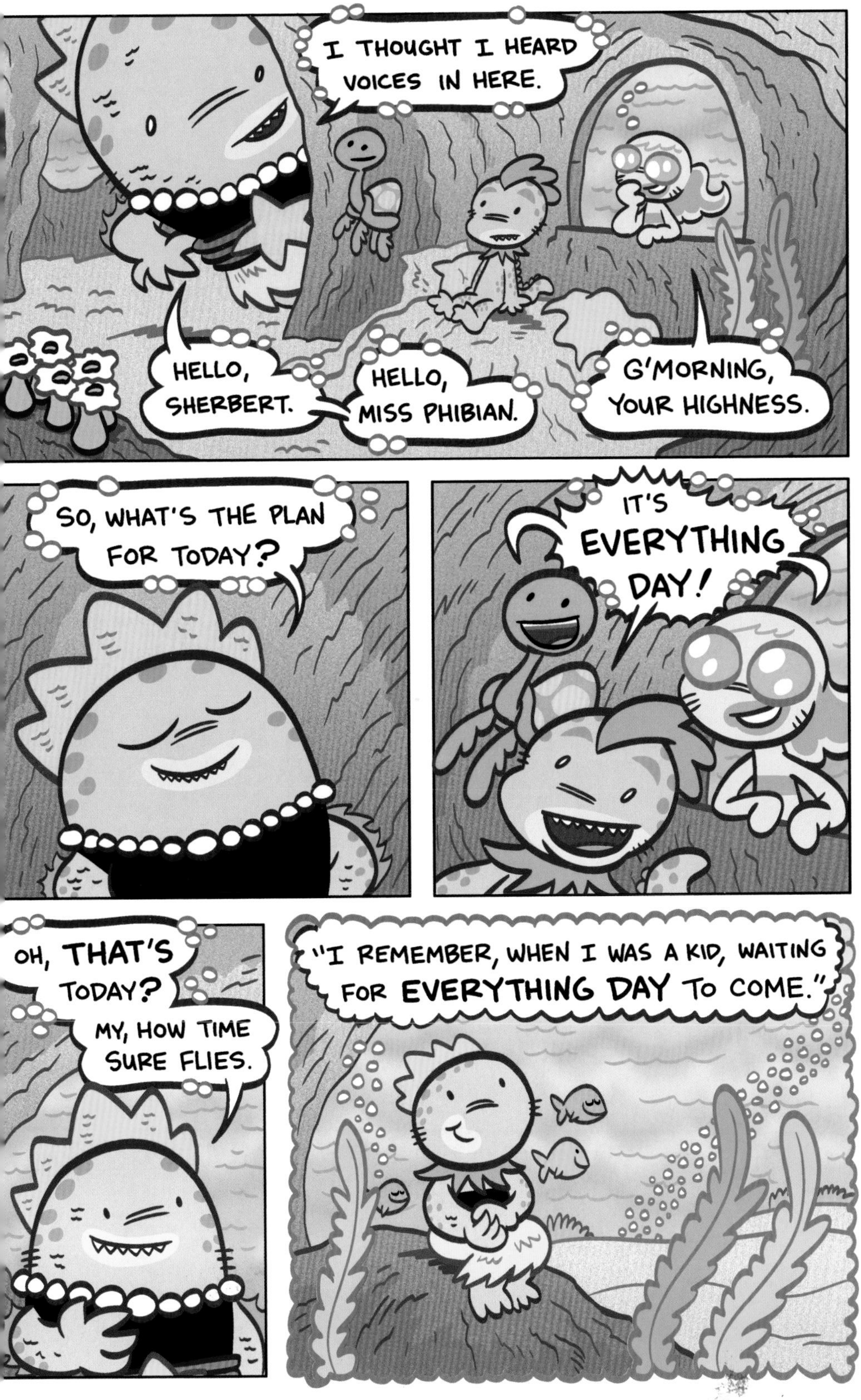
I THOUGHT I HEARD VOICES IN HERE.
HELLO, SHERBERT.
HELLO, MISS PHIBIAN.
G'MORNING, YOUR HIGHNESS.
SO, WHAT'S THE PLAN FOR TODAY?
IT'S EVERYTHING DAY!
OH, THAT'S TODAY?
MY, HOW TIME SURE FLIES.
"I REMEMBER, WHEN I WAS A KID, WAITING FOR EVERYTHING DAY TO COME."

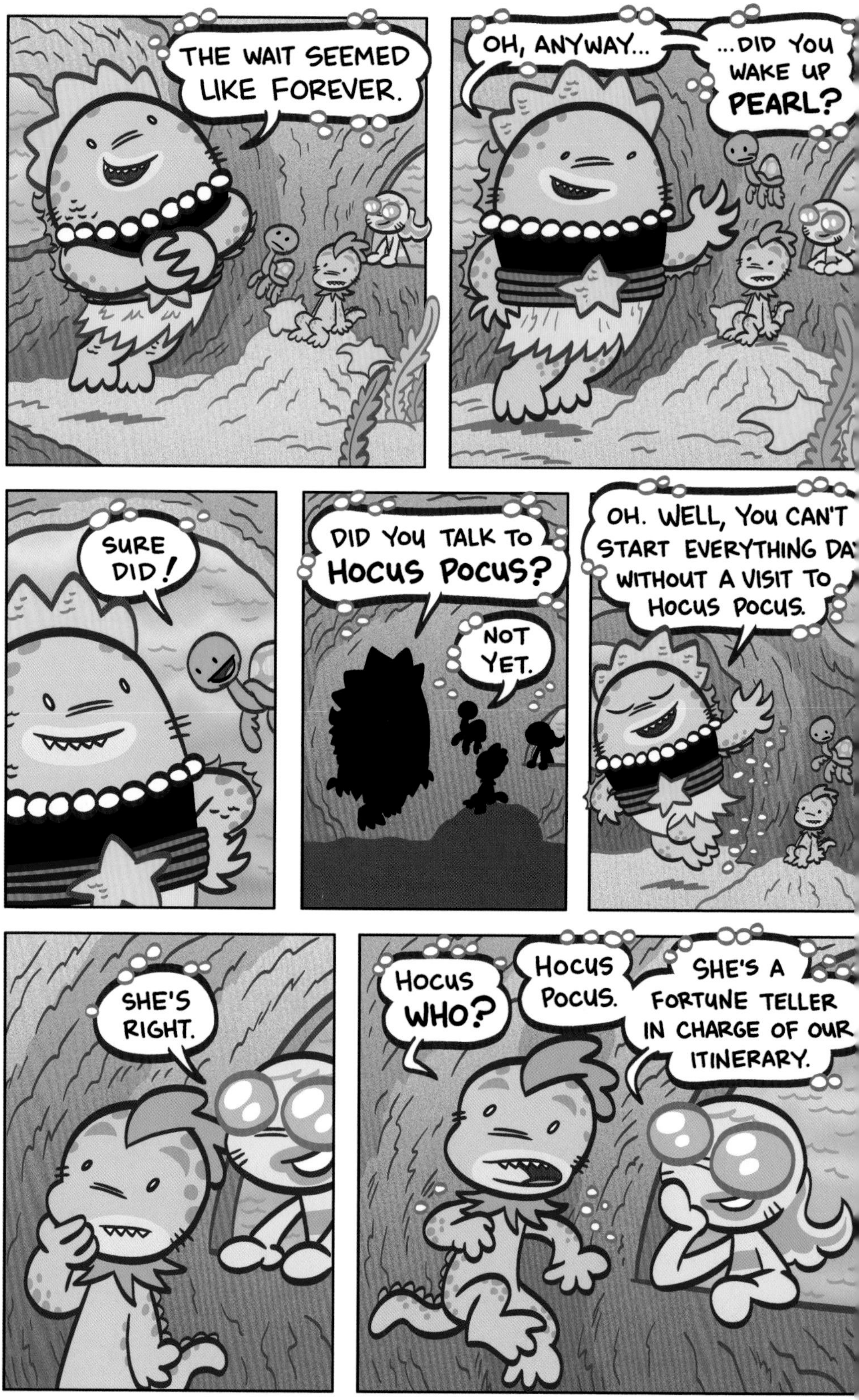
THE WAIT SEEMED LIKE FOREVER.
OH, ANYWAY...
...DID YOU WAKE UP PEARL?
SURE DID!
DID YOU TALK TO HOCUS POCUS?
NOT YET.
OH. WELL, YOU CAN'T START EVERYTHING DAY WITHOUT A VISIT TO HOCUS POCUS.
SHE'S RIGHT.
HOCUS WHO?
HOCUS POCUS.
SHE'S A FORTUNE TELLER IN CHARGE OF OUR ITINERARY.

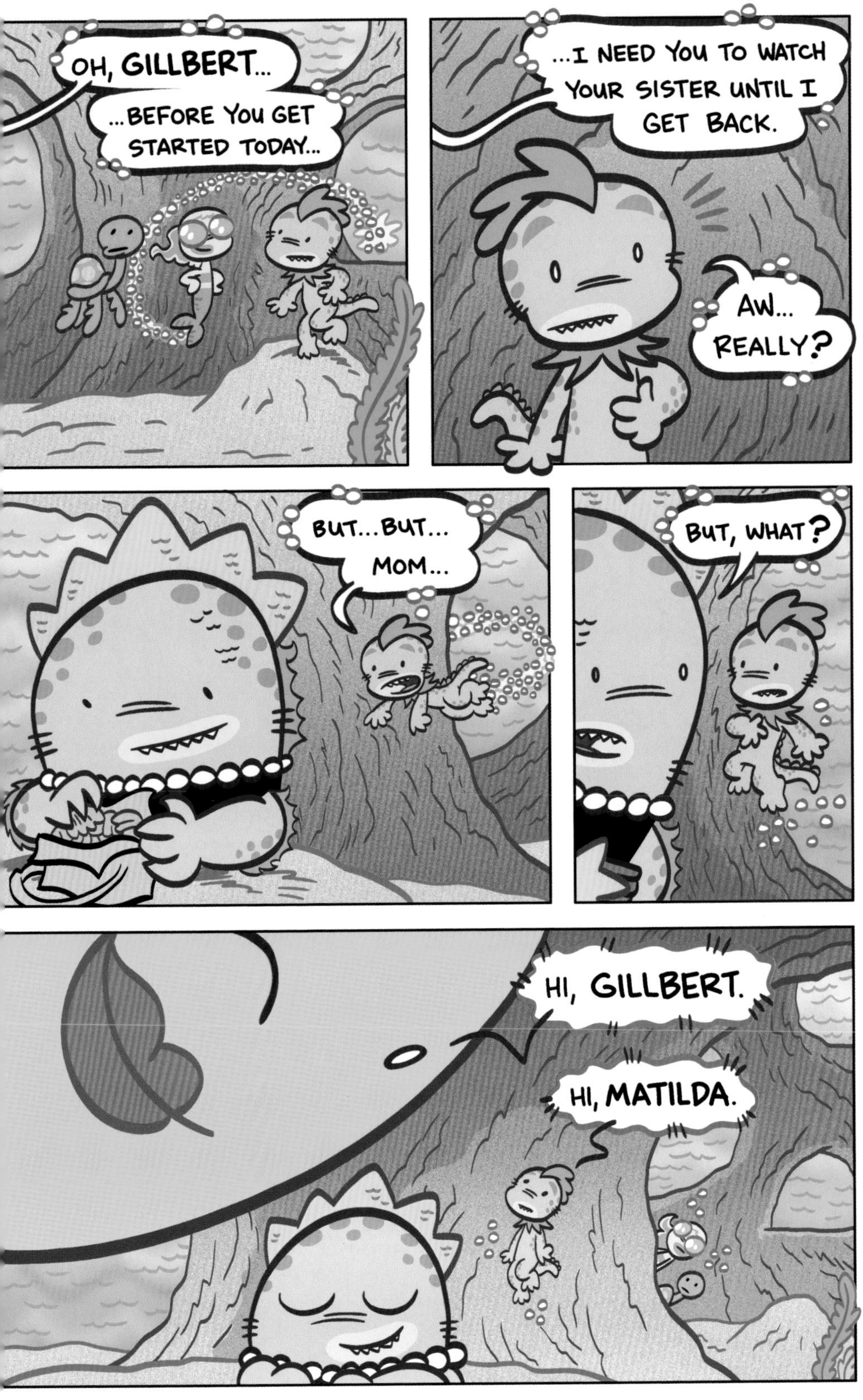
OH, GILLBERT...
...BEFORE YOU GET STARTED TODAY...
...I NEED YOU TO WATCH YOUR SISTER UNTIL I GET BACK.
AW... REALLY?
BUT...BUT... MOM...
BUT, WHAT?
HI, GILLBERT.
HI, MATILDA.

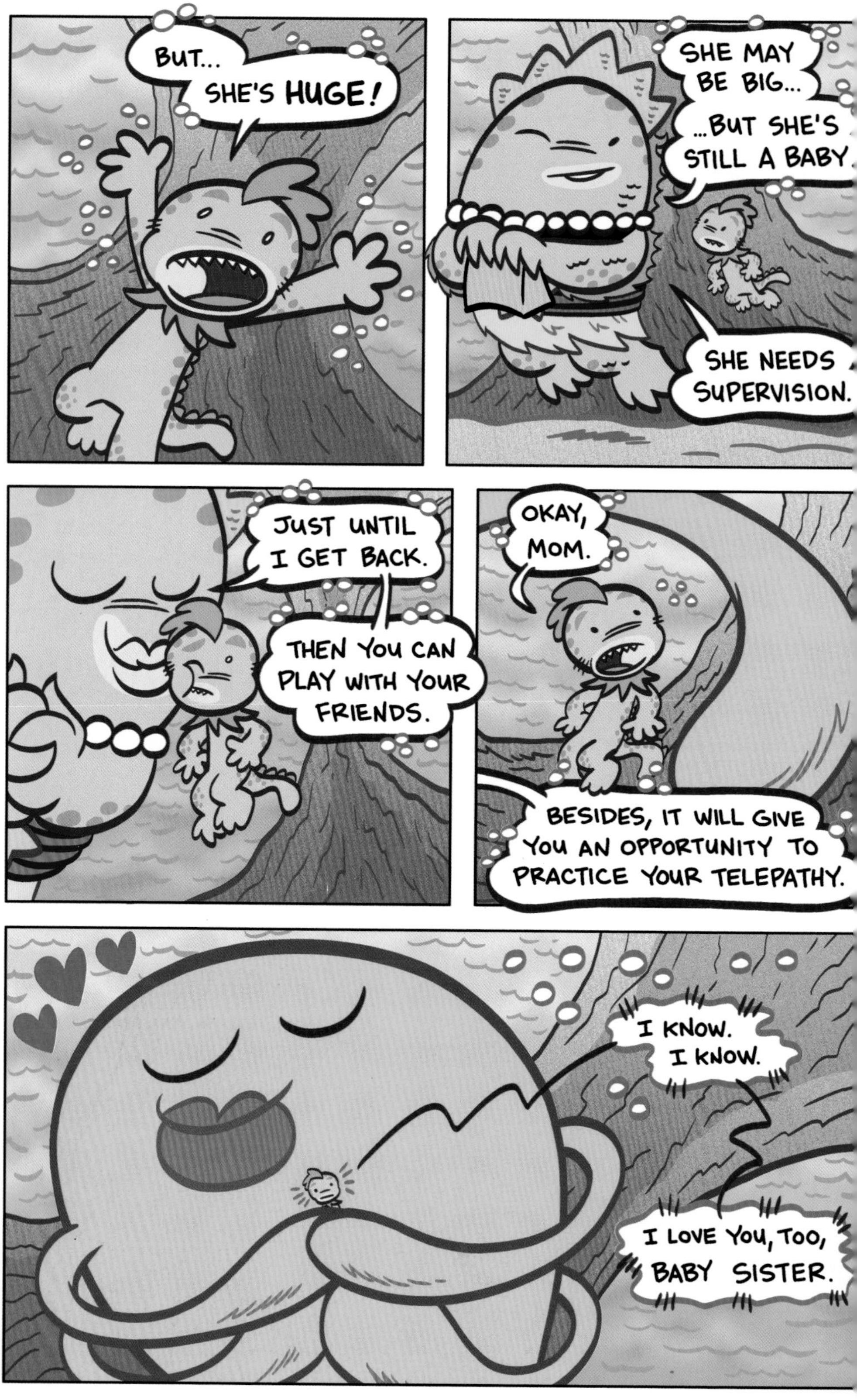
BUT...
SHE'S HUGE!
SHE MAY BE BIG...
...BUT SHE'S STILL A BABY.
SHE NEEDS SUPERVISION.
JUST UNTIL I GET BACK.
THEN YOU CAN PLAY WITH YOUR FRIENDS.
OKAY, MOM.
BESIDES, IT WILL GIVE YOU AN OPPORTUNITY TO PRACTICE YOUR TELEPATHY.
I KNOW. I KNOW.
I LOVE YOU, TOO, BABY SISTER.

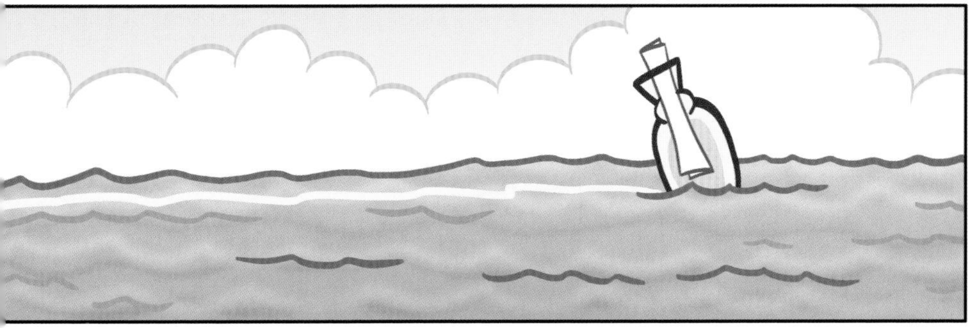

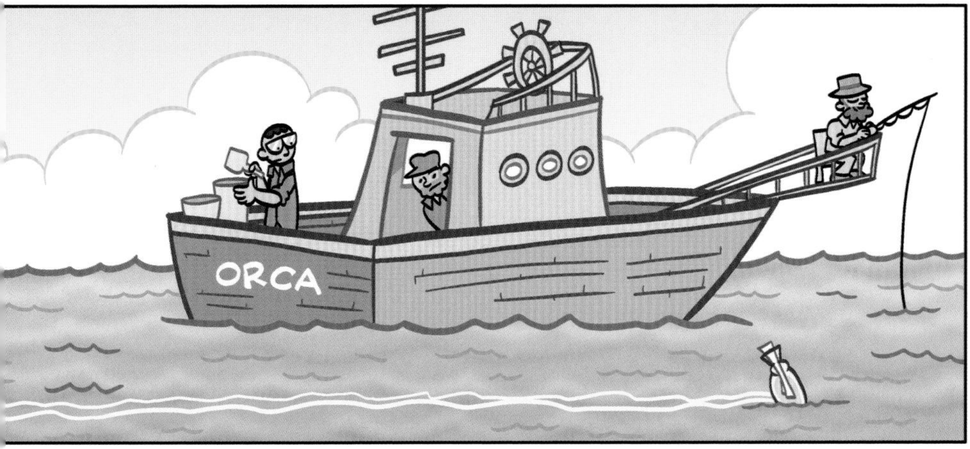
ORCA

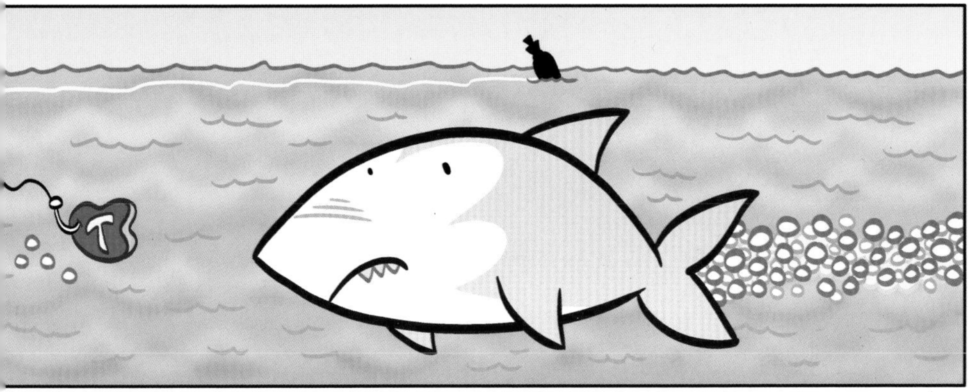
T

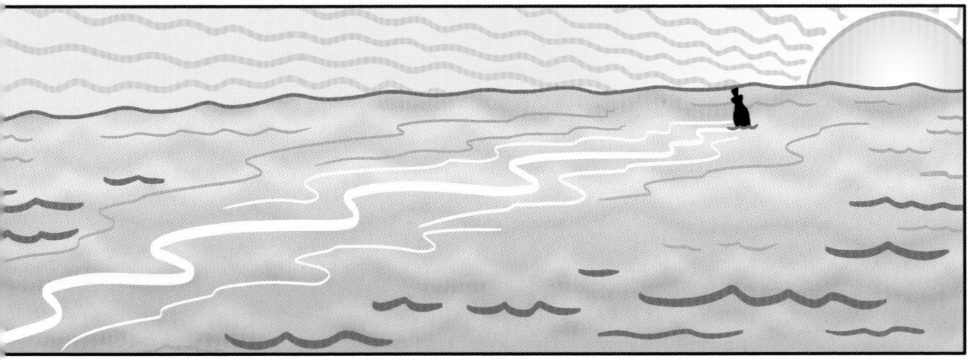

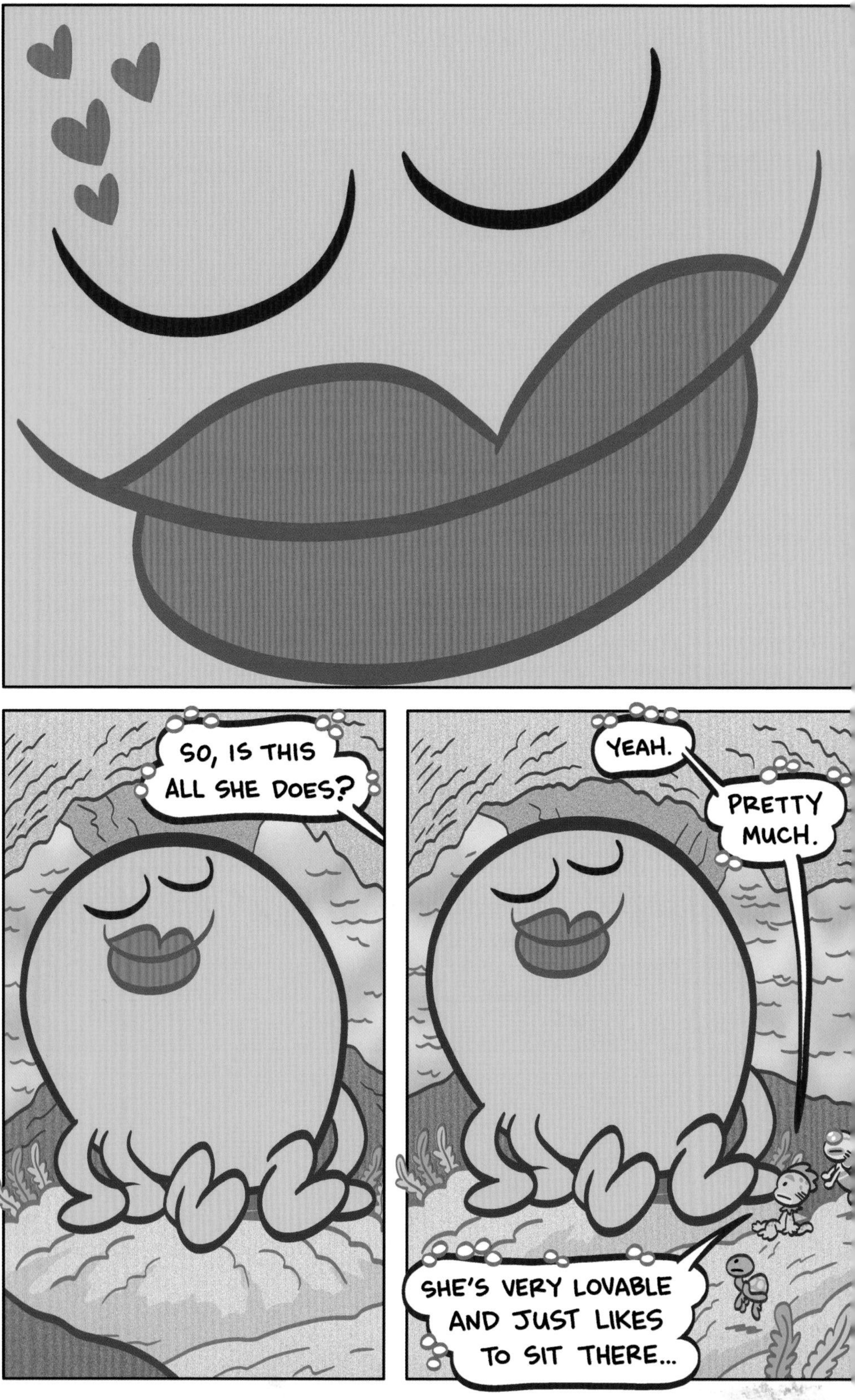
SO, IS THIS ALL SHE DOES?
YEAH.
PRETTY MUCH.
SHE'S VERY LOVABLE AND JUST LIKES TO SIT THERE...

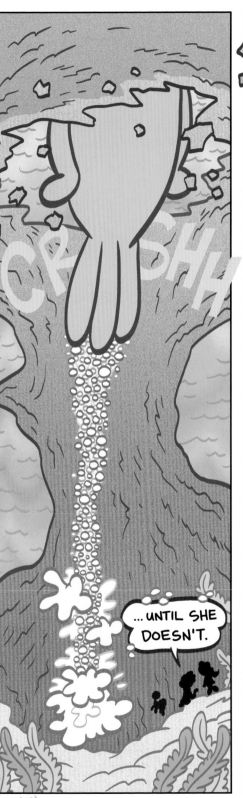

CR ISHH

...UNTIL SHE DOESN'T.

ANYTHING CAN HAPPEN ON **EVERYTHING DAY.**

YEP.

AND WITH **MATILDA,** ANYTHING IS VERY POSSIBLE.

C'MON, WE HAVE TO CATCH UP!

SHE'S QUITE FAST!

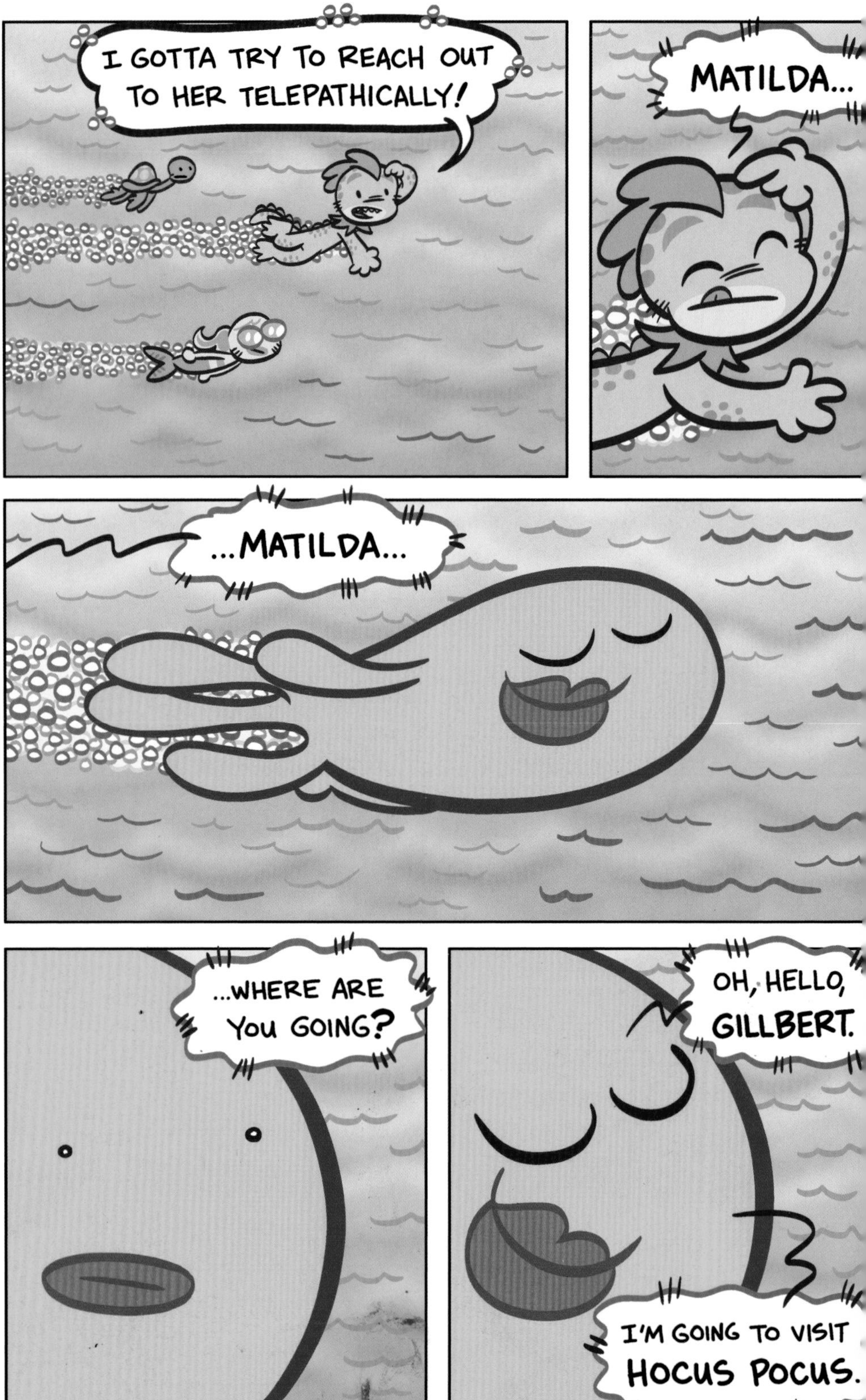
I GOTTA TRY TO REACH OUT TO HER TELEPATHICALLY!
MATILDA...
...MATILDA...
...WHERE ARE YOU GOING?
OH, HELLO, GILLBERT.
I'M GOING TO VISIT HOCUS POCUS.

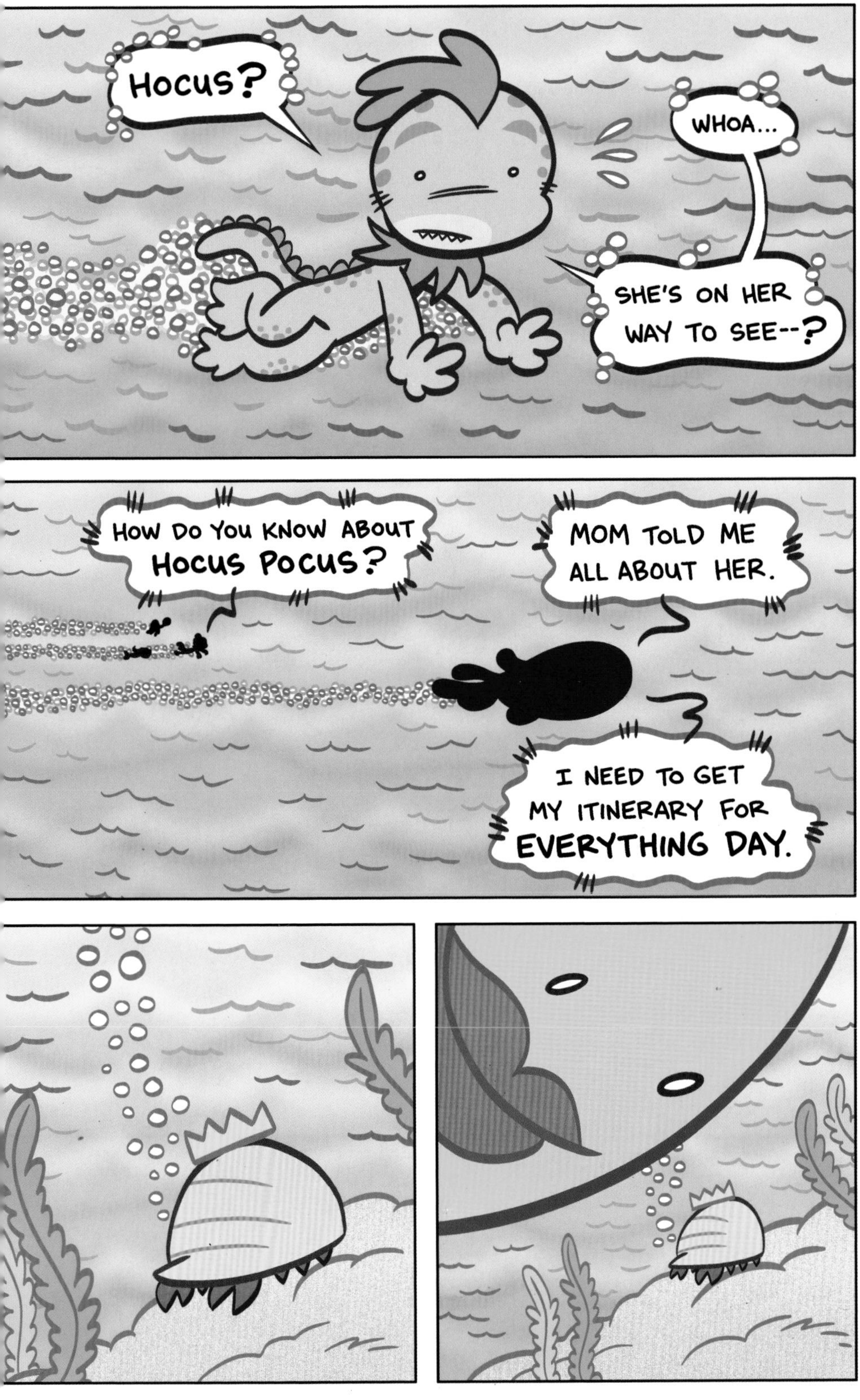
HOCUS?
WHOA...
SHE'S ON HER WAY TO SEE--?
HOW DO YOU KNOW ABOUT HOCUS POCUS?
MOM TOLD ME ALL ABOUT HER.
I NEED TO GET MY ITINERARY FOR EVERYTHING DAY.

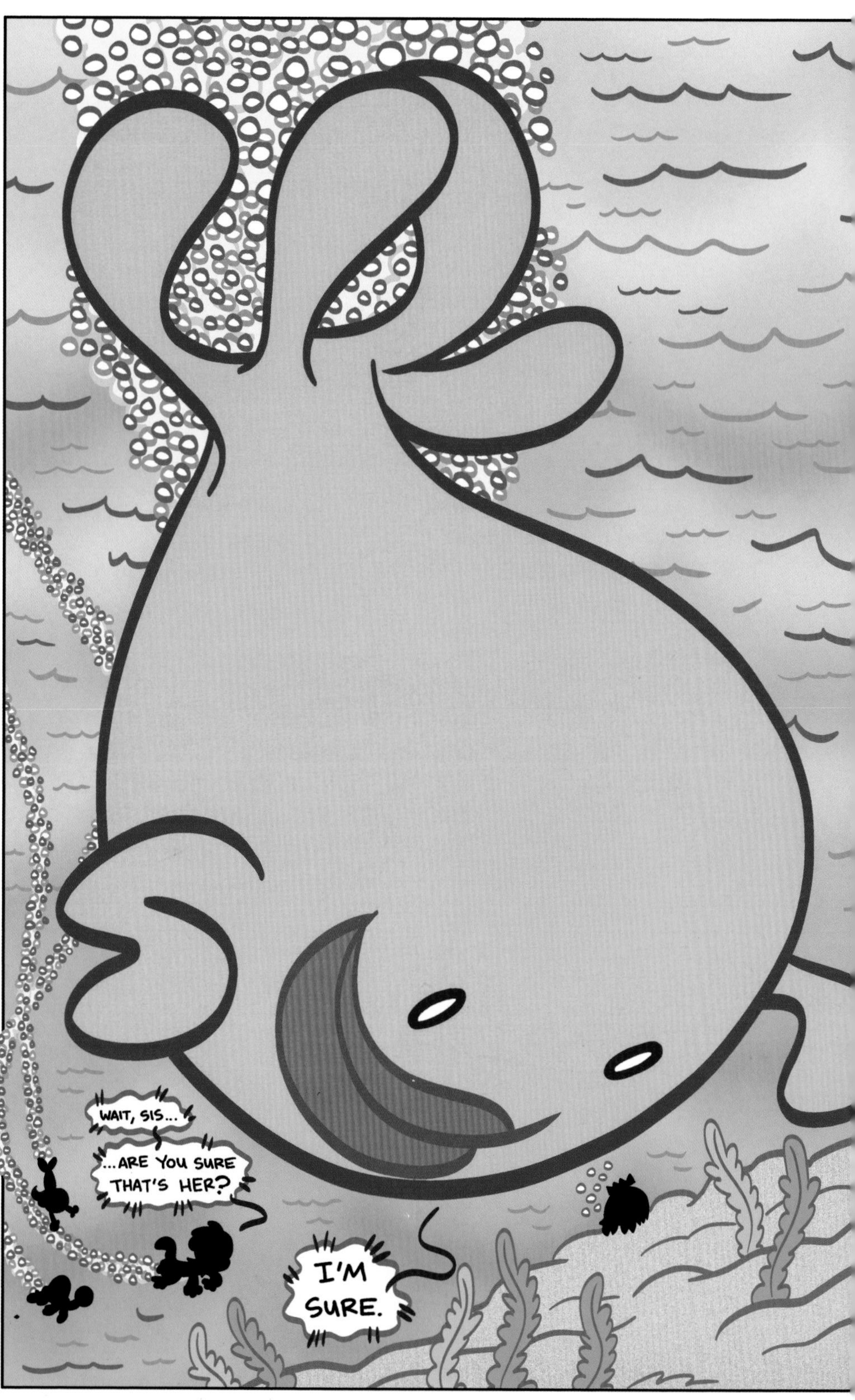
WAIT, SIS...
...ARE YOU SURE THAT'S HER?
I'M SURE.

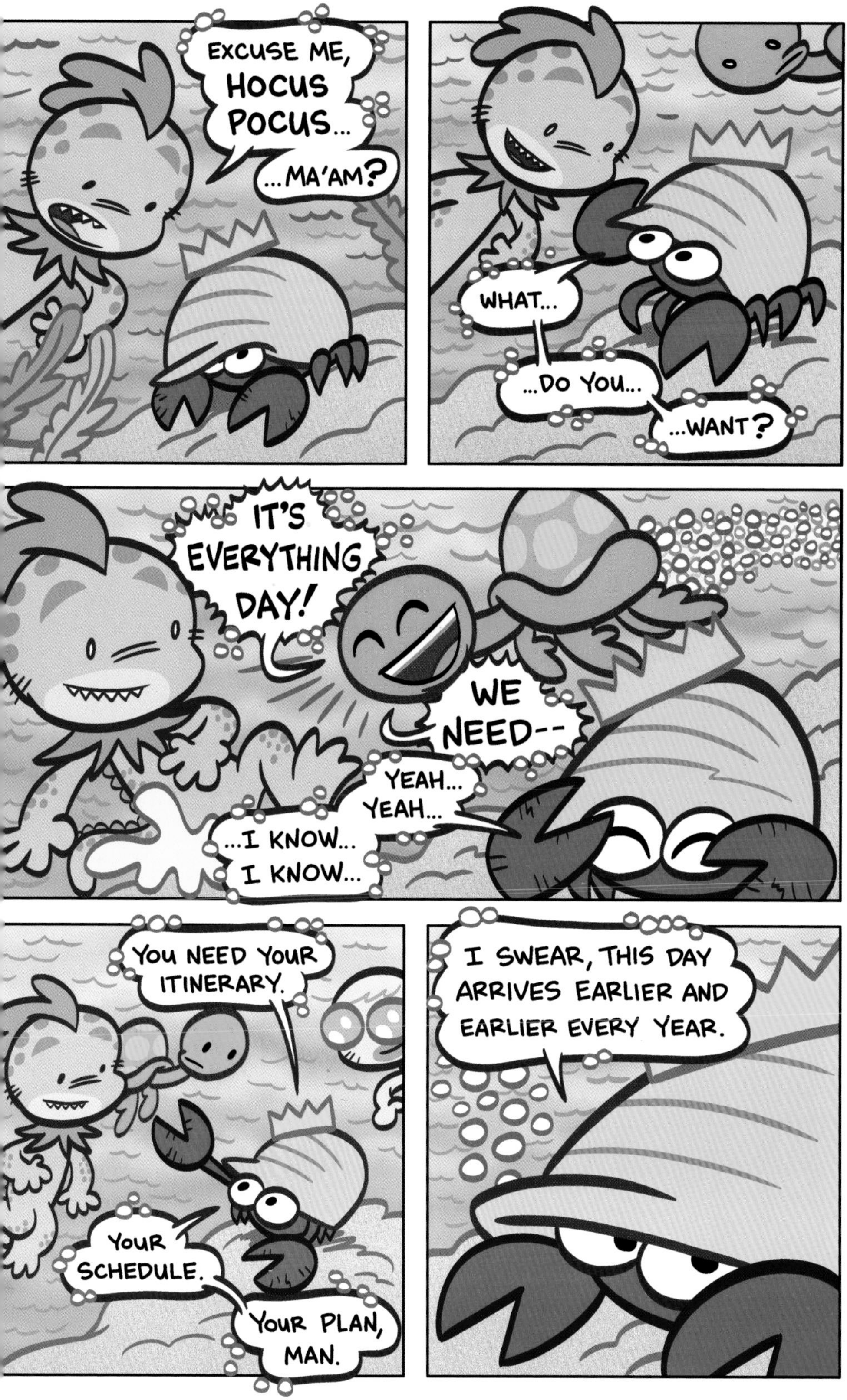
EXCUSE ME, HOCUS POCUS...
...MA'AM?
WHAT...
...DO YOU...
...WANT?
IT'S EVERYTHING DAY!
WE NEED--
YEAH... YEAH...
...I KNOW... I KNOW...
YOU NEED YOUR ITINERARY.
YOUR SCHEDULE.
YOUR PLAN, MAN.
I SWEAR, THIS DAY ARRIVES EARLIER AND EARLIER EVERY YEAR.

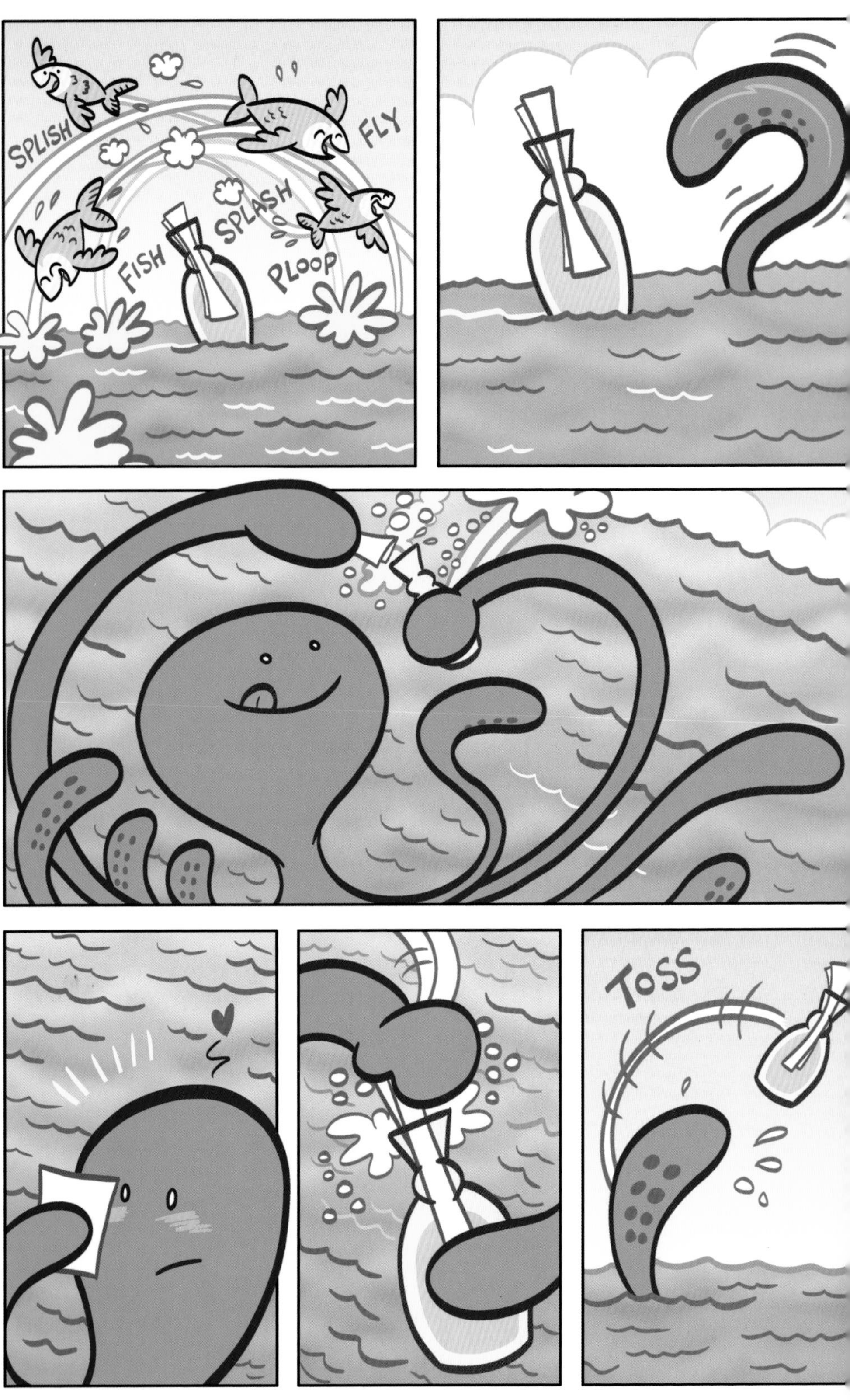
SPLISH
FLY
SPLASH
FISH
PLOOP
TOSS

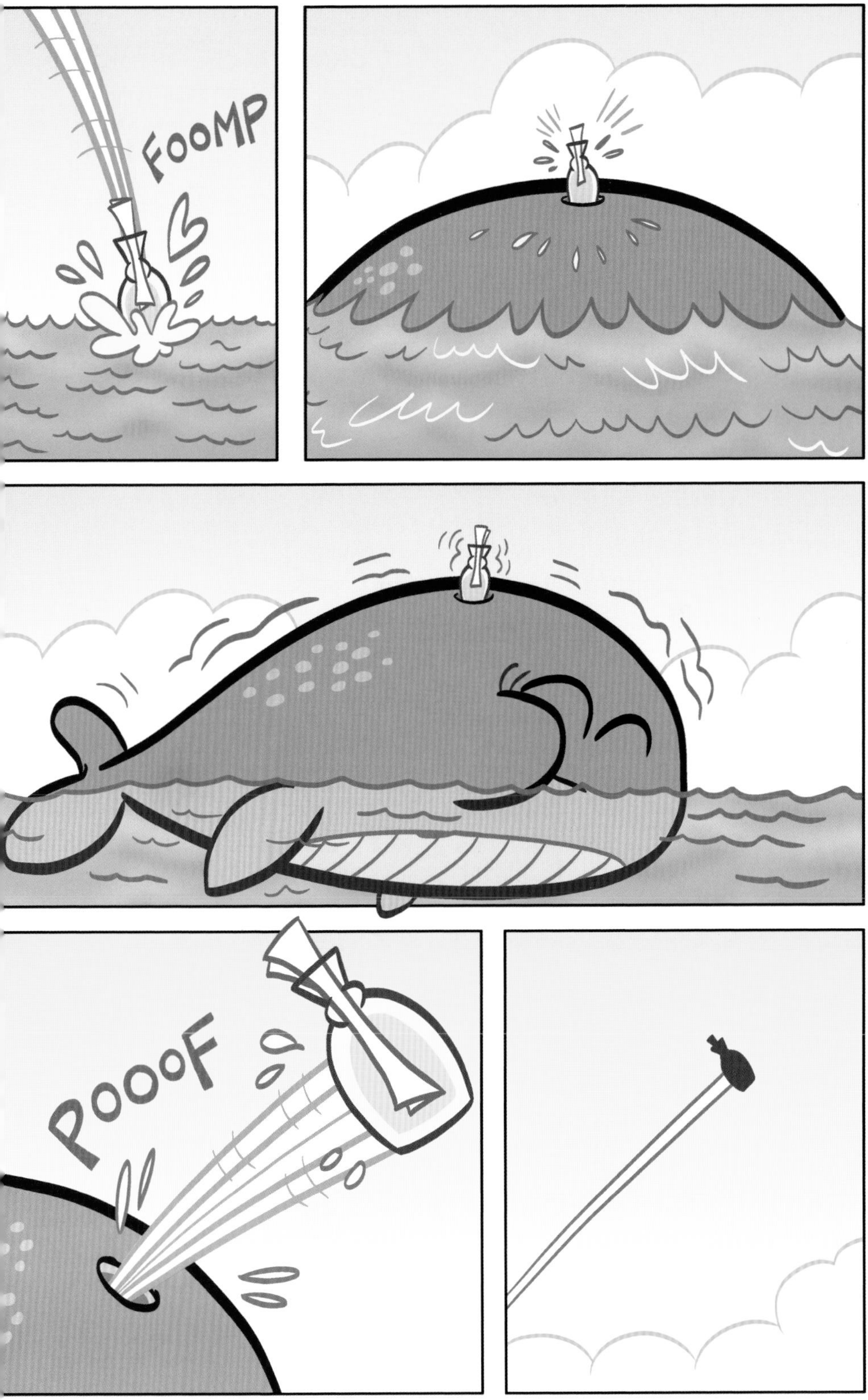
FOOMP
POOOF

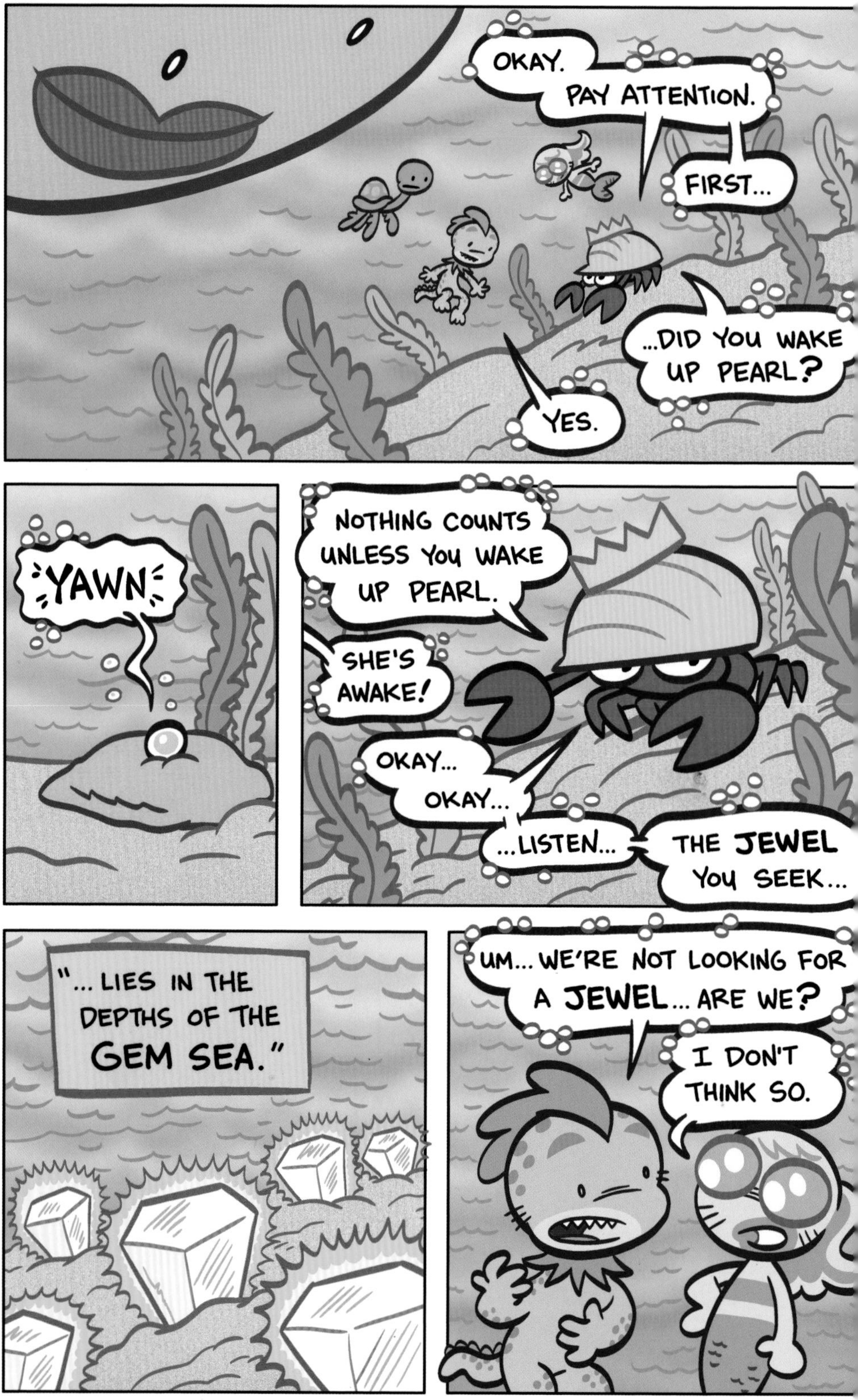
OKAY.
PAY ATTENTION.
FIRST...
...DID YOU WAKE UP PEARL?
YES.
YAWN
NOTHING COUNTS UNLESS YOU WAKE UP PEARL.
SHE'S AWAKE!
OKAY... OKAY...
...LISTEN...
THE JEWEL YOU SEEK...
"... LIES IN THE DEPTHS OF THE GEM SEA."
UM... WE'RE NOT LOOKING FOR A JEWEL... ARE WE?
I DON'T THINK SO.

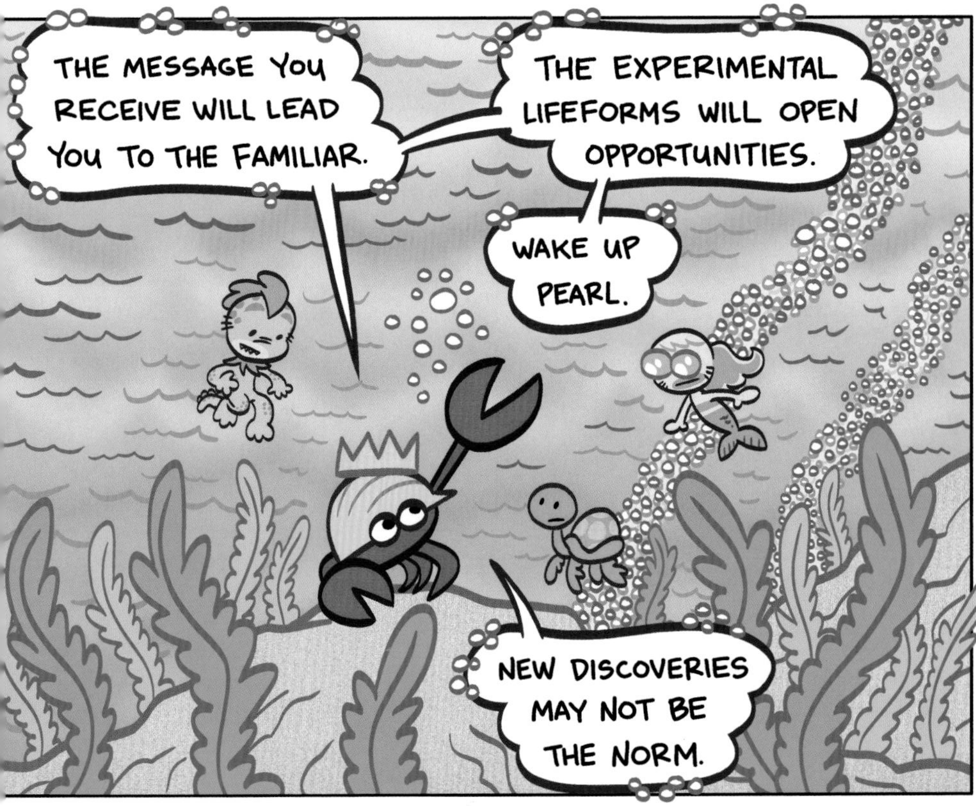
THE MESSAGE YOU RECEIVE WILL LEAD YOU TO THE FAMILIAR.
THE EXPERIMENTAL LIFEFORMS WILL OPEN OPPORTUNITIES.
WAKE UP PEARL.
NEW DISCOVERIES MAY NOT BE THE NORM.

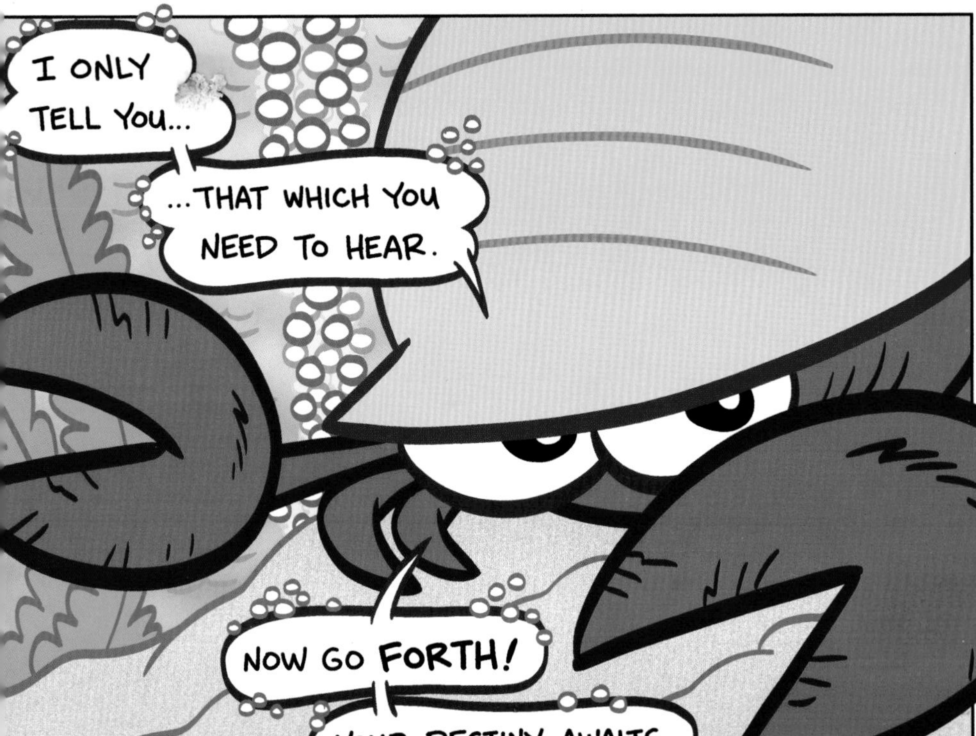
I ONLY TELL YOU...
...THAT WHICH YOU NEED TO HEAR.
NOW GO FORTH!
YOUR DESTINY AWAITS.

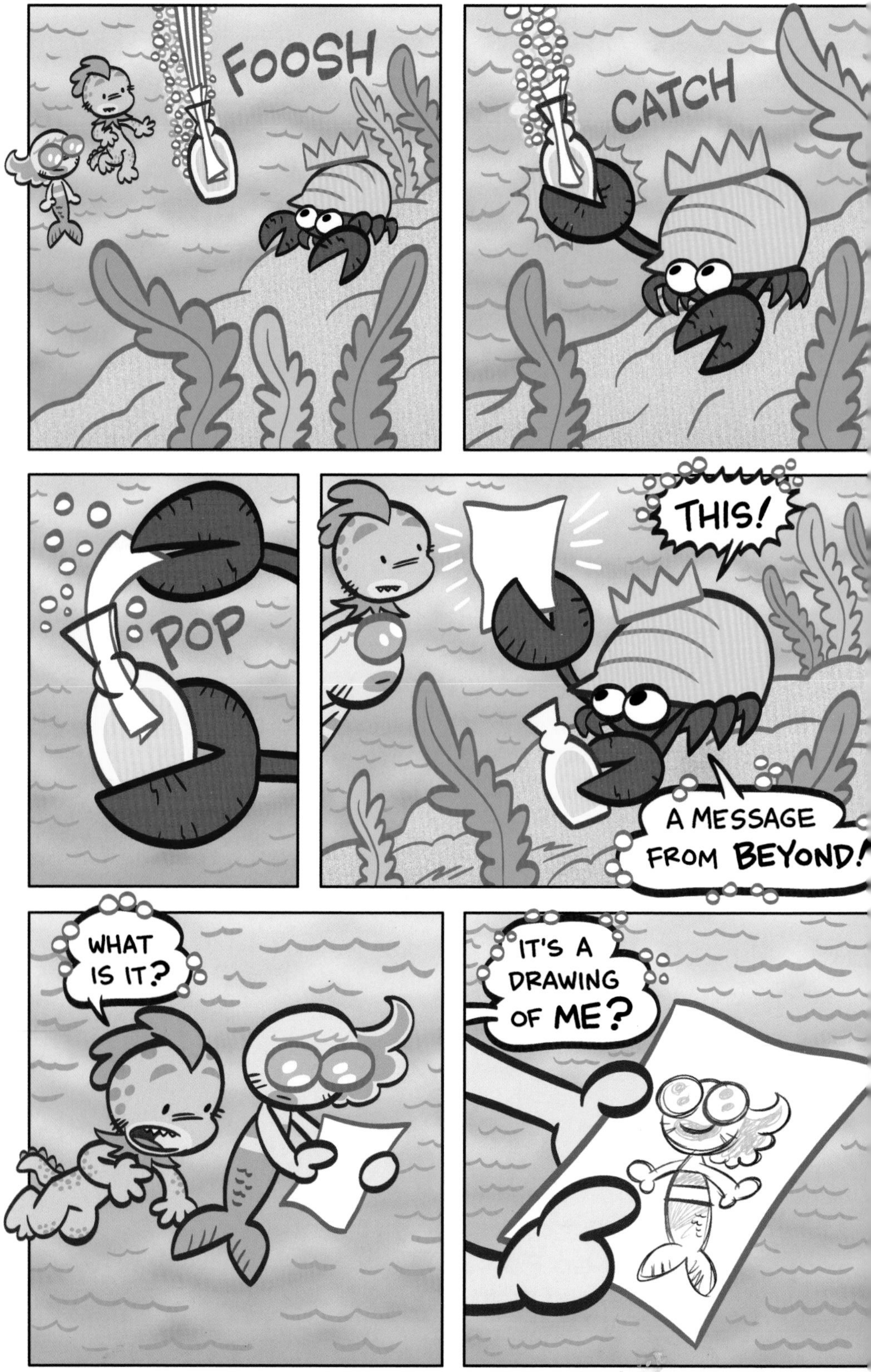
FOOSH
CATCH
POP
THIS!
A MESSAGE FROM BEYOND!
WHAT IS IT?
IT'S A DRAWING OF ME?

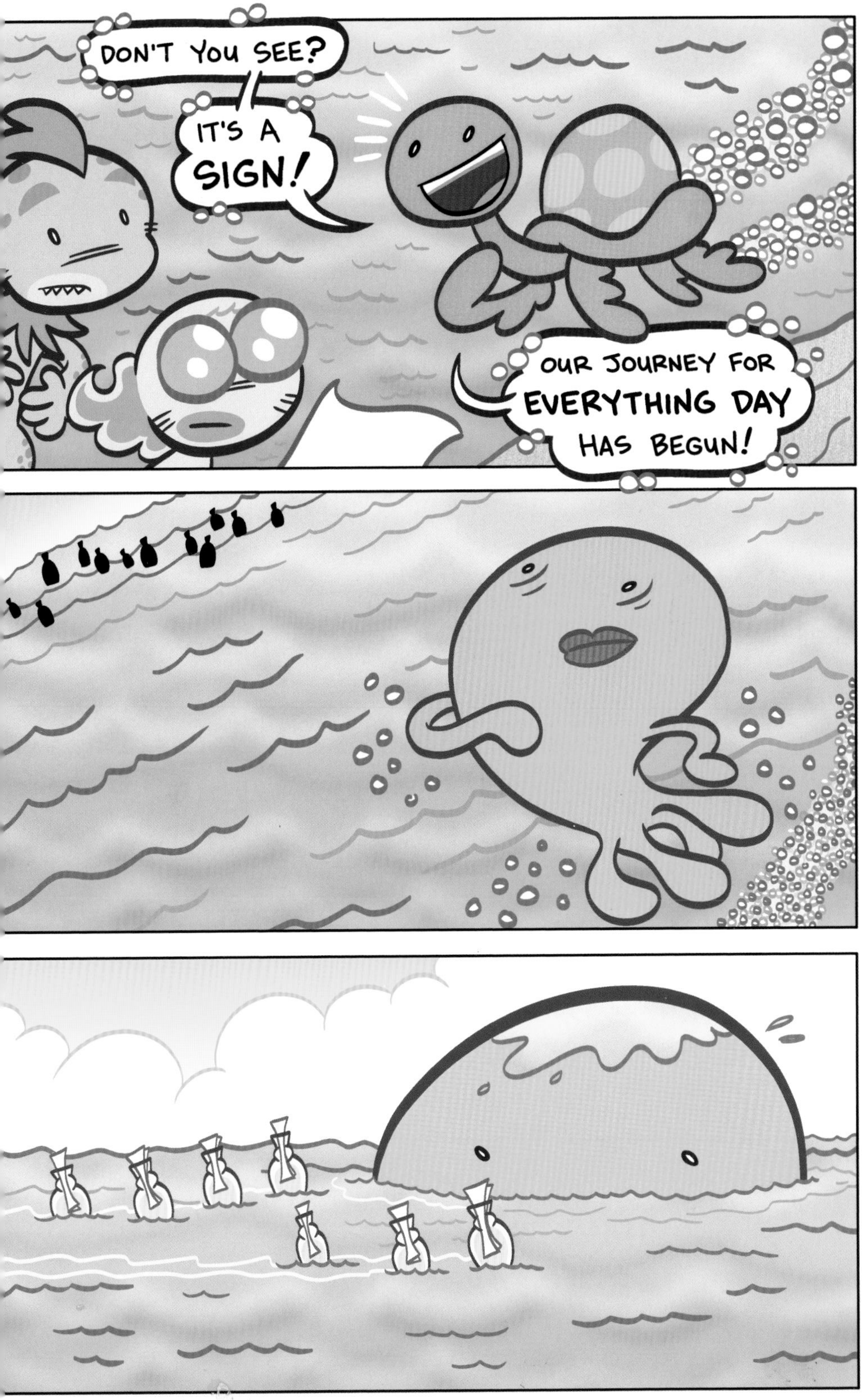
DON'T YOU SEE?
IT'S A SIGN!
OUR JOURNEY FOR EVERYTHING DAY HAS BEGUN!

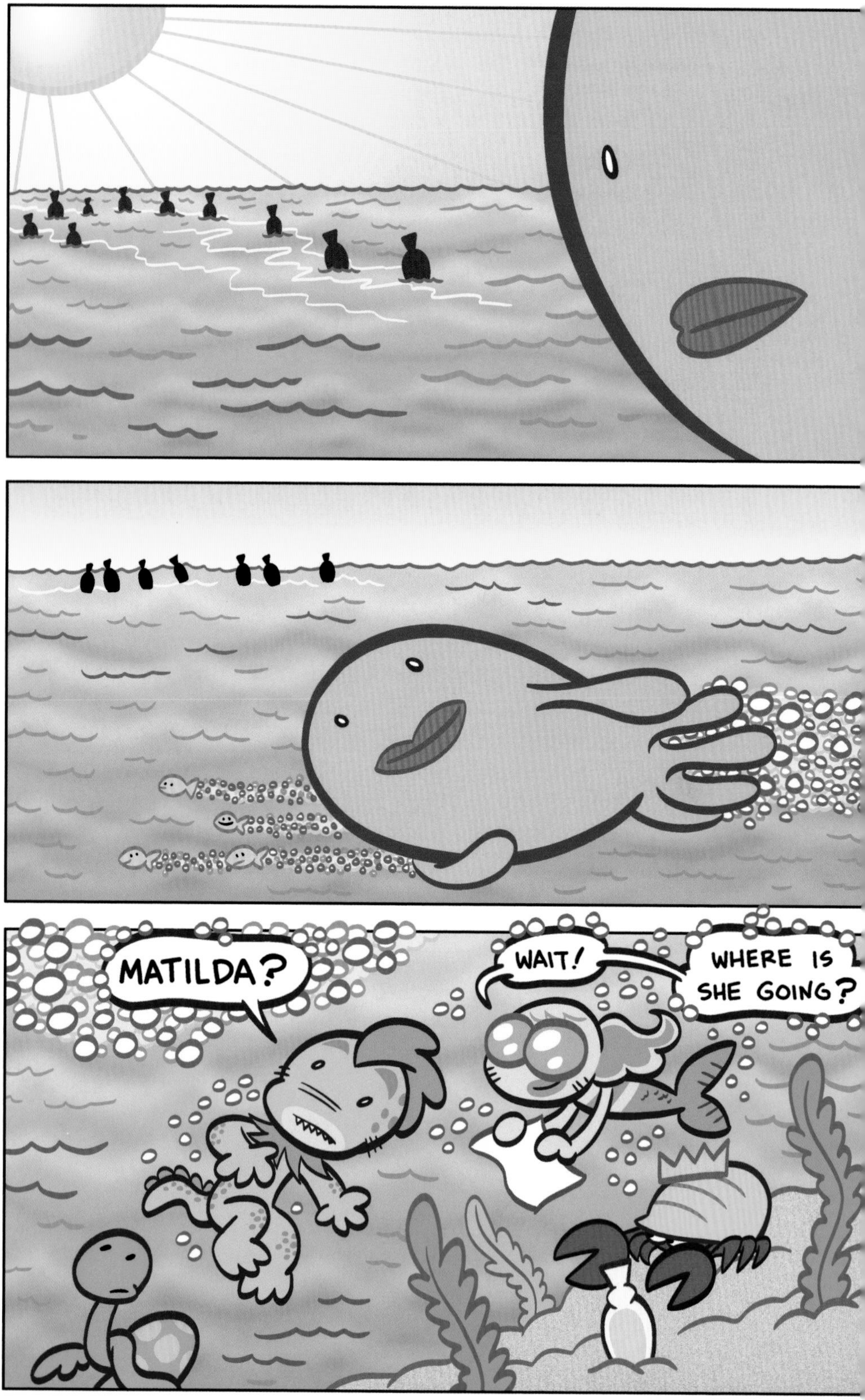
MATILDA?
WAIT!
WHERE IS SHE GOING?

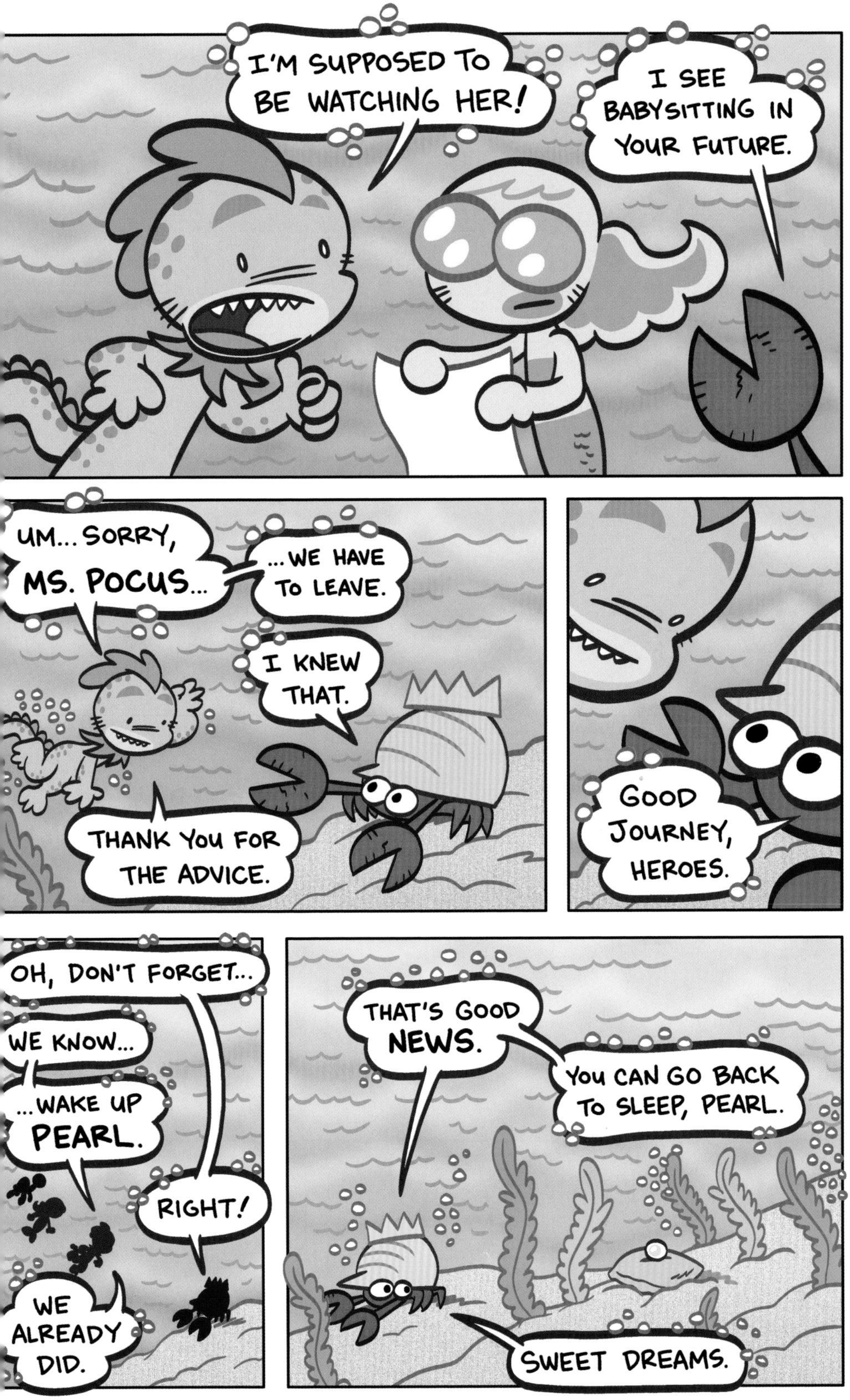
I'M SUPPOSED TO BE WATCHING HER!
I SEE BABYSITTING IN YOUR FUTURE.
UM... SORRY, MS. POCUS...
...WE HAVE TO LEAVE.
I KNEW THAT.
THANK YOU FOR THE ADVICE.
GOOD JOURNEY, HEROES.
OH, DON'T FORGET...
WE KNOW...
...WAKE UP PEARL.
RIGHT!
WE ALREADY DID.
THAT'S GOOD NEWS.
YOU CAN GO BACK TO SLEEP, PEARL.
SWEET DREAMS.

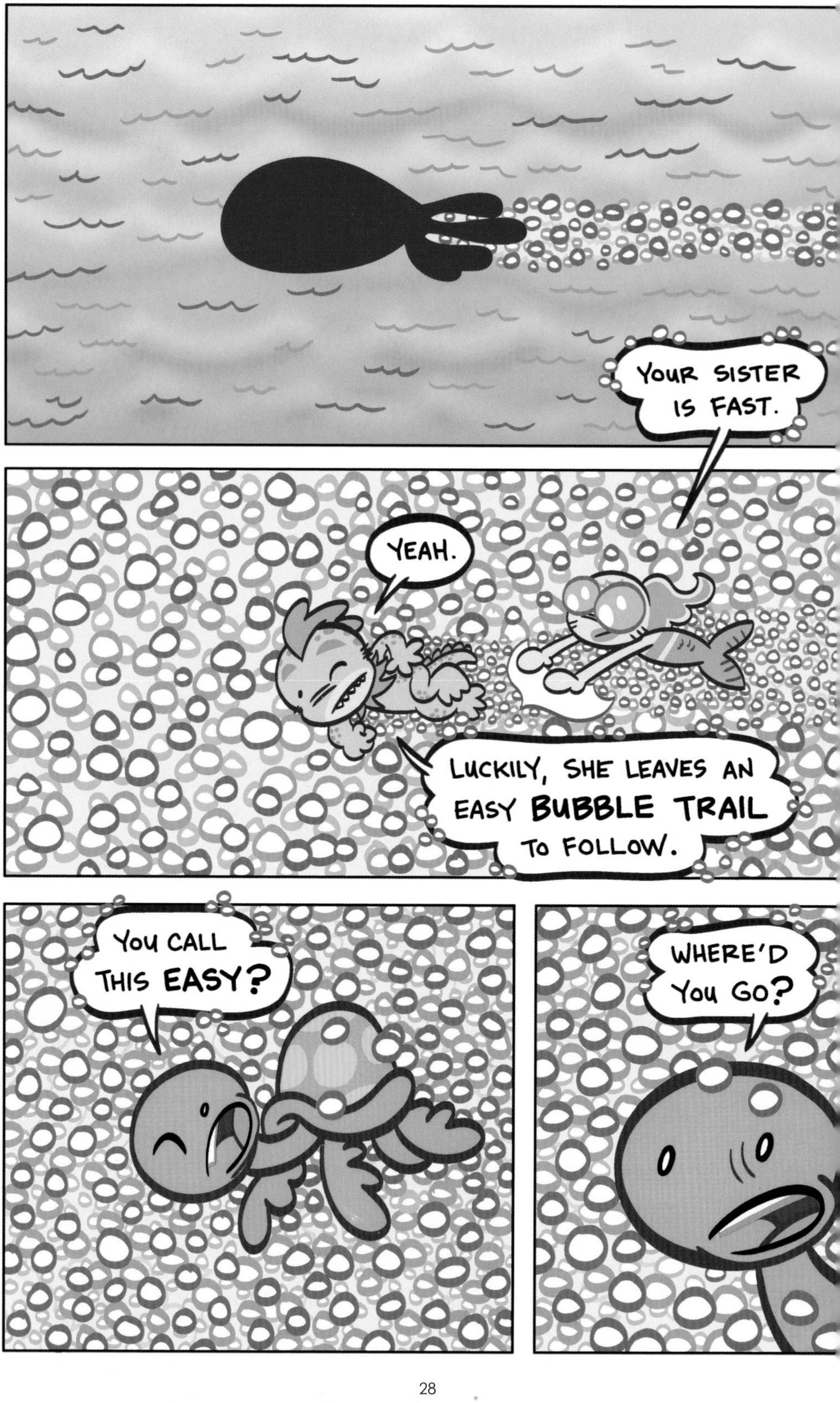
YOUR SISTER IS FAST.
YEAH.
LUCKILY, SHE LEAVES AN EASY BUBBLE TRAIL TO FOLLOW.
YOU CALL THIS EASY?
WHERE'D YOU GO?

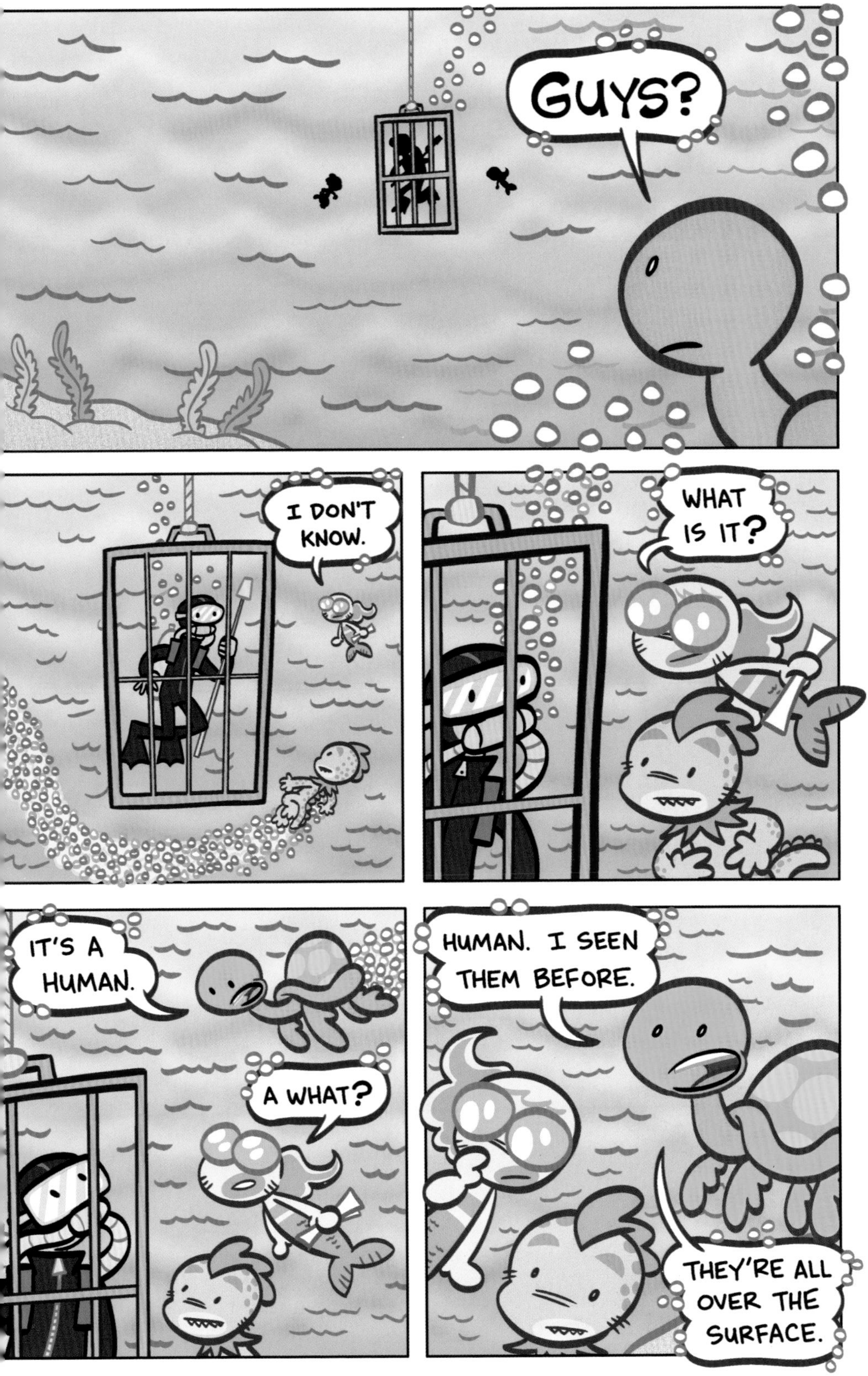
GUYS?
I DON'T KNOW.
WHAT IS IT?
IT'S A HUMAN.
A WHAT?
HUMAN. I SEEN THEM BEFORE.
THEY'RE ALL OVER THE SURFACE.

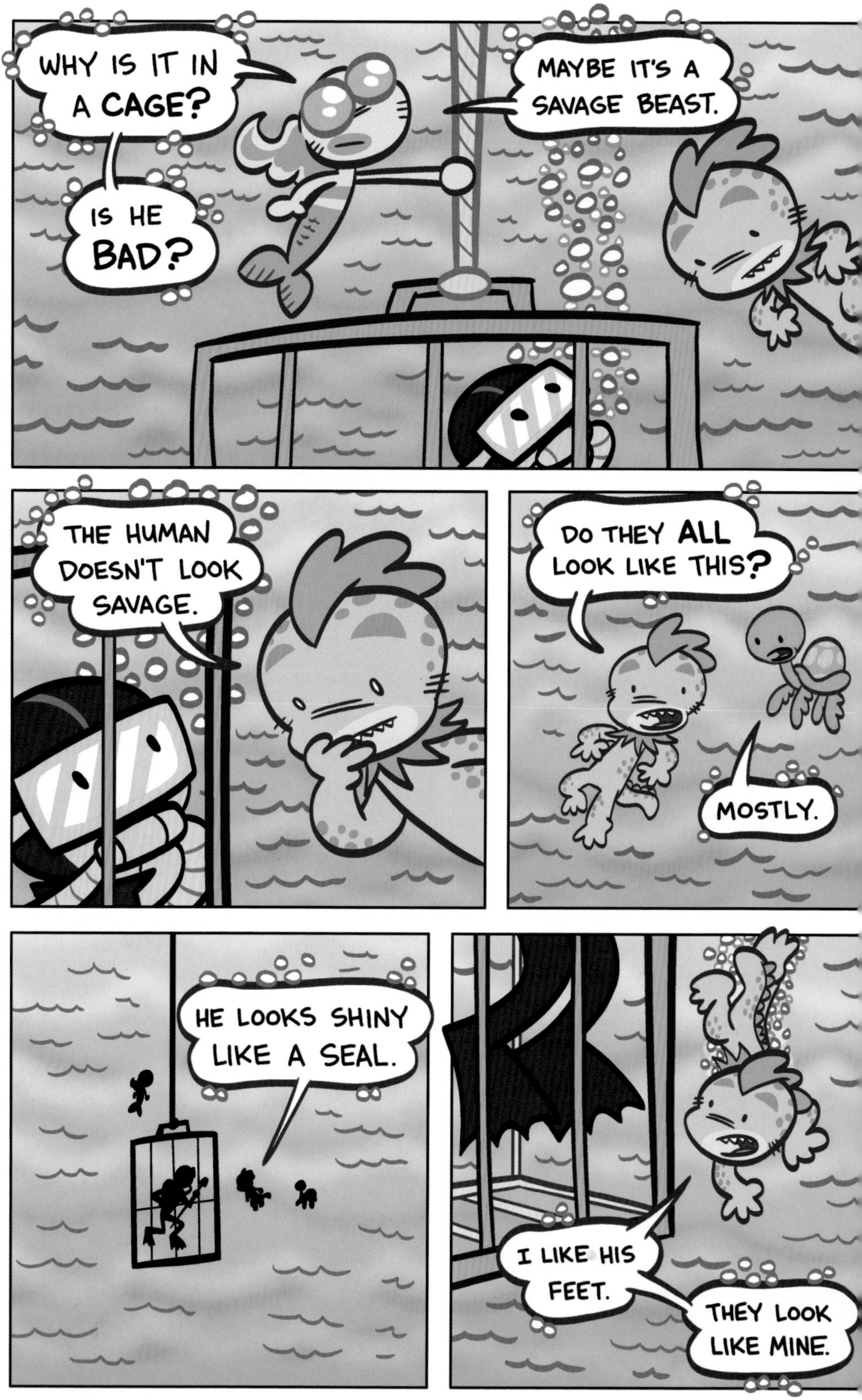
WHY IS IT IN A CAGE?
IS HE BAD?
MAYBE IT'S A SAVAGE BEAST.
THE HUMAN DOESN'T LOOK SAVAGE.
DO THEY ALL LOOK LIKE THIS?
MOSTLY.
HE LOOKS SHINY LIKE A SEAL.
I LIKE HIS FEET.
THEY LOOK LIKE MINE.

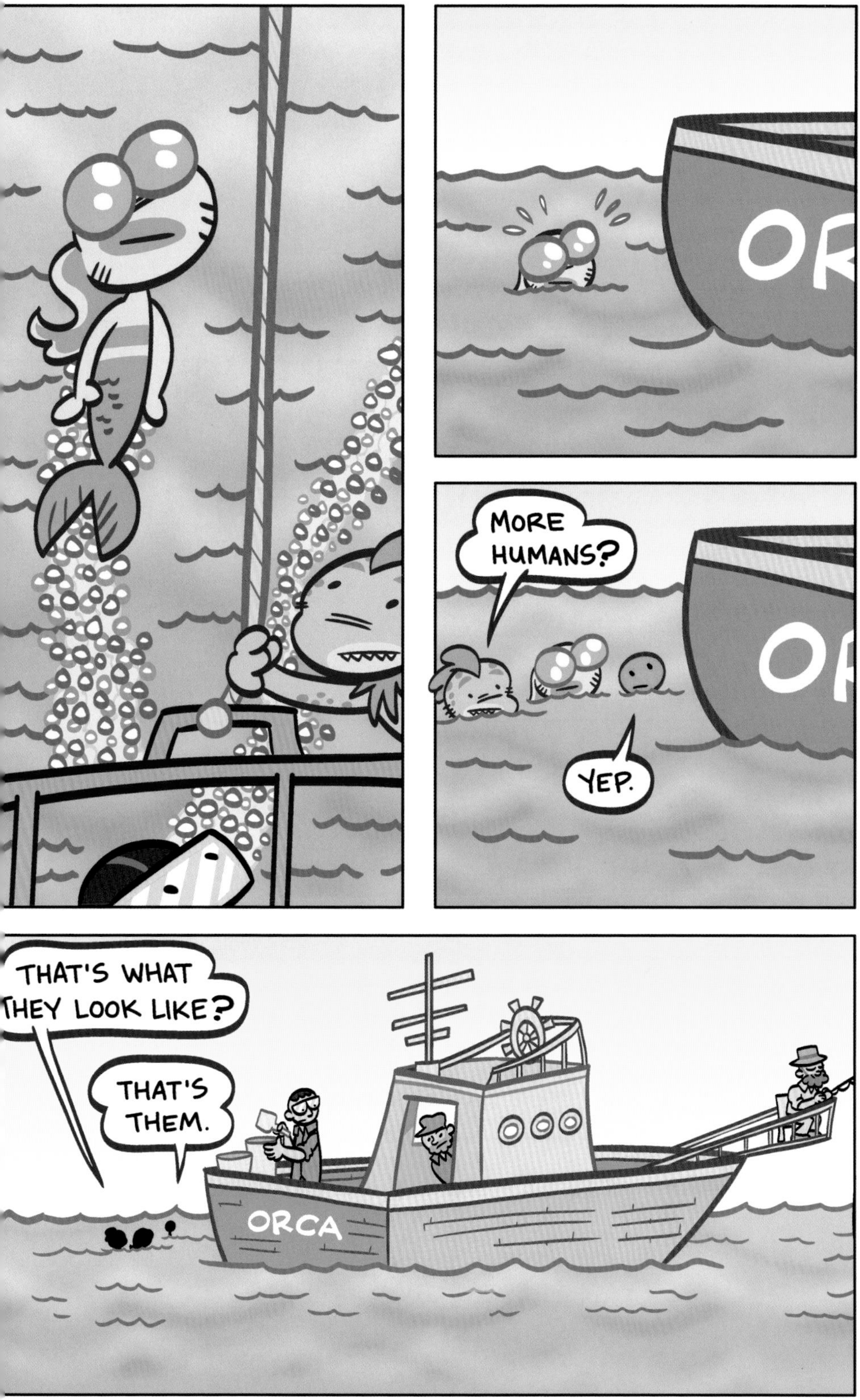

OR
MORE HUMANS?
OR
YEP.
THAT'S WHAT THEY LOOK LIKE?
THAT'S THEM.
ORCA

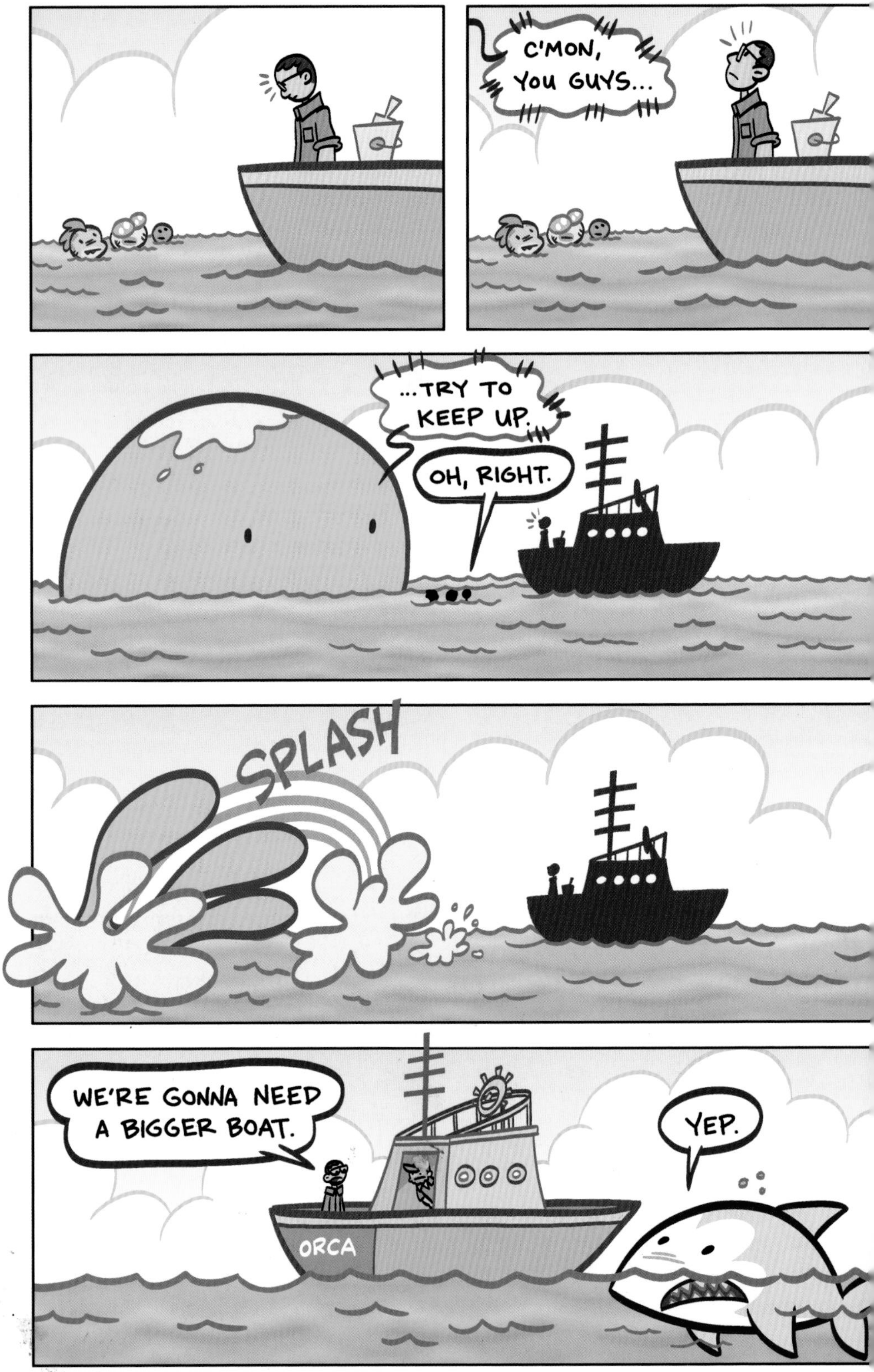
C'MON,
YOU GUYS...
...TRY TO
KEEP UP.
OH, RIGHT.
SPLASH
WE'RE GONNA NEED
A BIGGER BOAT.
ORCA
YEP.

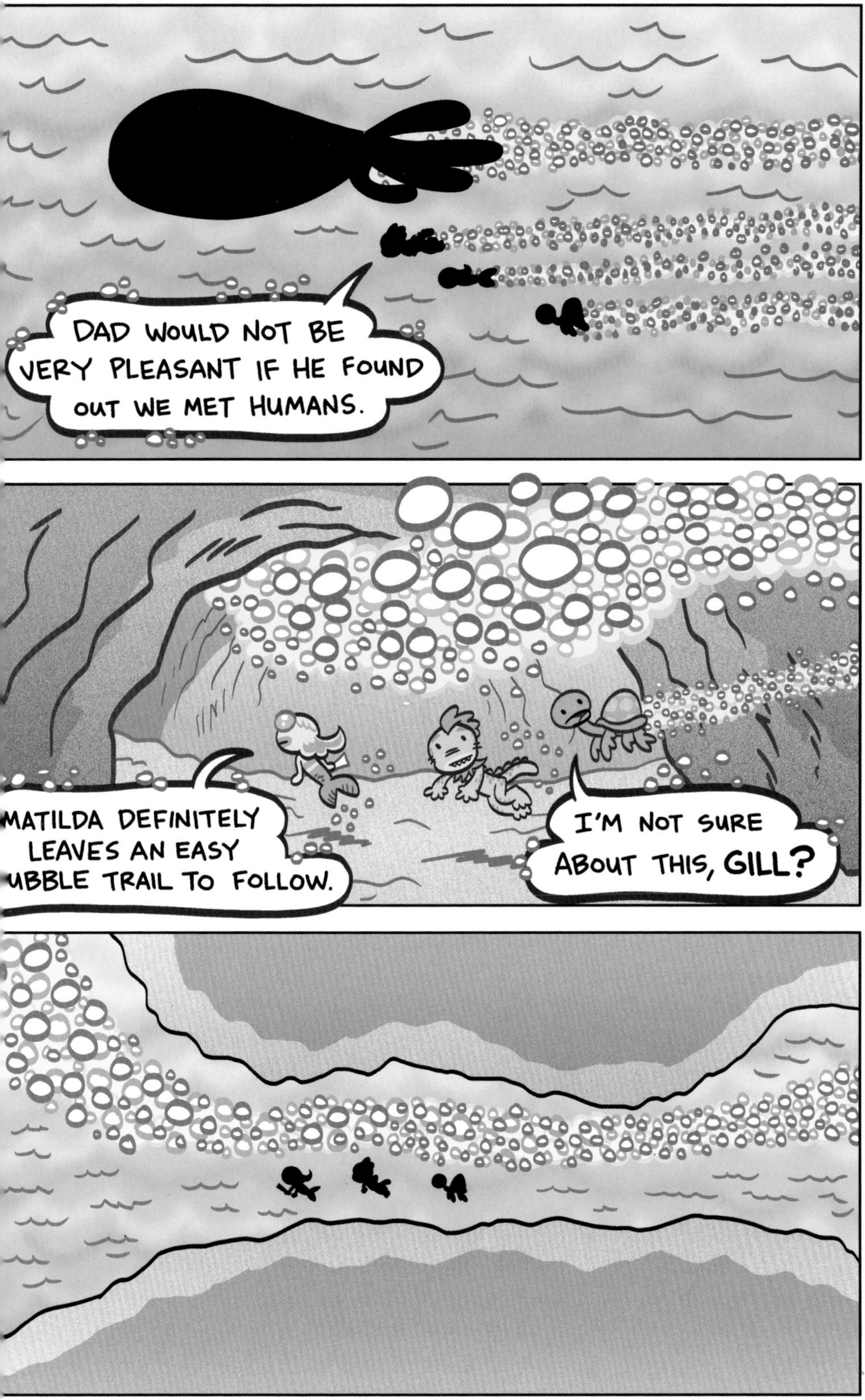
DAD WOULD NOT BE VERY PLEASANT IF HE FOUND OUT WE MET HUMANS.
MATILDA DEFINITELY LEAVES AN EASY UBBLE TRAIL TO FOLLOW.
I'M NOT SURE ABOUT THIS, GILL?

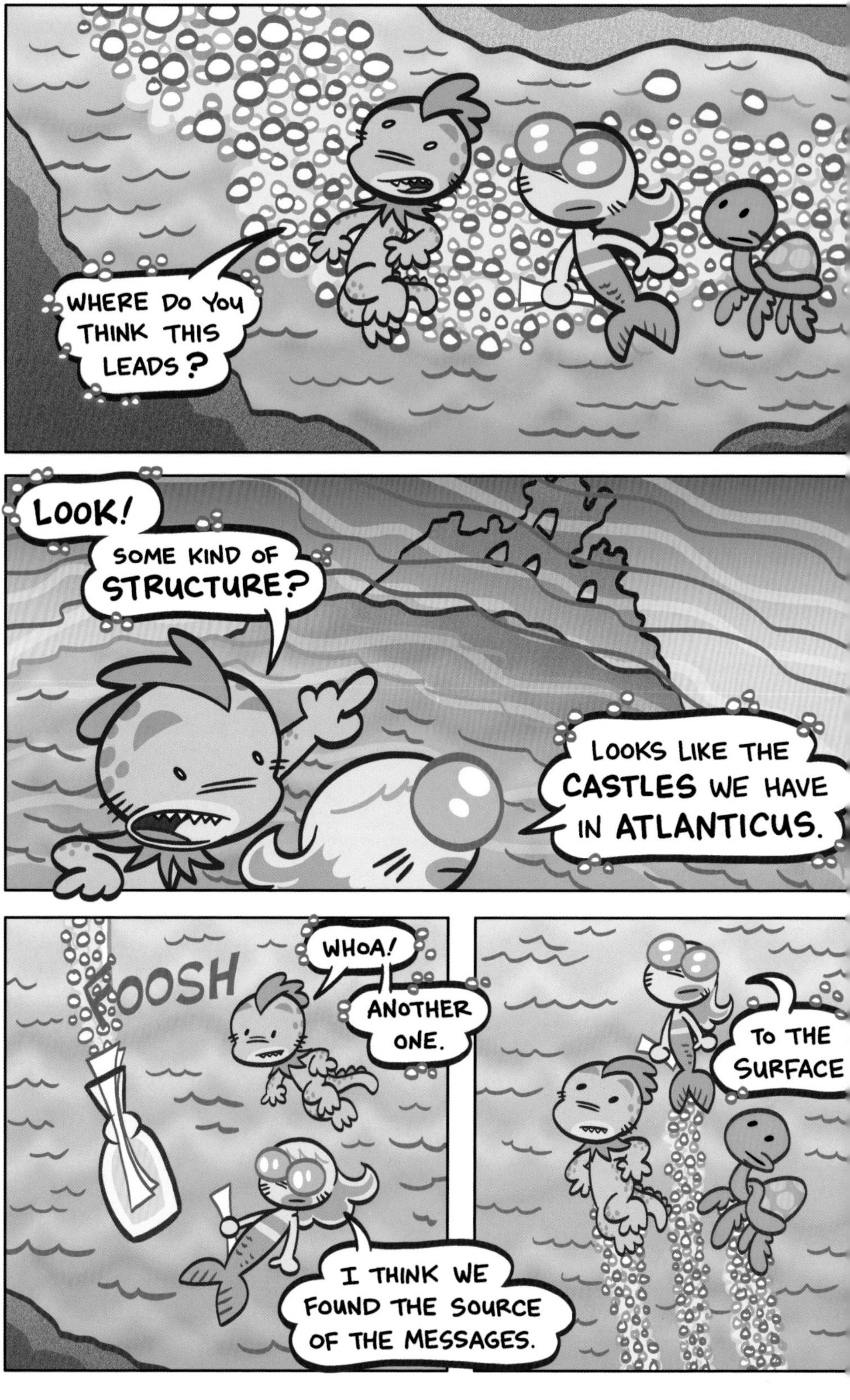
WHERE DO YOU THINK THIS LEADS?
LOOK!
SOME KIND OF STRUCTURE?
LOOKS LIKE THE CASTLES WE HAVE IN ATLANTICUS.
FOOSH
WHOA!
ANOTHER ONE.
I THINK WE FOUND THE SOURCE OF THE MESSAGES.
TO THE SURFACE

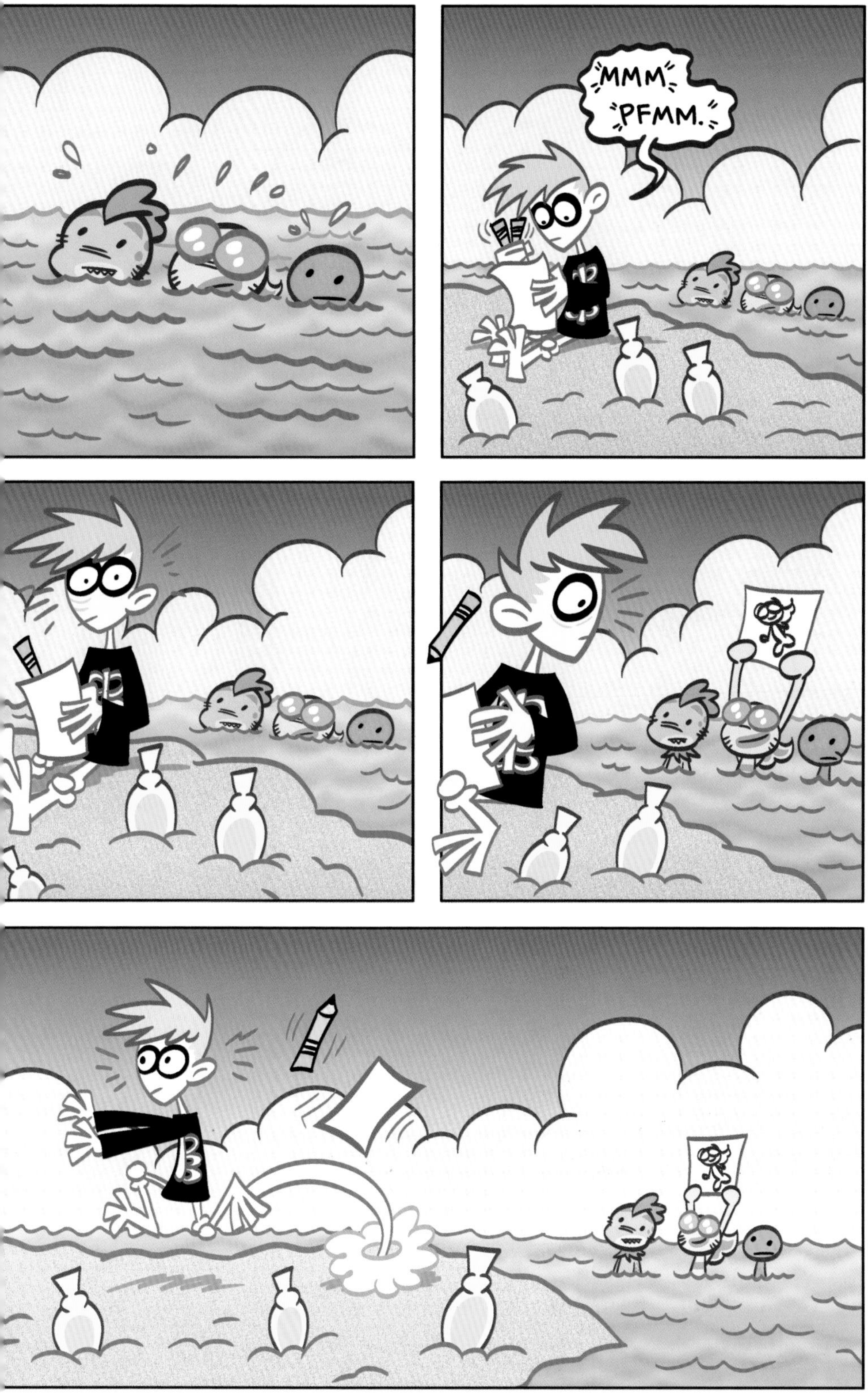
MMM PFMM.

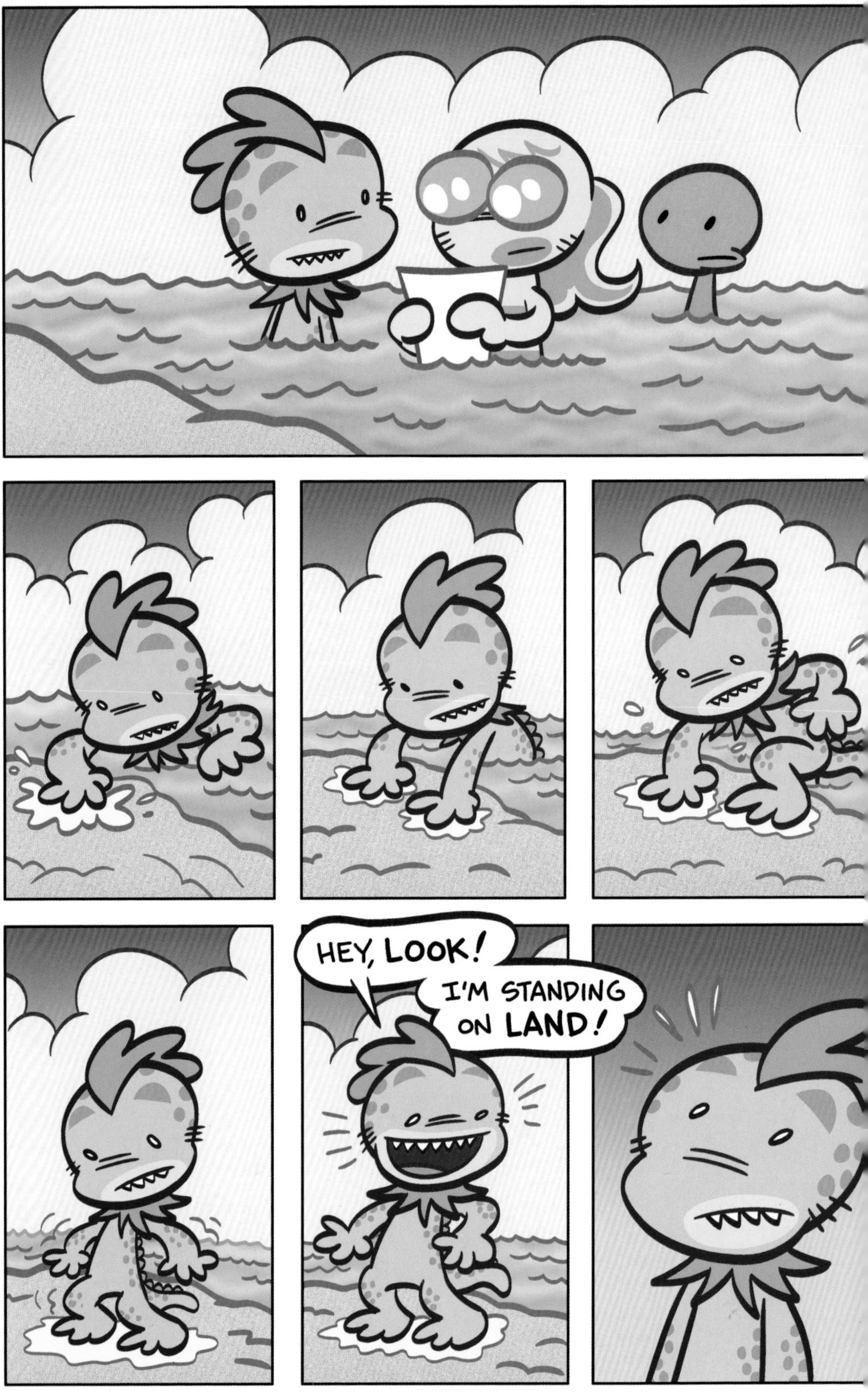
HEY, LOOK!
I'M STANDING ON LAND!

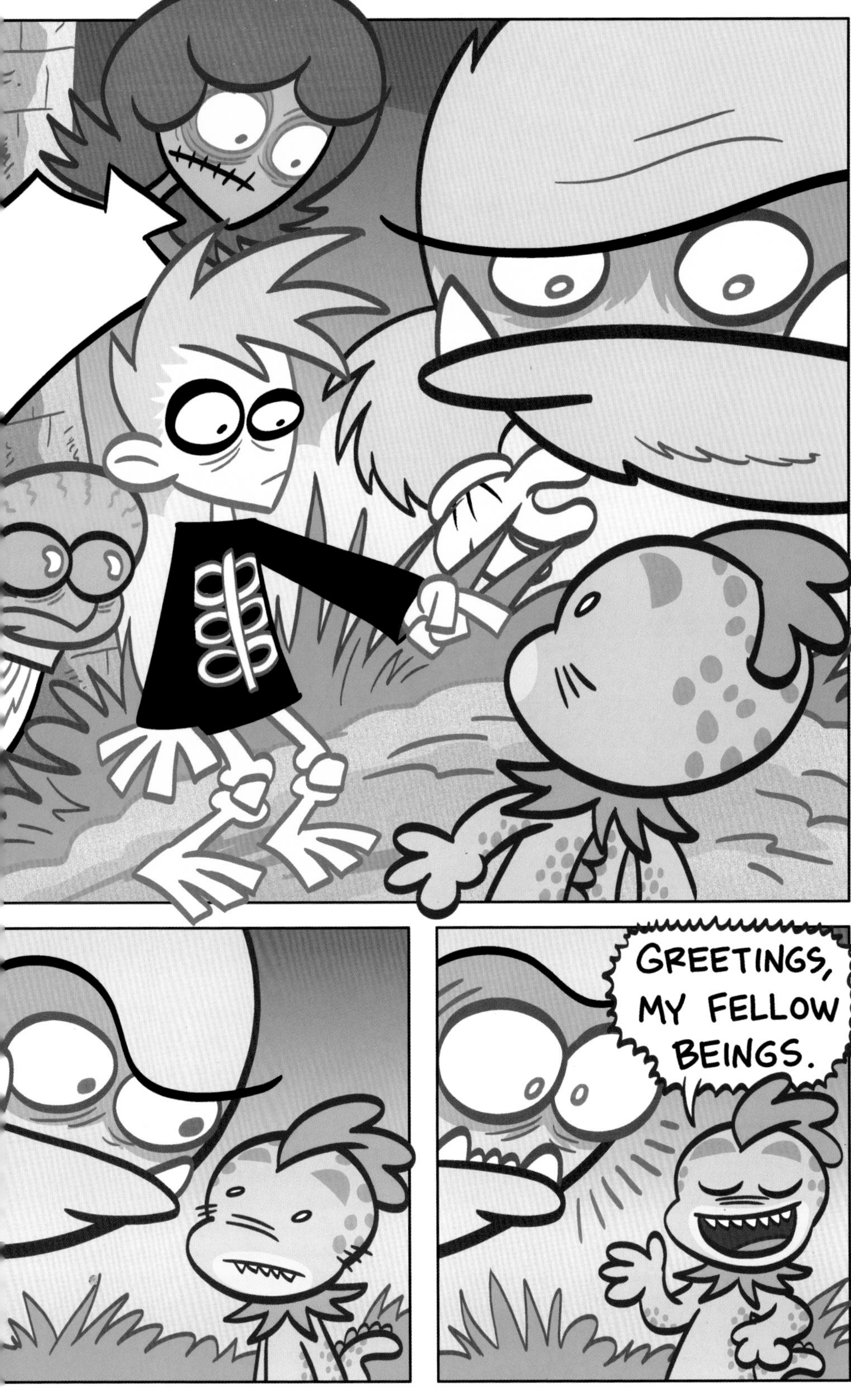
GREETINGS, MY FELLOW BEINGS.

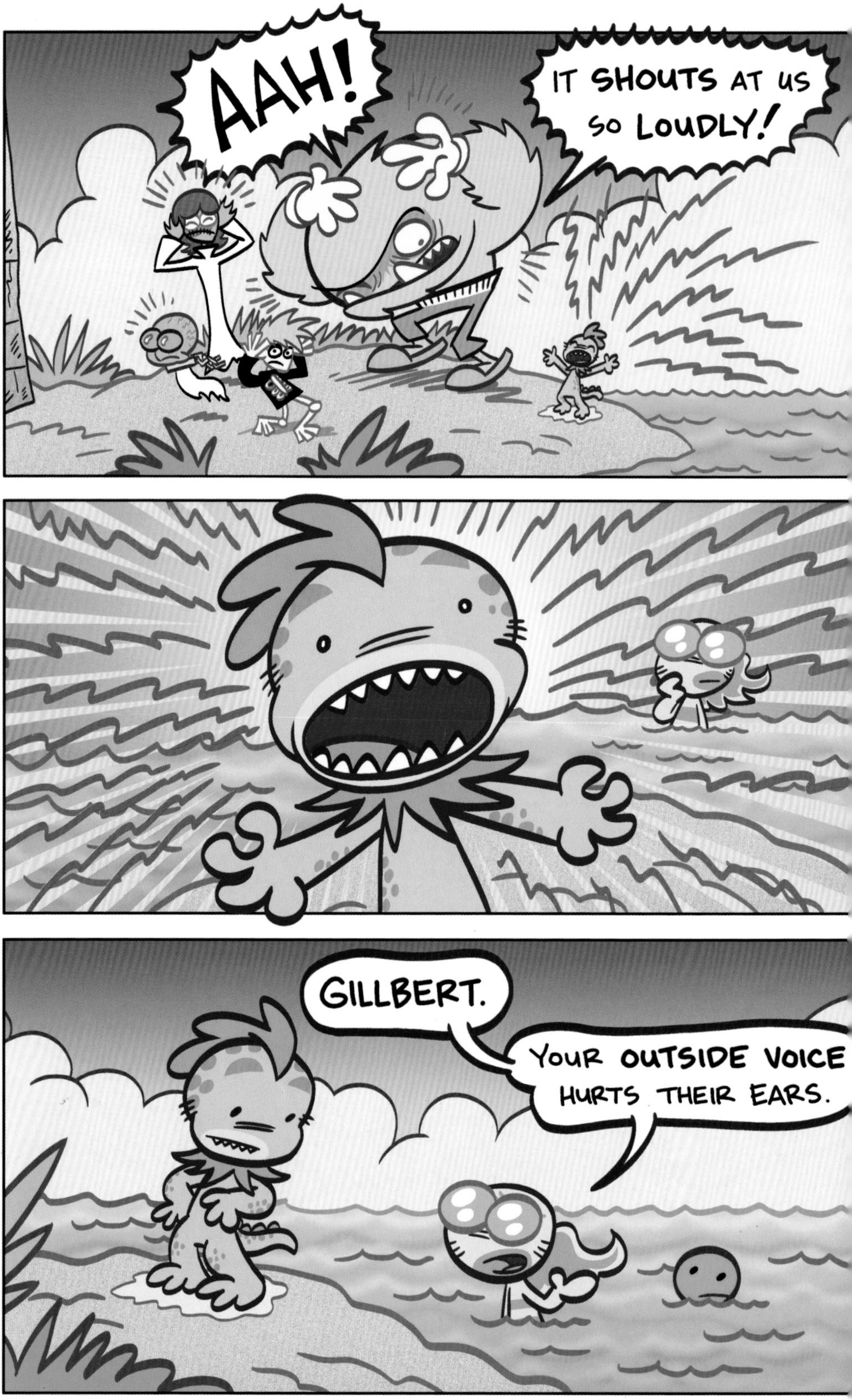
AAH!
IT SHOUTS AT US SO LOUDLY!
GILLBERT.
YOUR OUTSIDE VOICE HURTS THEIR EARS.

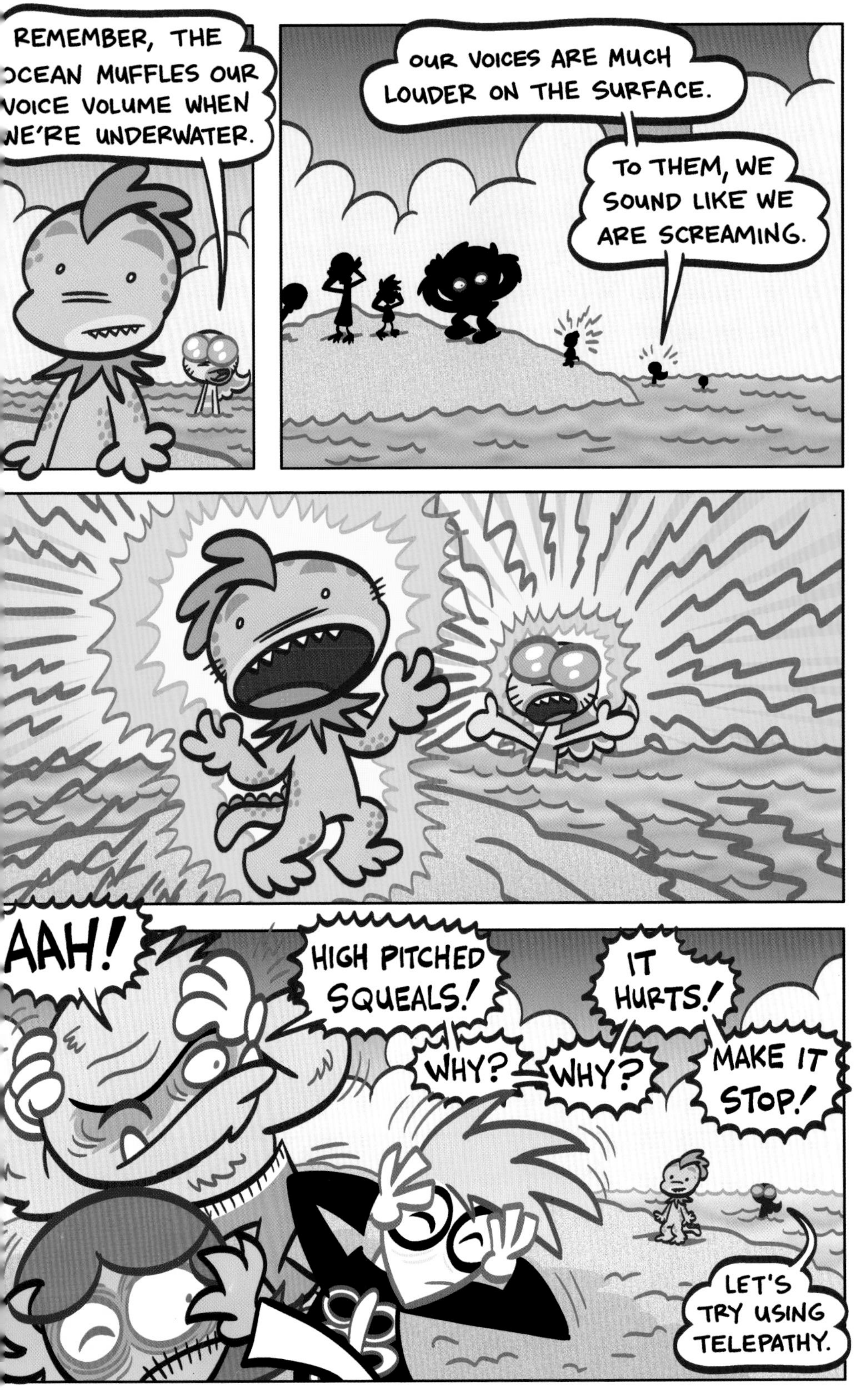
REMEMBER, THE OCEAN MUFFLES OUR VOICE VOLUME WHEN WE'RE UNDERWATER.
OUR VOICES ARE MUCH LOUDER ON THE SURFACE.
TO THEM, WE SOUND LIKE WE ARE SCREAMING.
AAH!
HIGH PITCHED SQUEALS!
WHY?
IT HURTS!
WHY?
MAKE IT STOP!
LET'S TRY USING TELEPATHY.

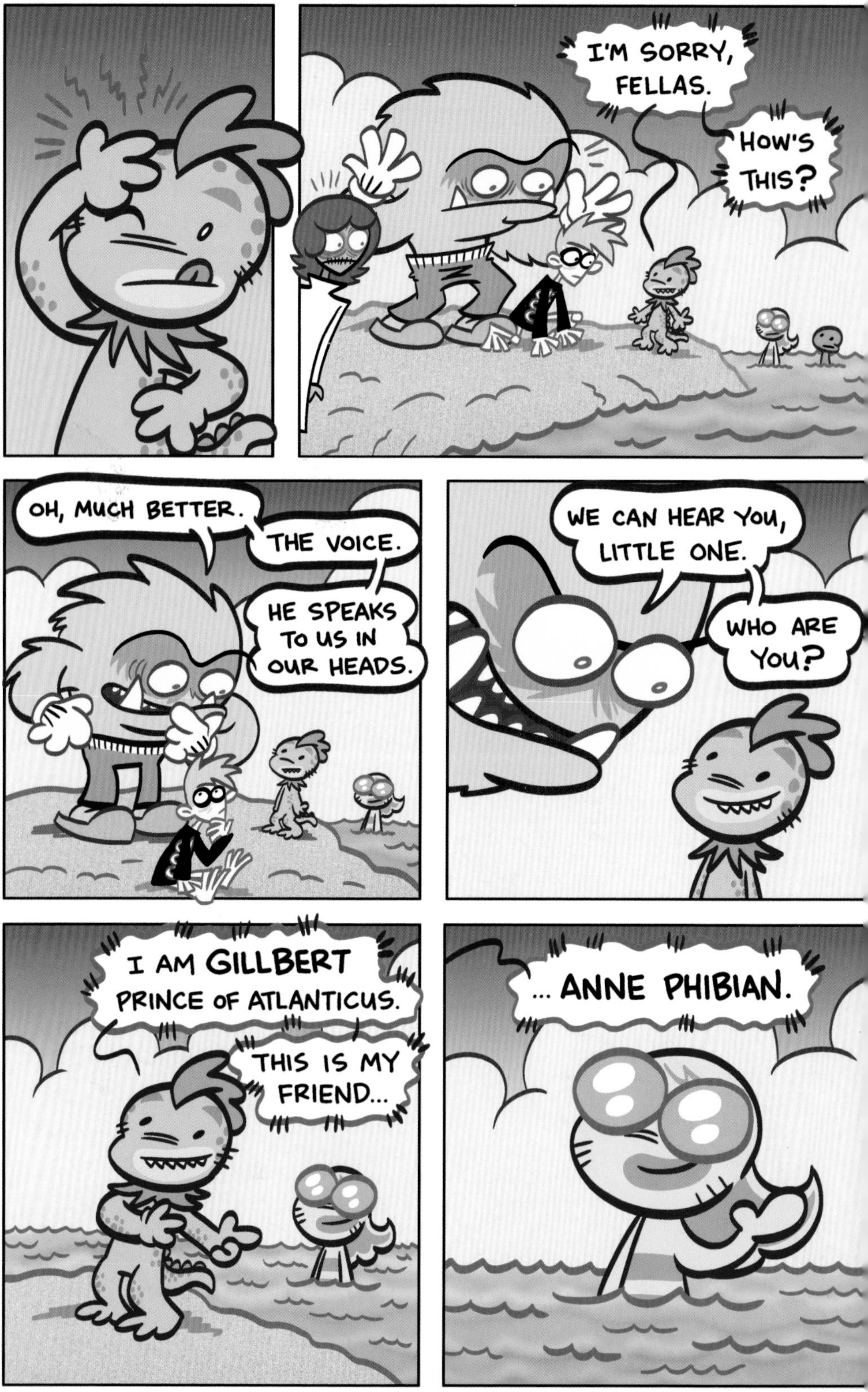

I'M SORRY, FELLAS.
HOW'S THIS?
OH, MUCH BETTER.
THE VOICE.
HE SPEAKS TO US IN OUR HEADS.
WE CAN HEAR YOU, LITTLE ONE.
WHO ARE YOU?
I AM GILLBERT PRINCE OF ATLANTICUS.
THIS IS MY FRIEND...
... ANNE PHIBIAN.

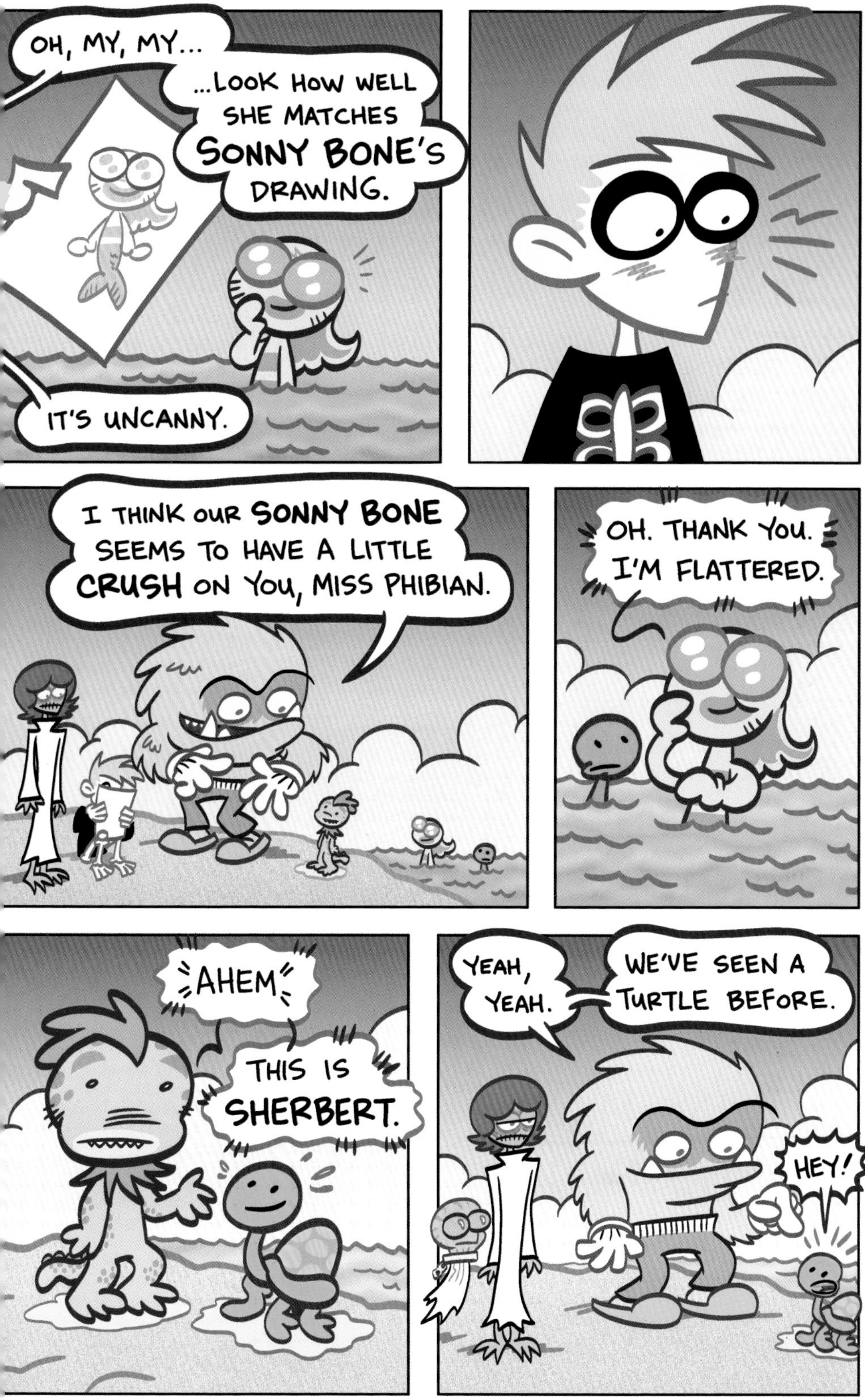
OH, MY, MY...
...LOOK HOW WELL SHE MATCHES SONNY BONE'S DRAWING.
IT'S UNCANNY.
I THINK OUR SONNY BONE SEEMS TO HAVE A LITTLE CRUSH ON YOU, MISS PHIBIAN.
OH. THANK YOU. I'M FLATTERED.
AHEM
THIS IS SHERBERT.
YEAH, YEAH.
WE'VE SEEN A TURTLE BEFORE.
HEY!

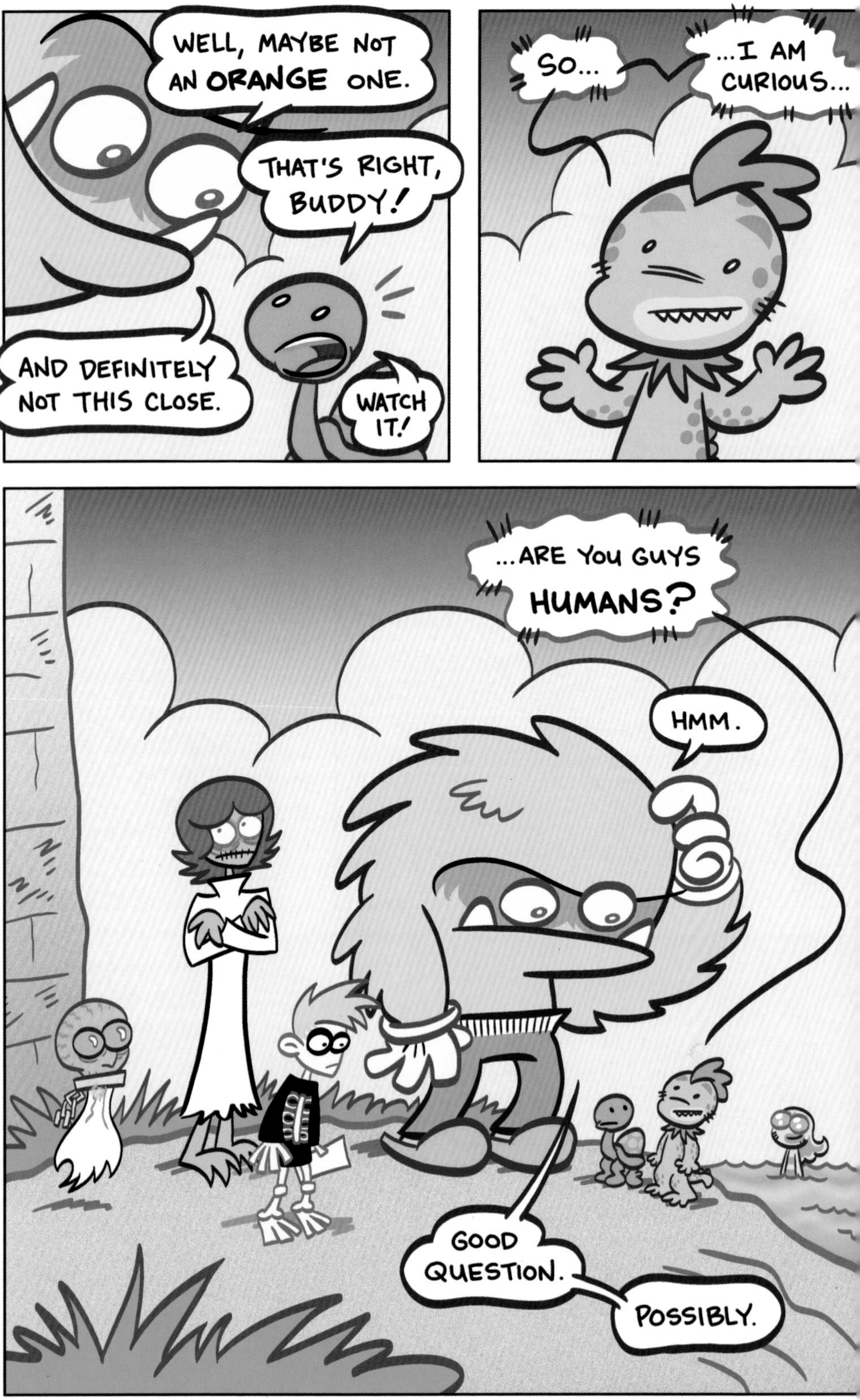

WELL, MAYBE NOT AN ORANGE ONE.
THAT'S RIGHT, BUDDY!
AND DEFINITELY NOT THIS CLOSE.
WATCH IT!
SO...
...I AM CURIOUS...
...ARE YOU GUYS HUMANS?
HMM.
GOOD QUESTION.
POSSIBLY.

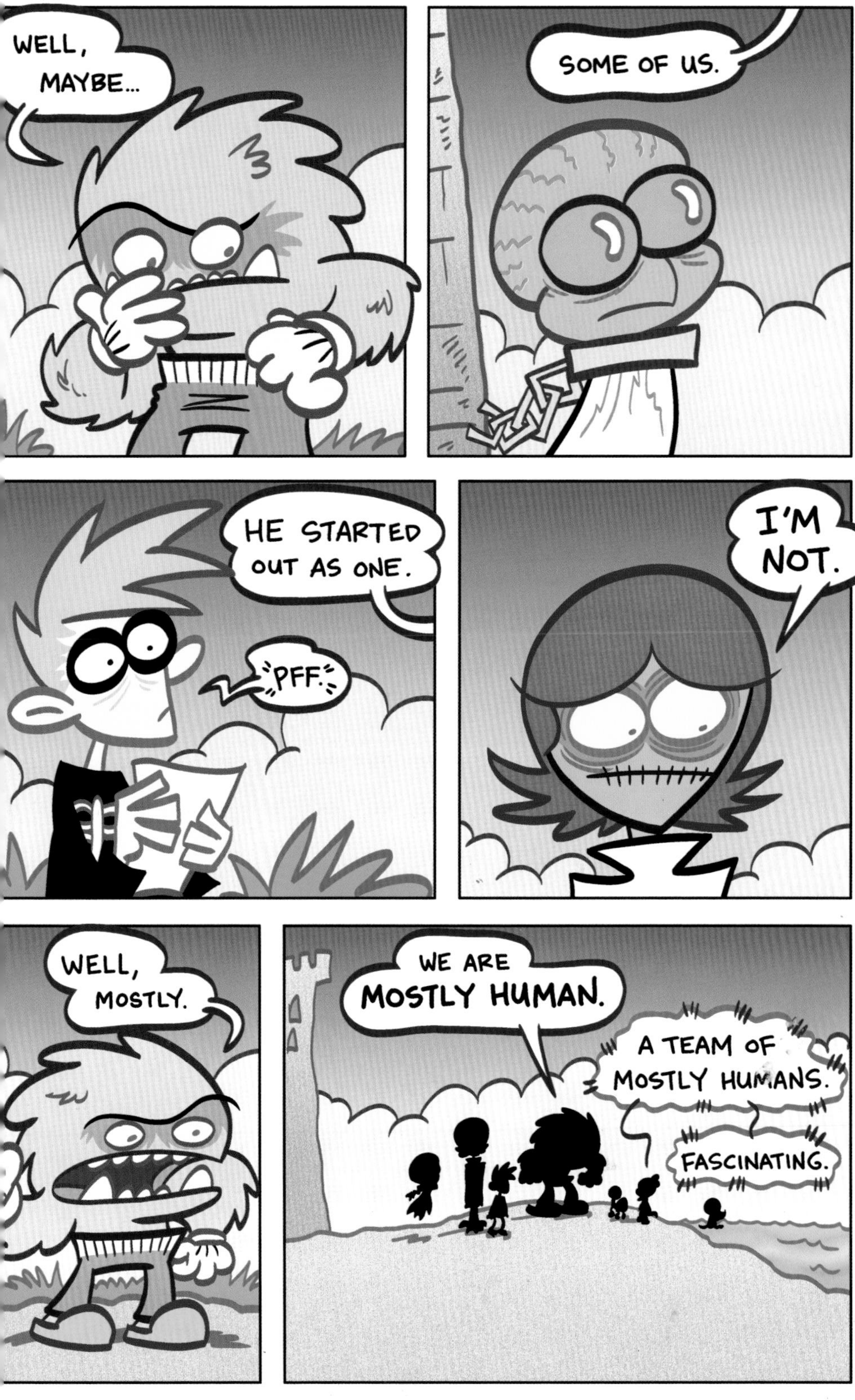
WELL,
MAYBE...
SOME OF US.
HE STARTED OUT AS ONE.
PFF.
I'M NOT.
WELL, MOSTLY.
WE ARE MOSTLY HUMAN.
A TEAM OF MOSTLY HUMANS.
FASCINATING.

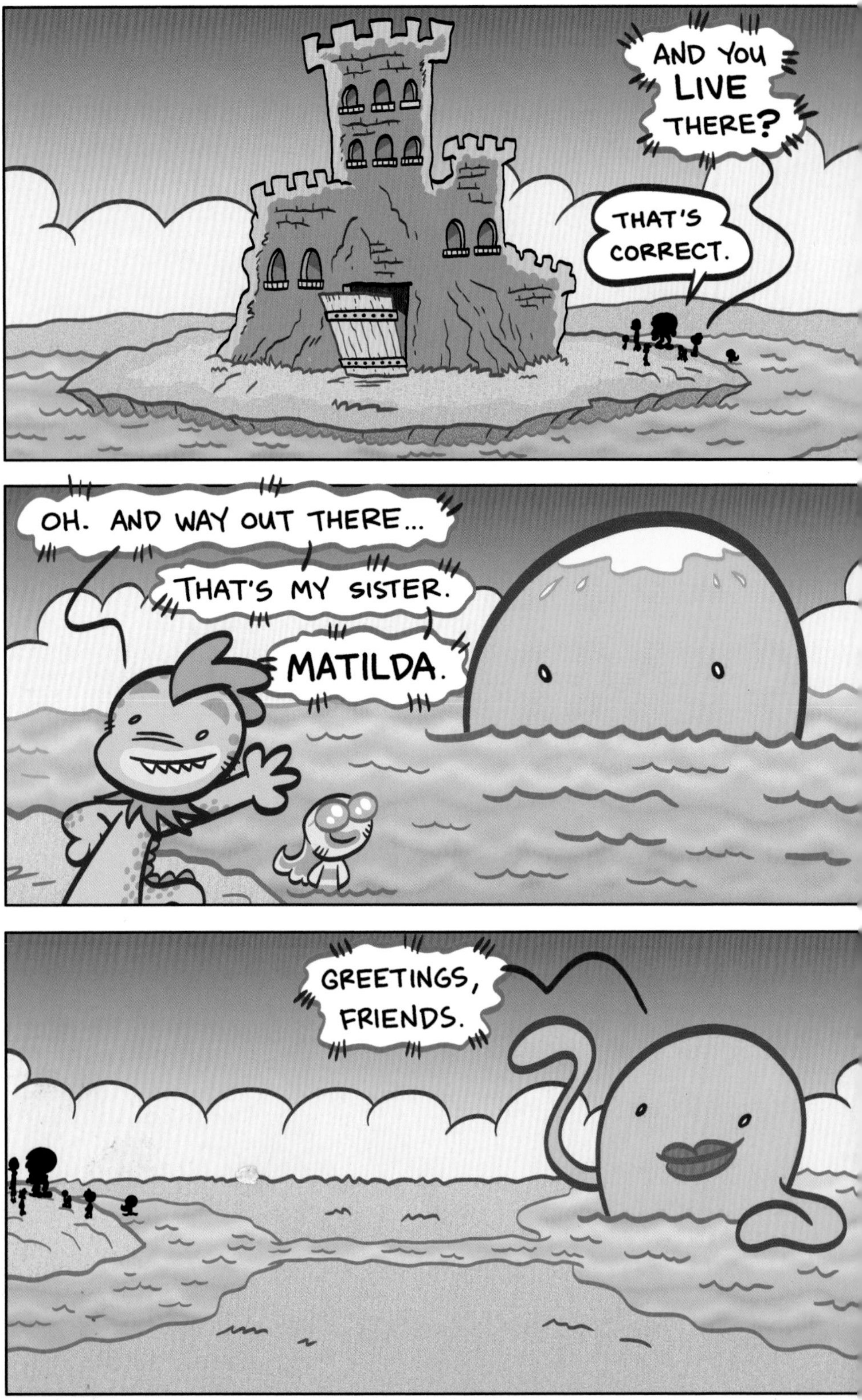
AND YOU LIVE THERE?
THAT'S CORRECT.
OH. AND WAY OUT THERE...
THAT'S MY SISTER.
MATILDA.
GREETINGS, FRIENDS.

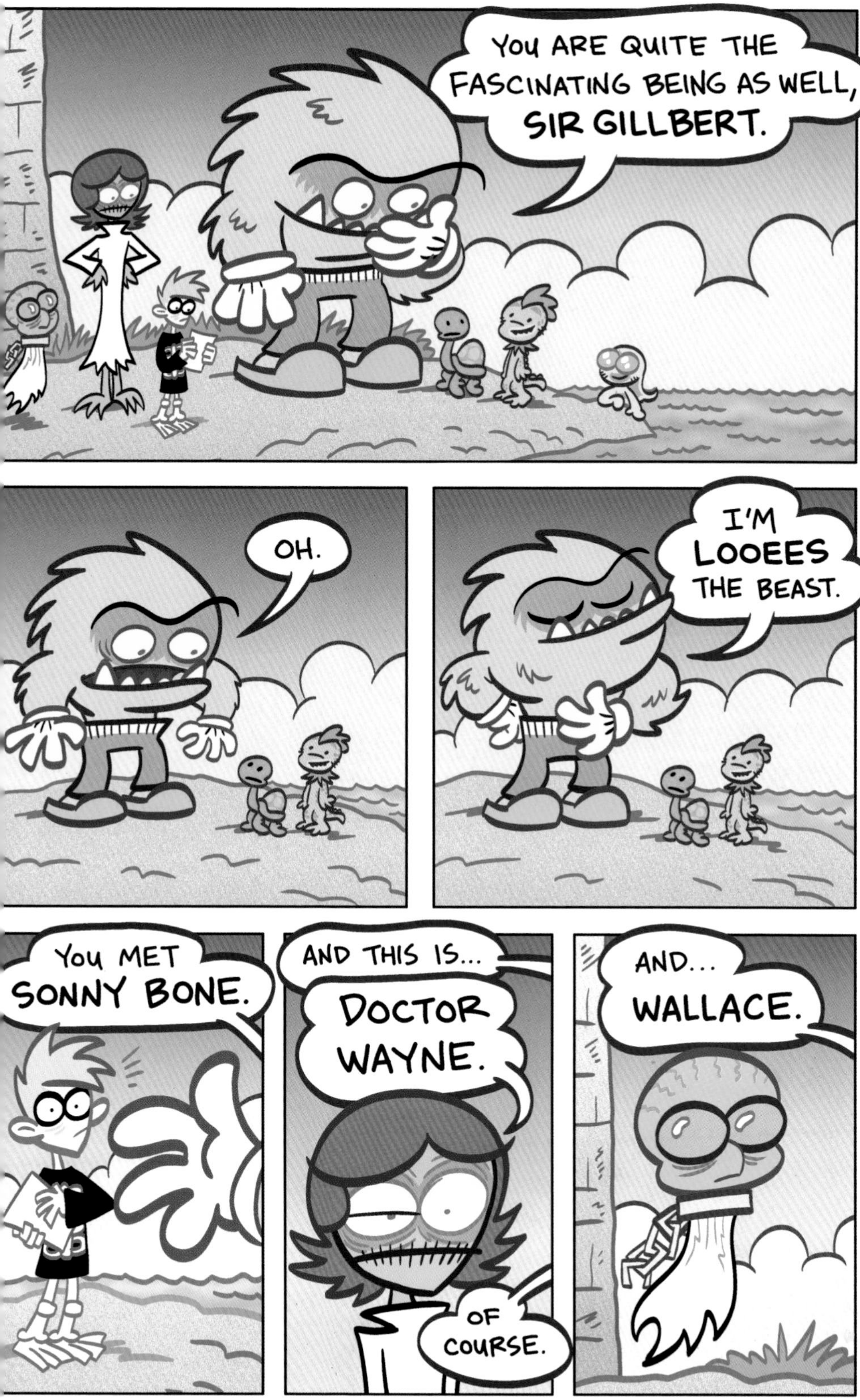

YOU ARE QUITE THE FASCINATING BEING AS WELL, SIR GILLBERT.
OH.
I'M LOOEES THE BEAST.
YOU MET SONNY BONE.
AND THIS IS...
DOCTOR WAYNE.
OF COURSE.
AND...
WALLACE.

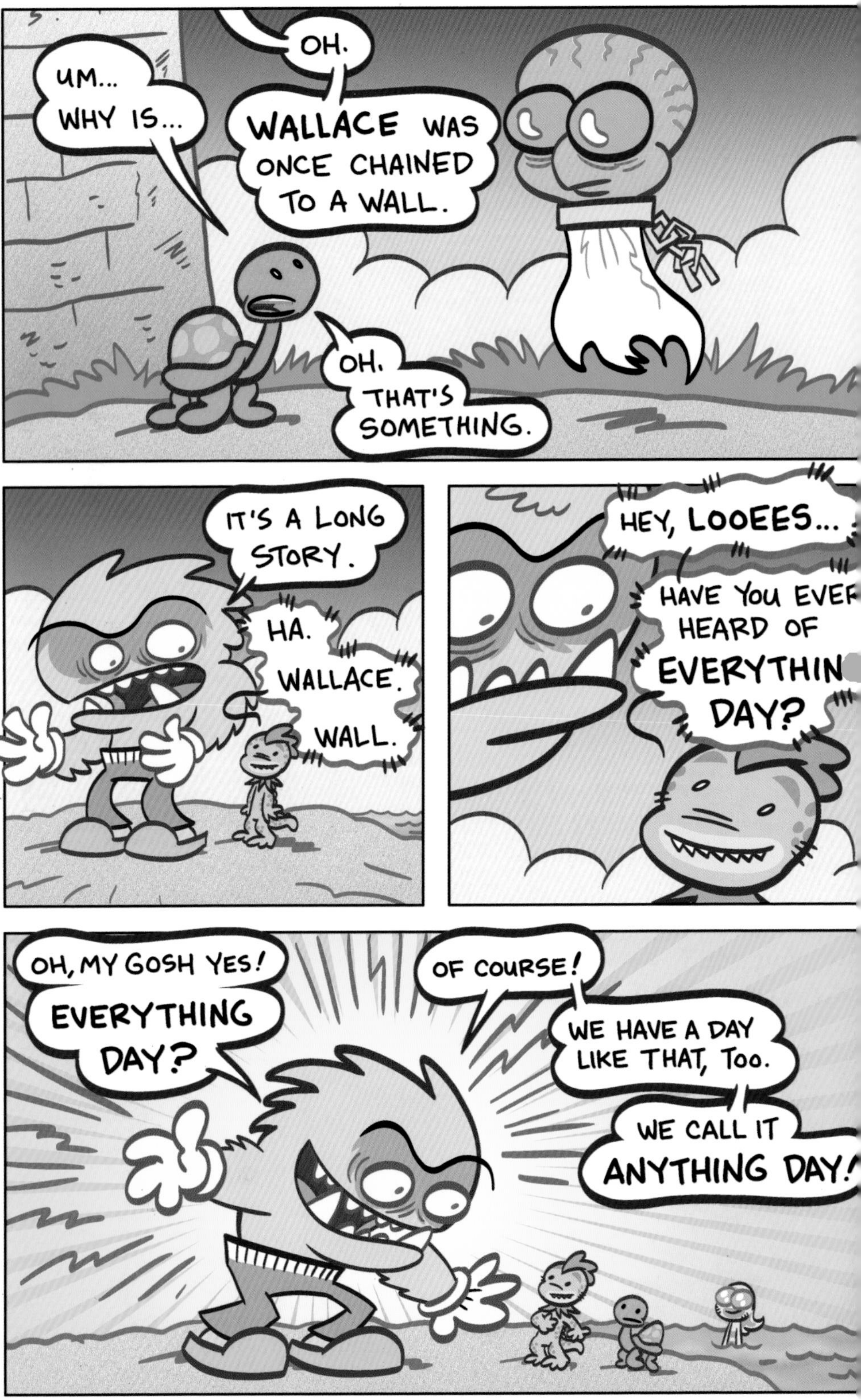
UM... WHY IS...
OH.
WALLACE WAS ONCE CHAINED TO A WALL.
OH. THAT'S SOMETHING.
IT'S A LONG STORY.
HA. WALLACE. WALL.
HEY, LOOEES...
HAVE YOU EVER HEARD OF EVERYTHIN DAY?
OH, MY GOSH YES! EVERYTHING DAY?
OF COURSE!
WE HAVE A DAY LIKE THAT, TOO.
WE CALL IT ANYTHING DAY!

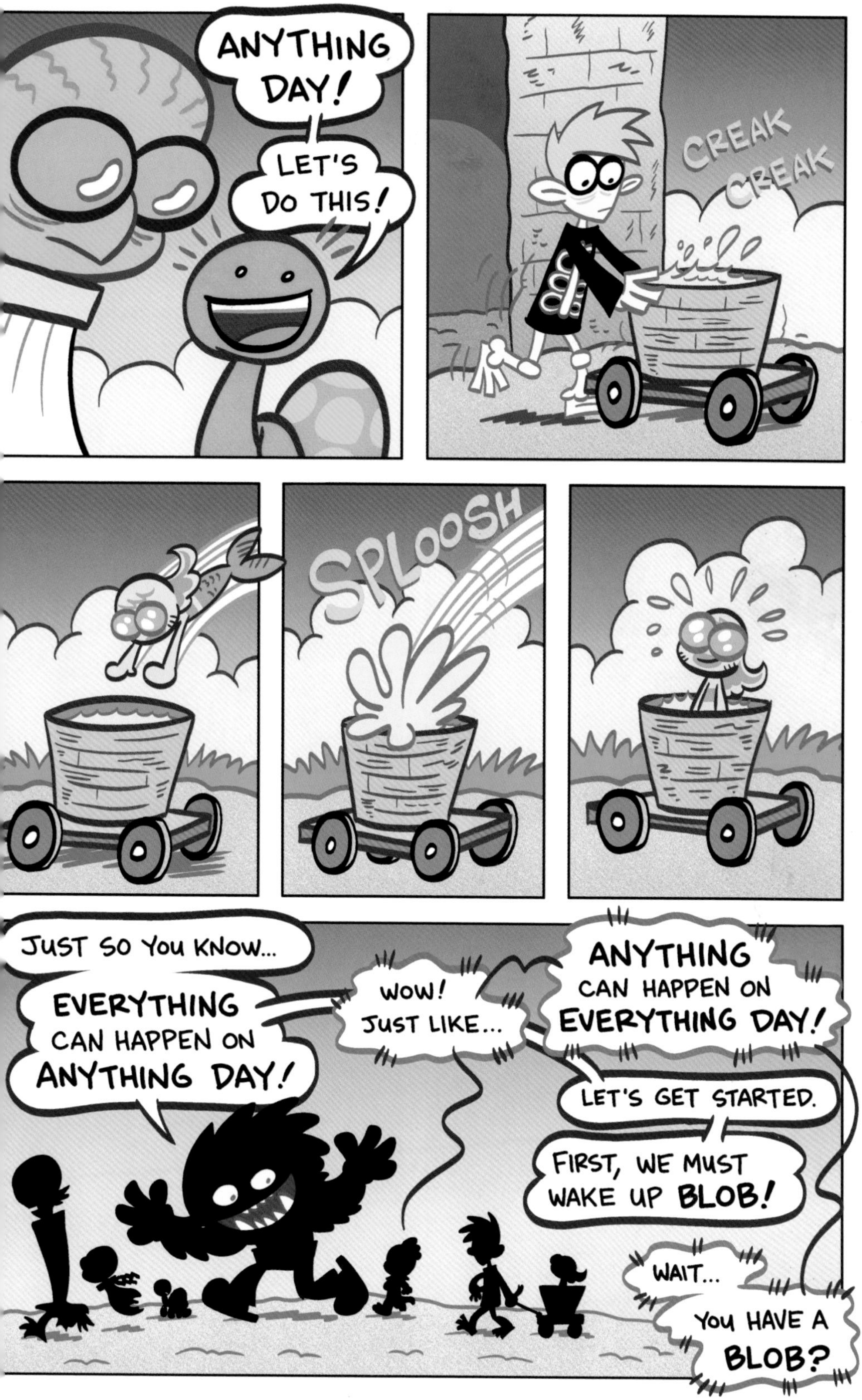
ANYTHING DAY!
LET'S DO THIS!
CREAK CREAK
SPLOOSH
JUST SO YOU KNOW...
EVERYTHING CAN HAPPEN ON ANYTHING DAY!
WOW! JUST LIKE...
ANYTHING CAN HAPPEN ON EVERYTHING DAY!
LET'S GET STARTED.
FIRST, WE MUST WAKE UP BLOB!
WAIT...
YOU HAVE A BLOB?

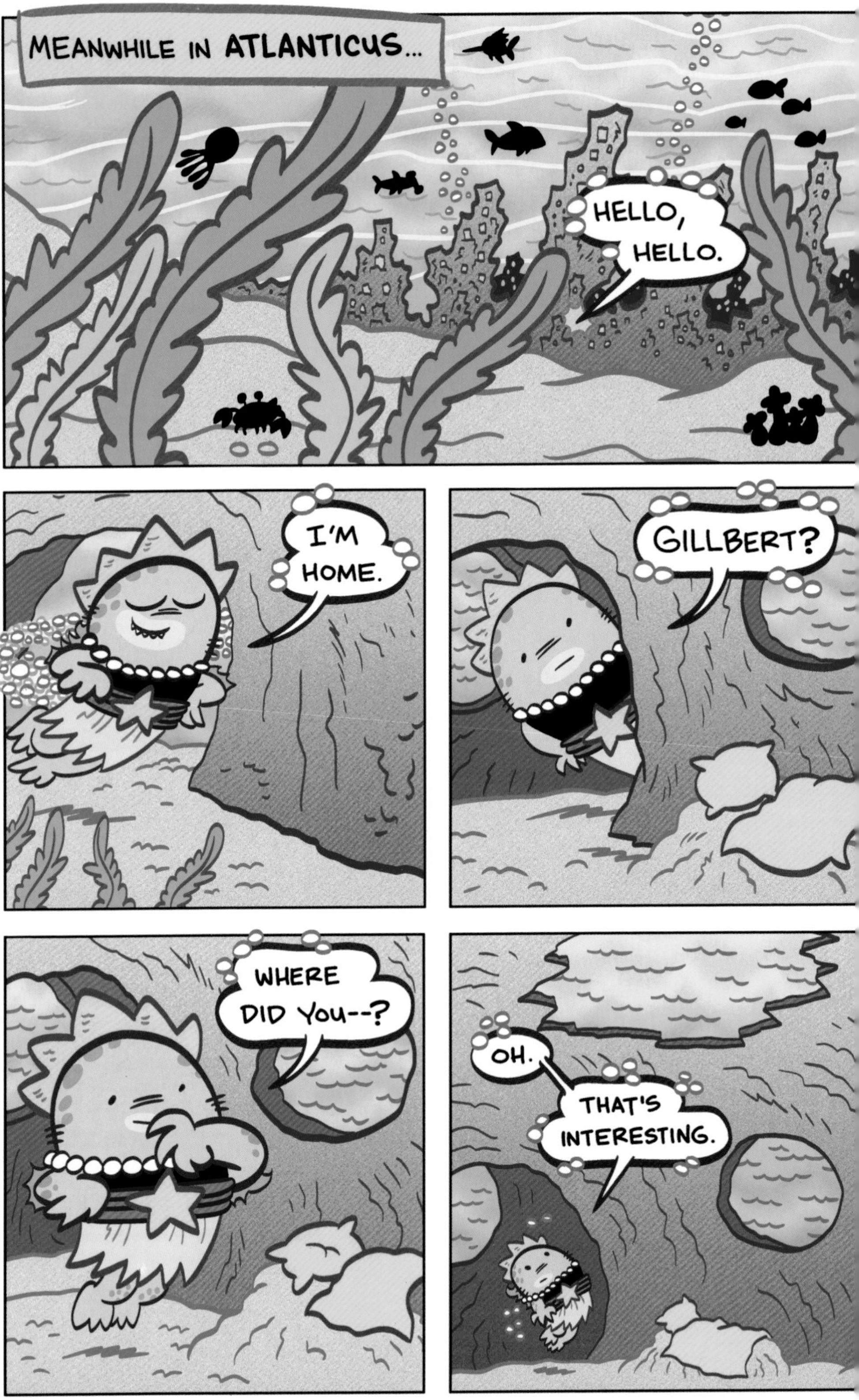
MEANWHILE IN ATLANTICUS...
HELLO, HELLO.
I'M HOME.
GILLBERT?
WHERE DID YOU--?
OH.
THAT'S INTERESTING.

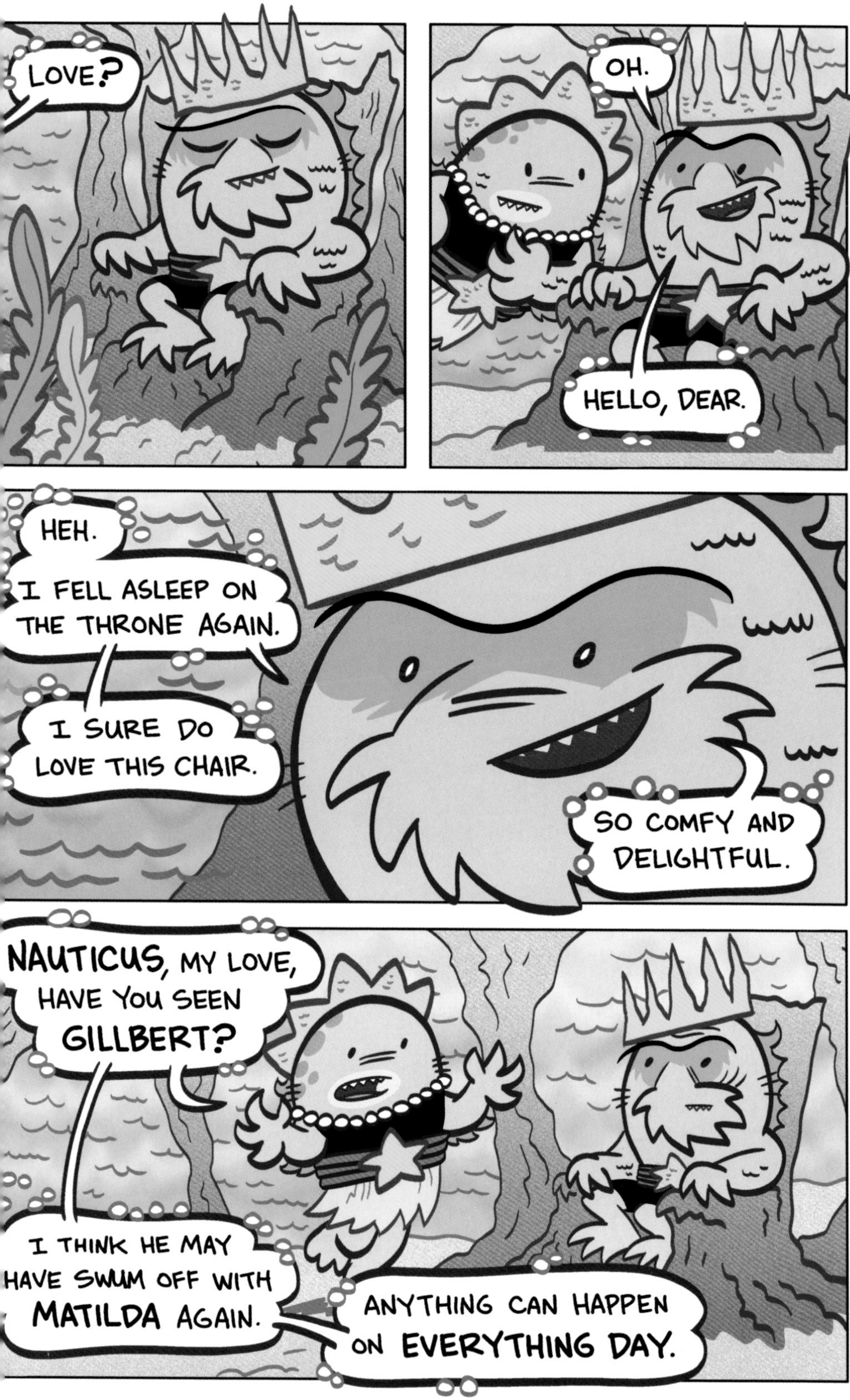

LOVE?
OH.
HELLO, DEAR.
HEH.
I FELL ASLEEP ON THE THRONE AGAIN.
I SURE DO LOVE THIS CHAIR.
SO COMFY AND DELIGHTFUL.
NAUTICUS, MY LOVE, HAVE YOU SEEN GILLBERT?
I THINK HE MAY HAVE SWUM OFF WITH MATILDA AGAIN.
ANYTHING CAN HAPPEN ON EVERYTHING DAY.

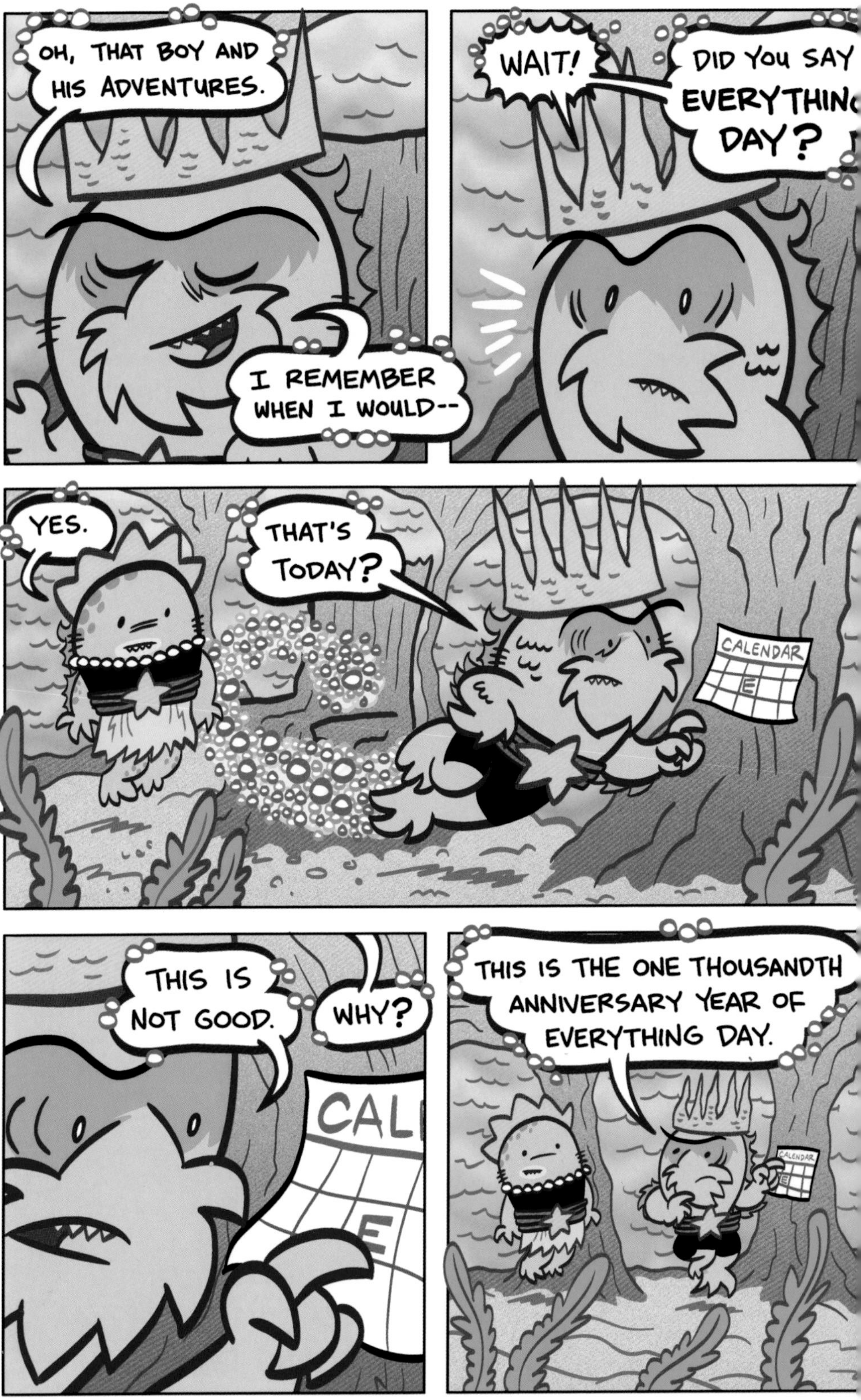
OH, THAT BOY AND HIS ADVENTURES.
I REMEMBER WHEN I WOULD--
WAIT!
DID YOU SAY EVERYTHING DAY?
YES.
THAT'S TODAY?
CALENDAR
THIS IS NOT GOOD.
WHY?
THIS IS THE ONE THOUSANDTH ANNIVERSARY YEAR OF EVERYTHING DAY.
CALENDAR

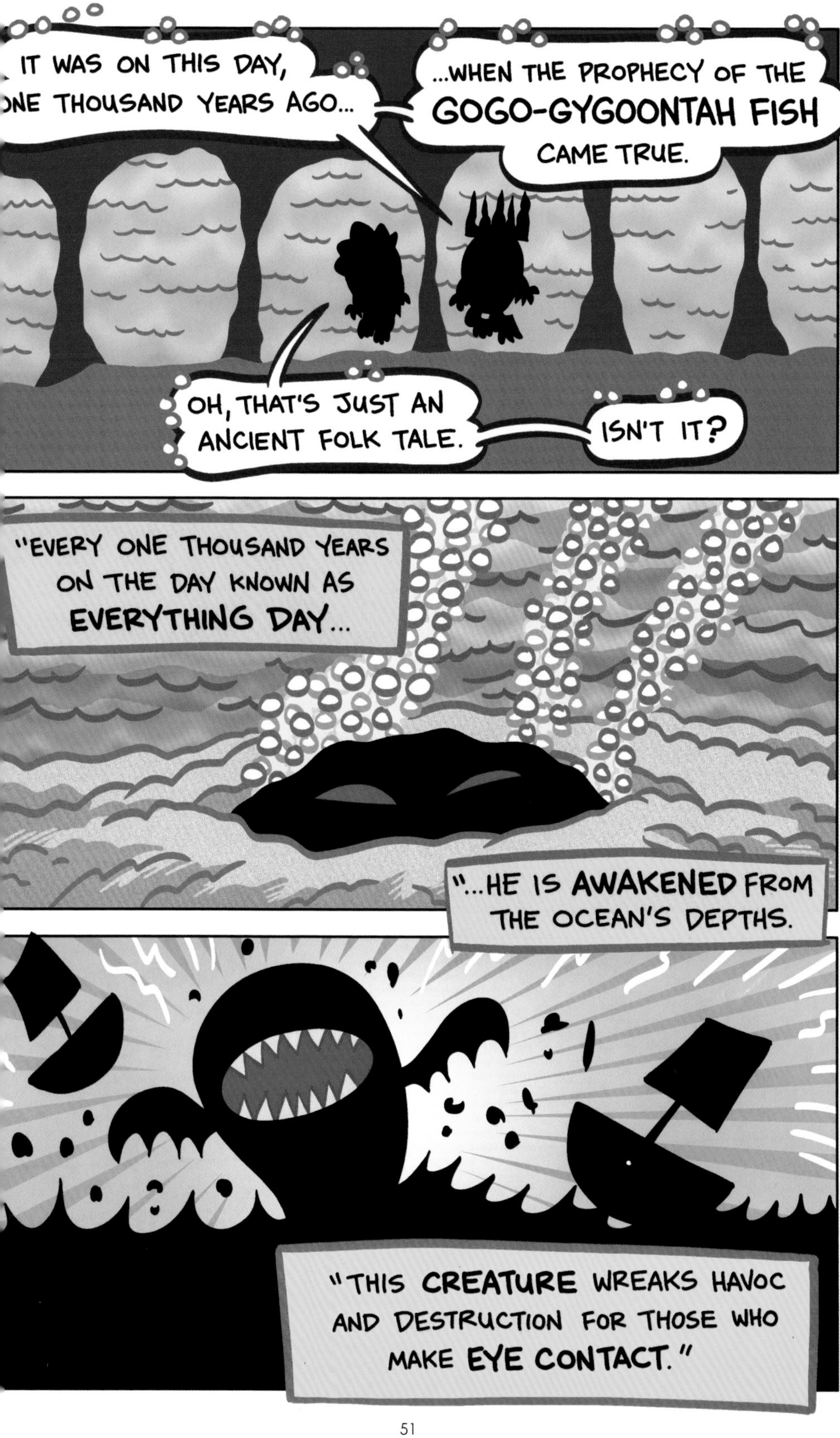
IT WAS ON THIS DAY, ONE THOUSAND YEARS AGO...
...WHEN THE PROPHECY OF THE GOGO-GYGOONTAH FISH CAME TRUE.
OH, THAT'S JUST AN ANCIENT FOLK TALE.
ISN'T IT?
"EVERY ONE THOUSAND YEARS ON THE DAY KNOWN AS EVERYTHING DAY...
"...HE IS AWAKENED FROM THE OCEAN'S DEPTHS.
"THIS CREATURE WREAKS HAVOC AND DESTRUCTION FOR THOSE WHO MAKE EYE CONTACT."

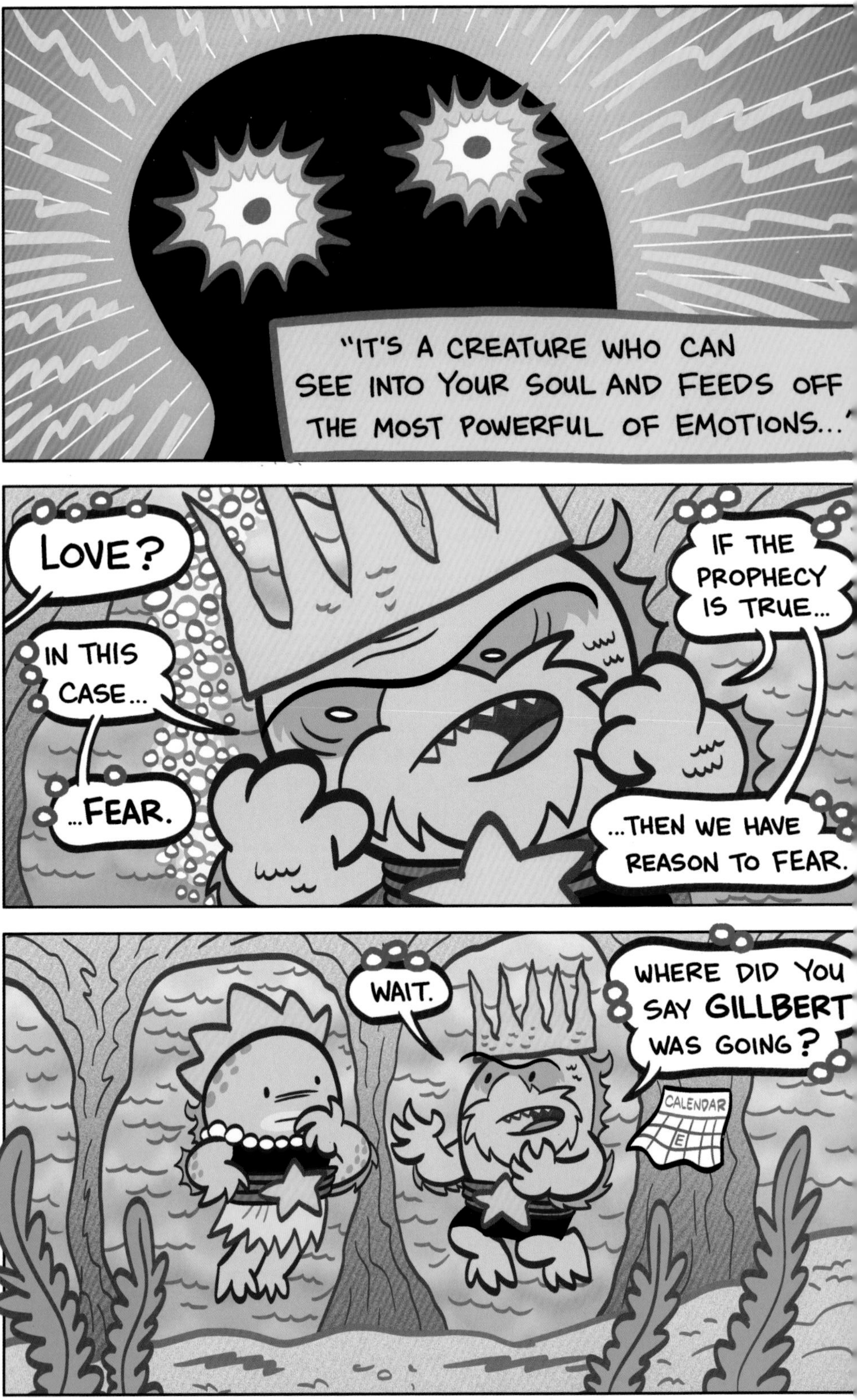
"IT'S A CREATURE WHO CAN SEE INTO YOUR SOUL AND FEEDS OFF THE MOST POWERFUL OF EMOTIONS..."
LOVE?
IN THIS CASE...
...FEAR.
IF THE PROPHECY IS TRUE...
...THEN WE HAVE REASON TO FEAR.
WAIT.
WHERE DID YOU SAY GILLBERT WAS GOING?
CALENDAR

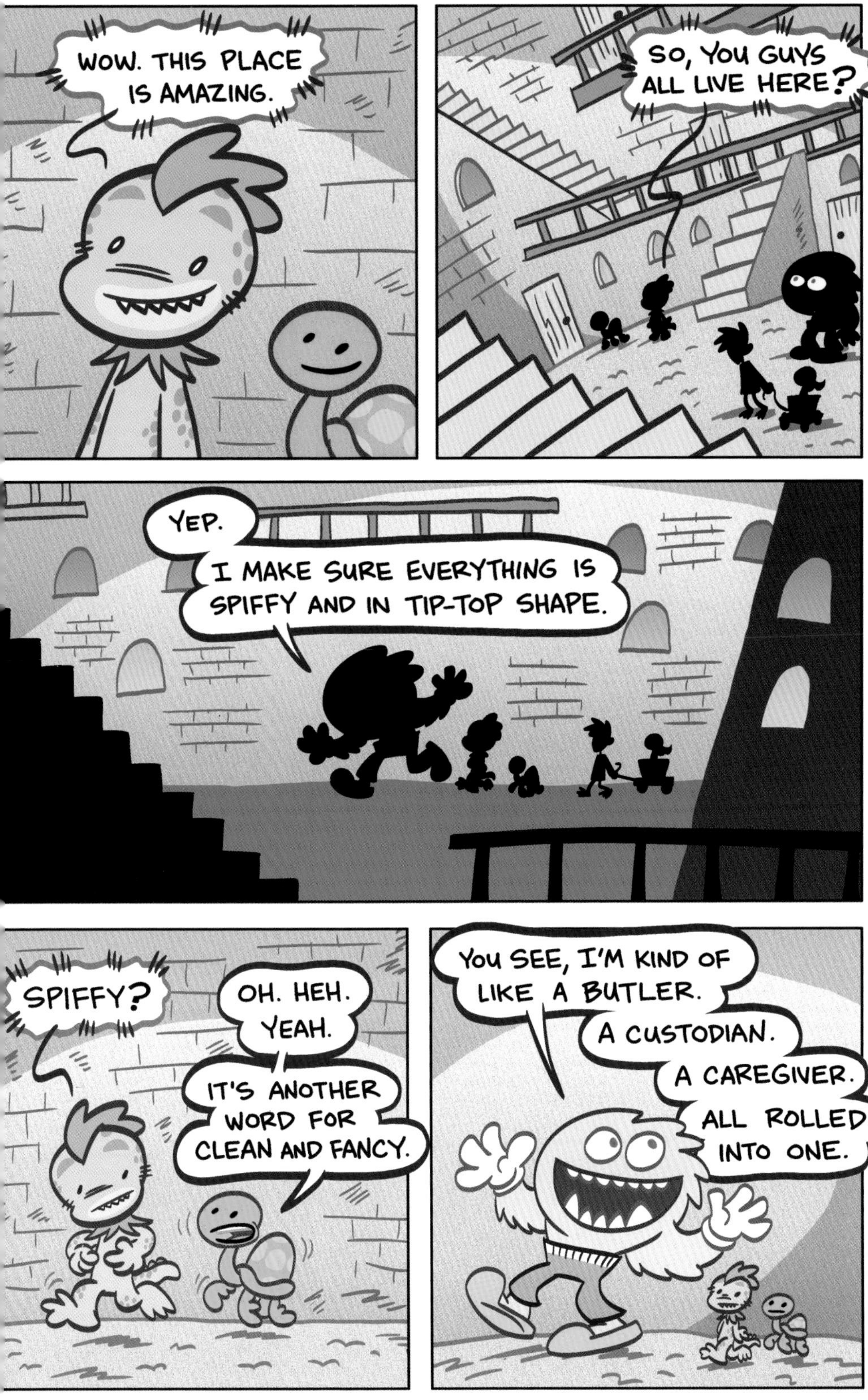
WOW. THIS PLACE IS AMAZING.
SO, YOU GUYS ALL LIVE HERE?
YEP.
I MAKE SURE EVERYTHING IS SPIFFY AND IN TIP-TOP SHAPE.
SPIFFY?
OH. HEH. YEAH.
IT'S ANOTHER WORD FOR CLEAN AND FANCY.
YOU SEE, I'M KIND OF LIKE A BUTLER.
A CUSTODIAN.
A CAREGIVER.
ALL ROLLED INTO ONE.

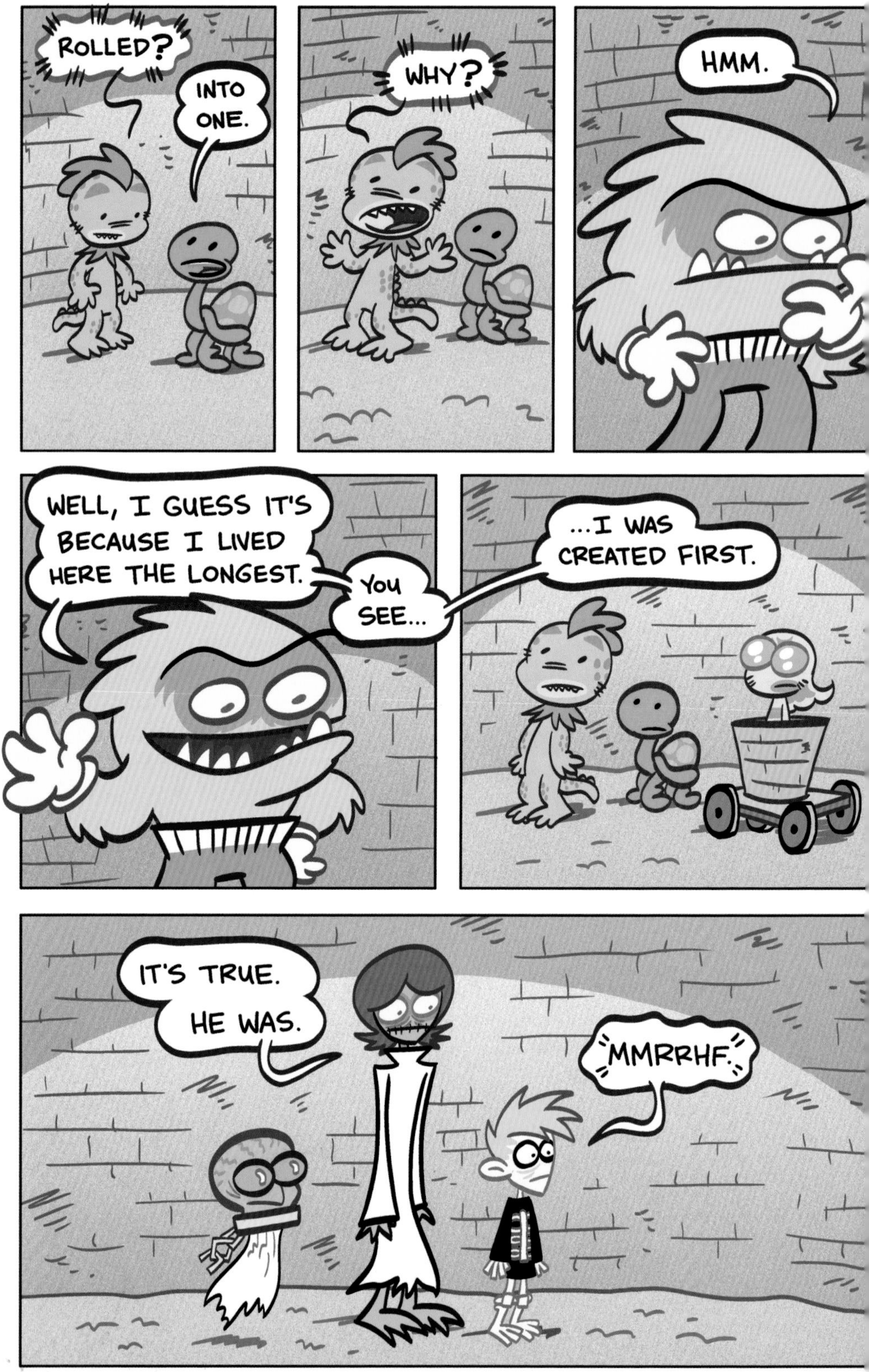

ROLLED?
INTO ONE.
WHY?
HMM.
WELL, I GUESS IT'S BECAUSE I LIVED HERE THE LONGEST.
YOU SEE...
...I WAS CREATED FIRST.
IT'S TRUE.
HE WAS.
MMRRHF.

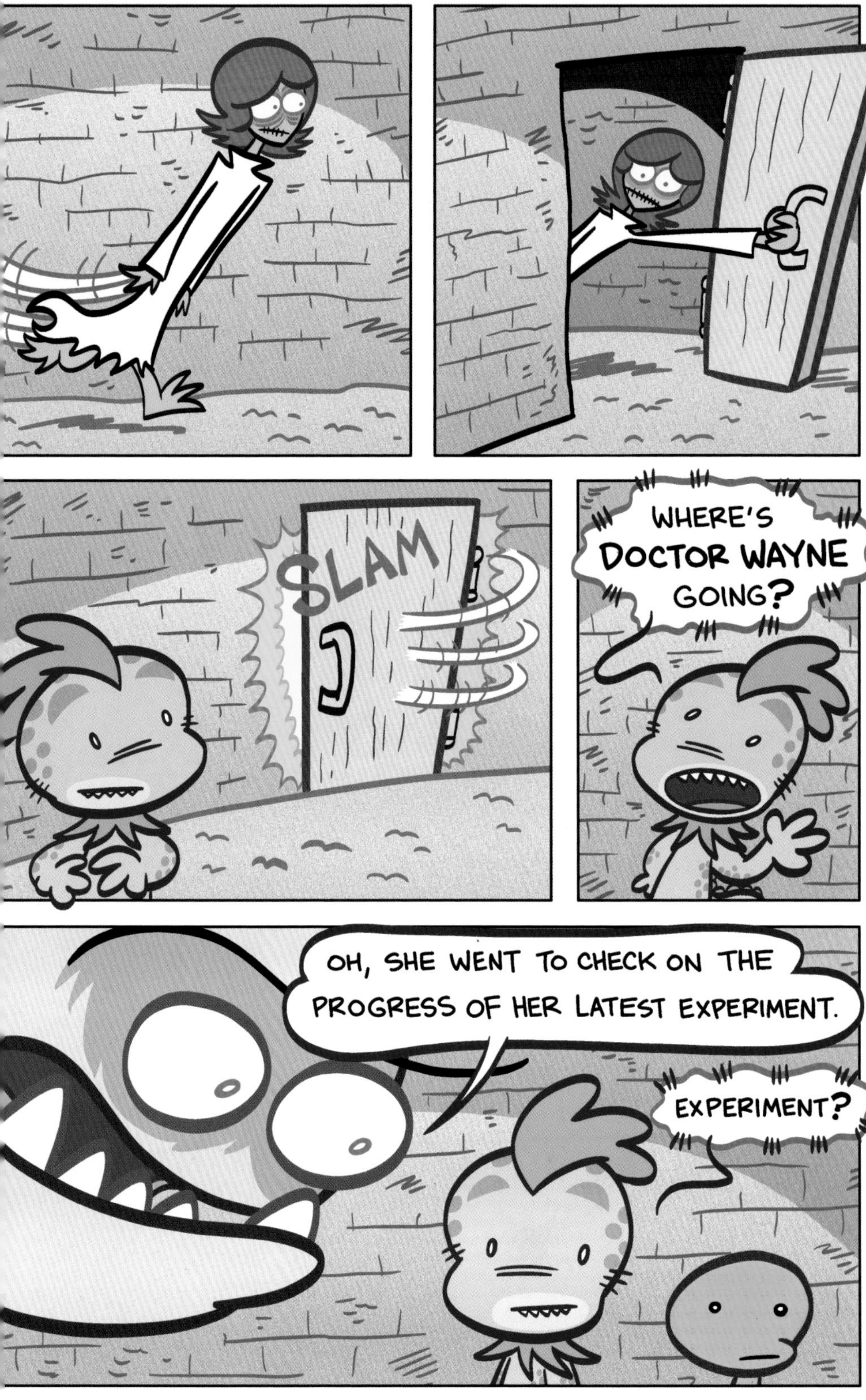
SLAM
WHERE'S DOCTOR WAYNE GOING?
OH, SHE WENT TO CHECK ON THE PROGRESS OF HER LATEST EXPERIMENT.
EXPERIMENT?

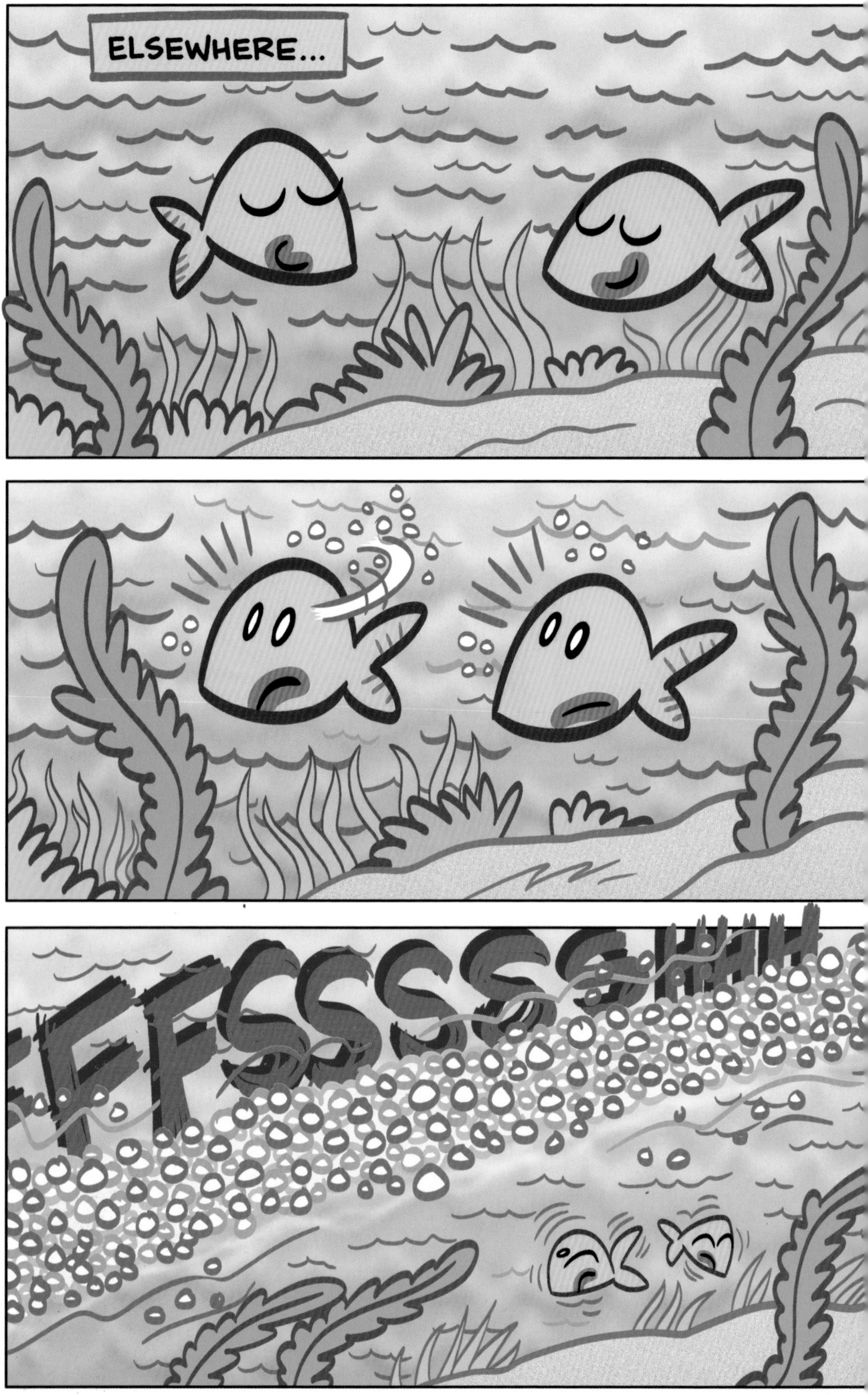
ELSEWHERE...
FFSSSSSHHHH

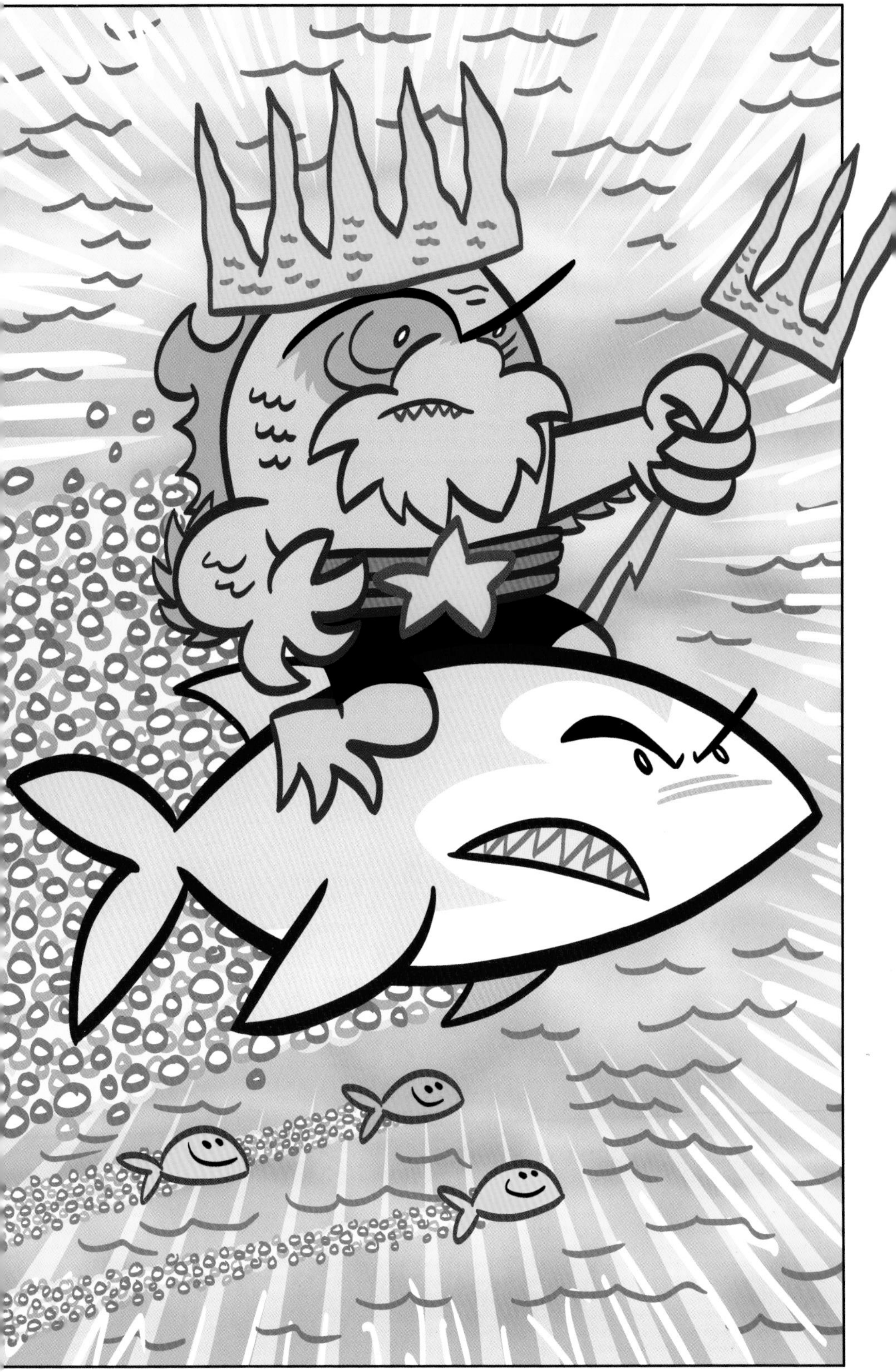

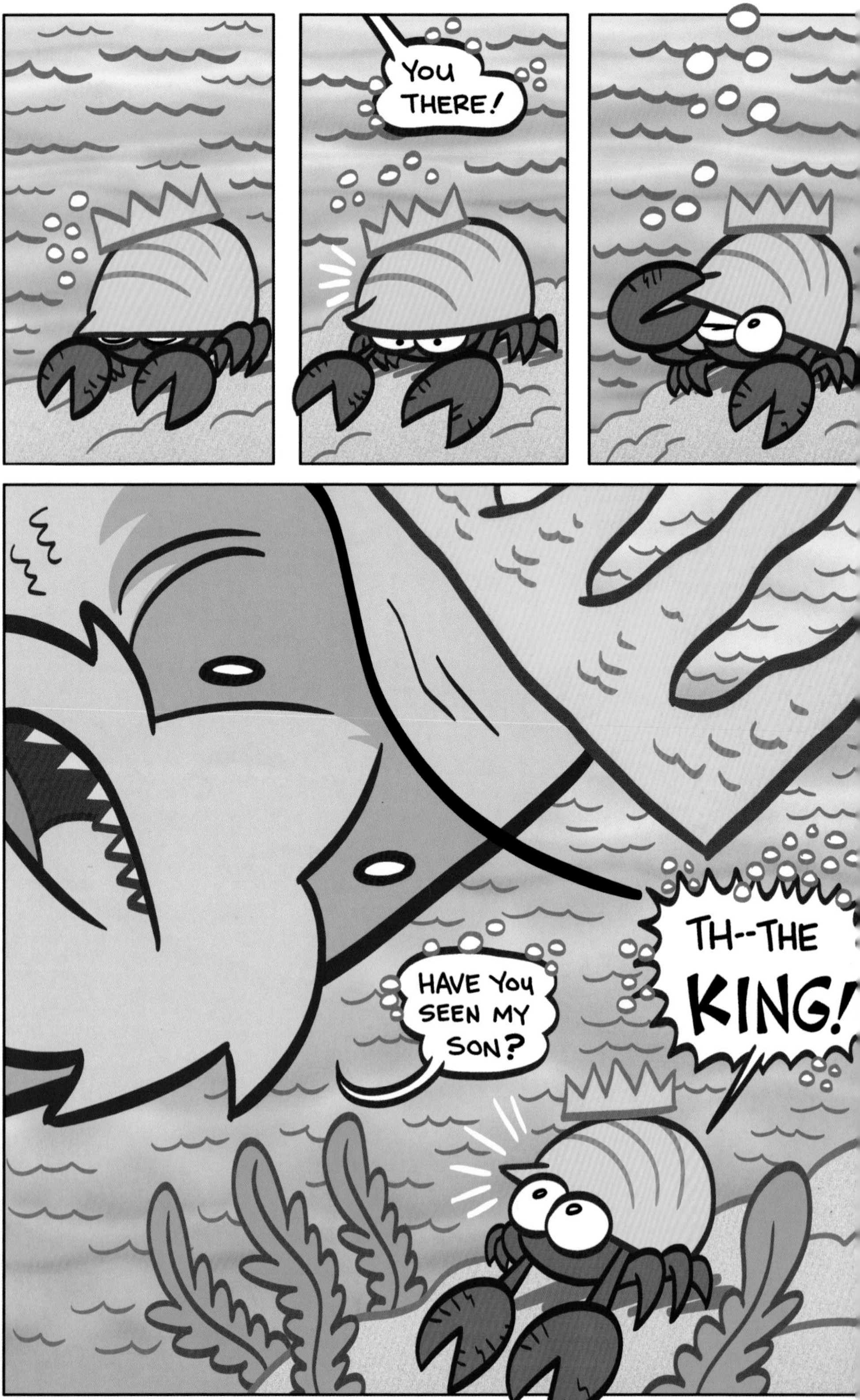
YOU THERE!
HAVE YOU SEEN MY SON?
TH--THE KING!

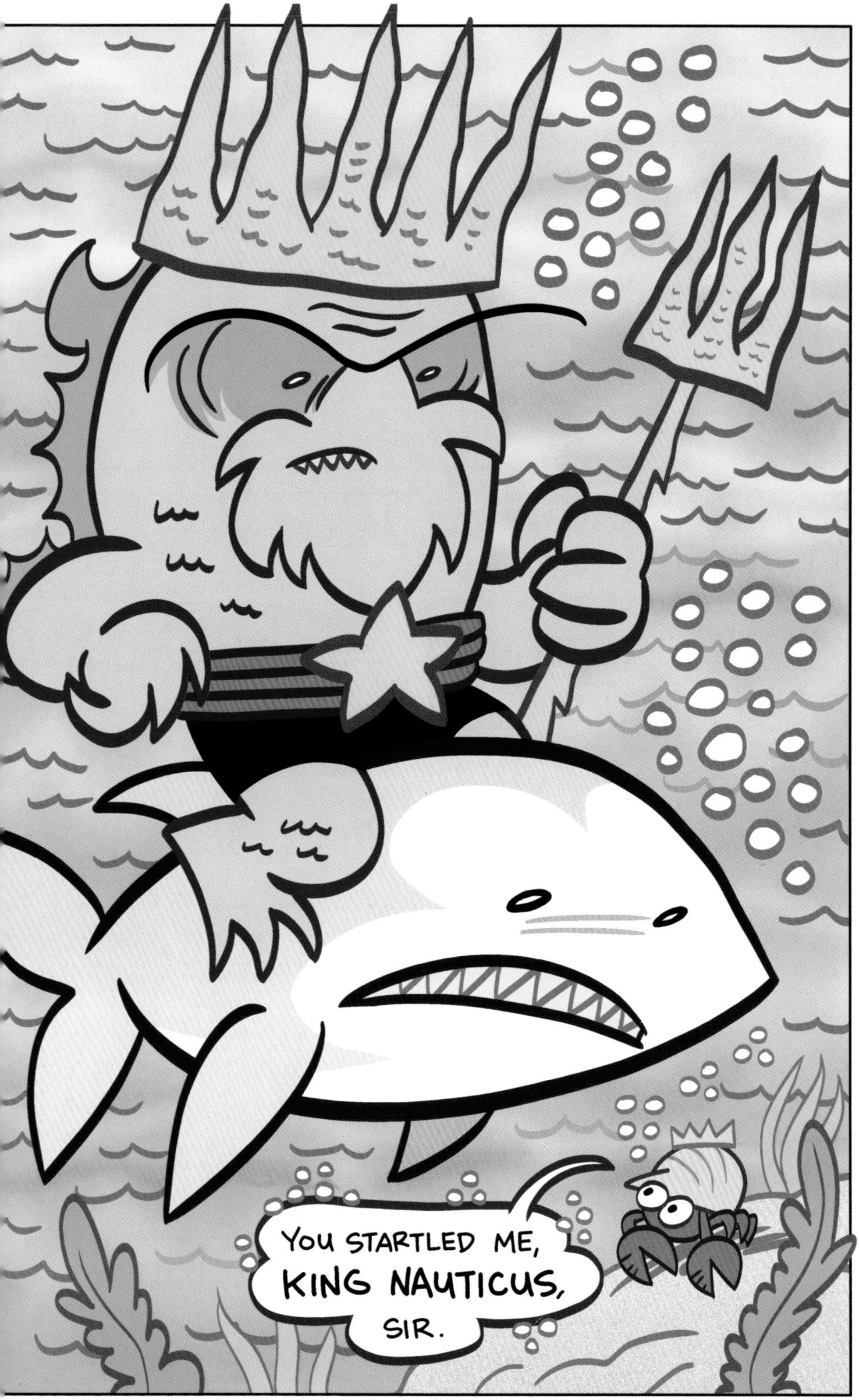
YOU STARTLED ME, KING NAUTICUS, SIR.

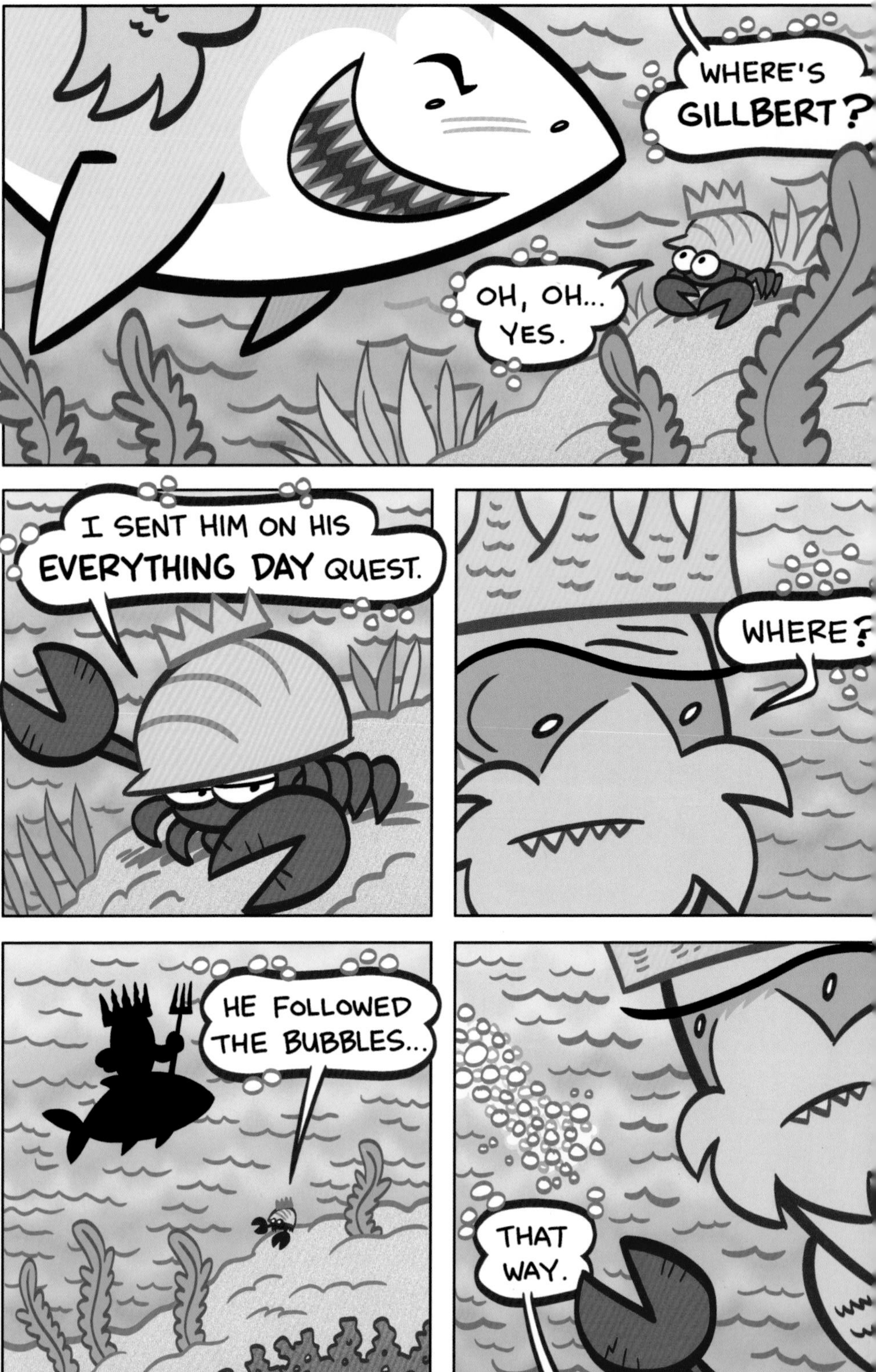
WHERE'S GILLBERT?
OH, OH... YES.
I SENT HIM ON HIS EVERYTHING DAY QUEST.
WHERE?
HE FOLLOWED THE BUBBLES...
THAT WAY.

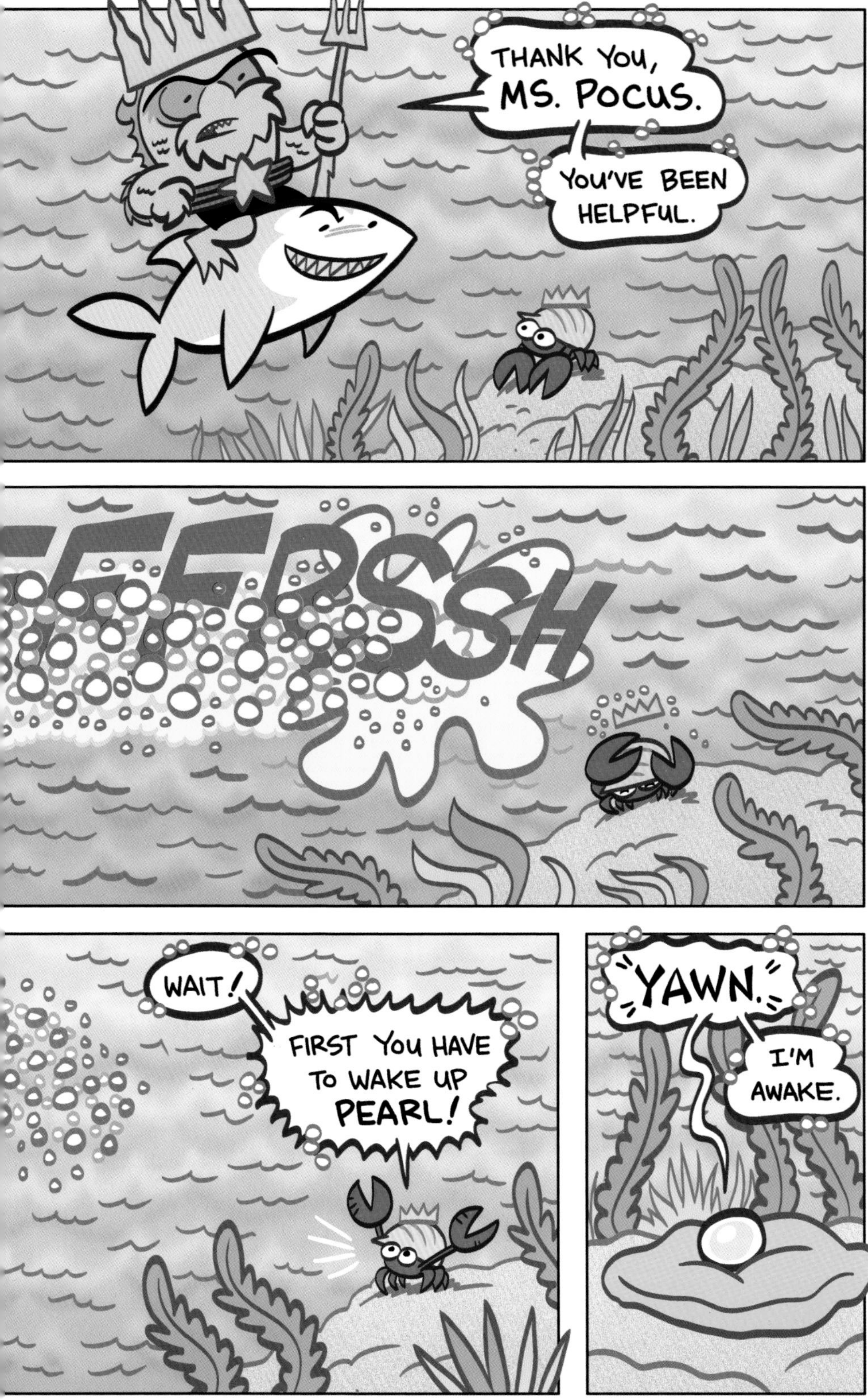

THANK YOU, MS. POCUS.
YOU'VE BEEN HELPFUL.
FFRSSH
WAIT!
FIRST YOU HAVE TO WAKE UP PEARL!
YAWN.
I'M AWAKE.

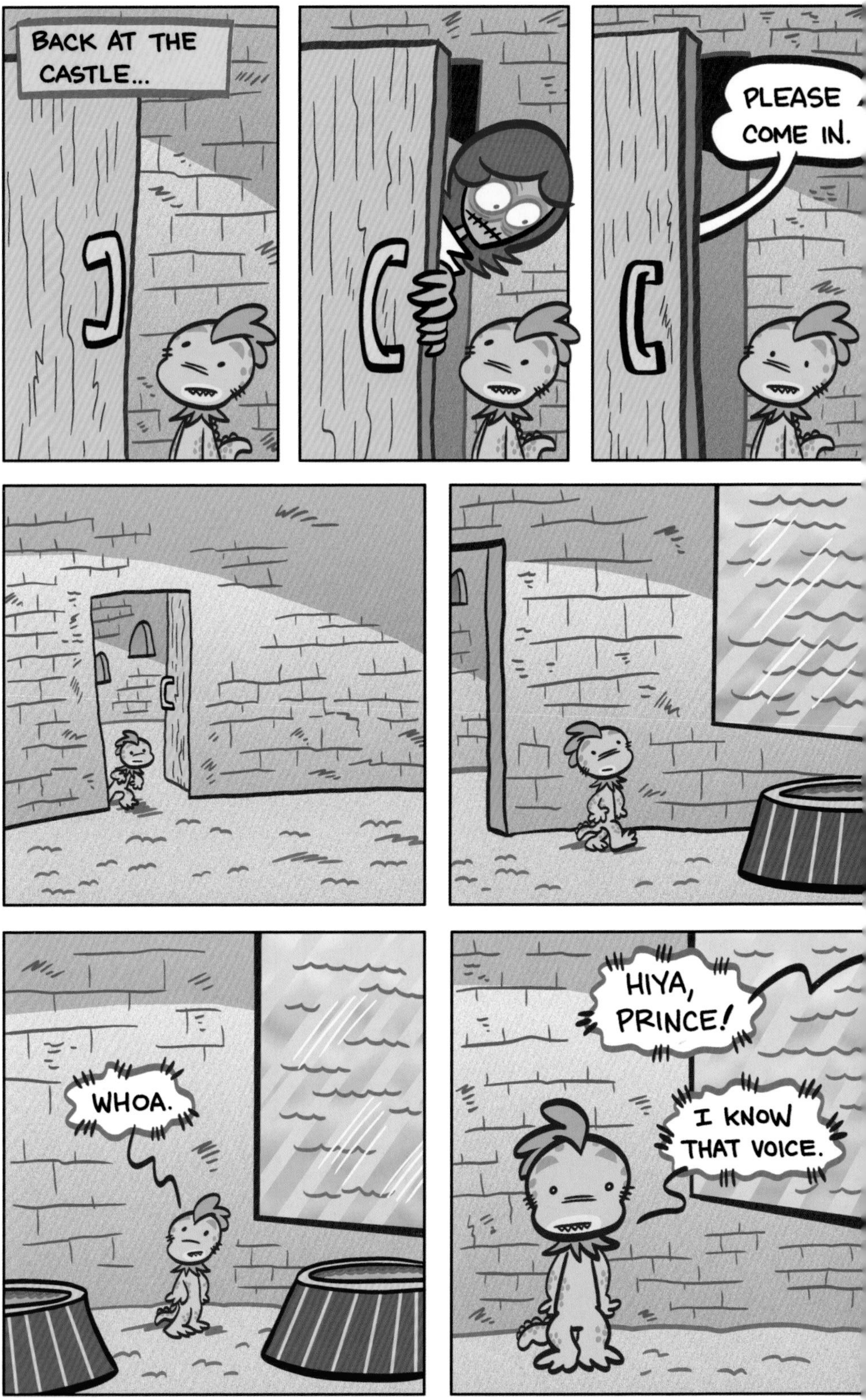
BACK AT THE CASTLE...
PLEASE COME IN.
WHOA.
HIYA, PRINCE!
I KNOW THAT VOICE.

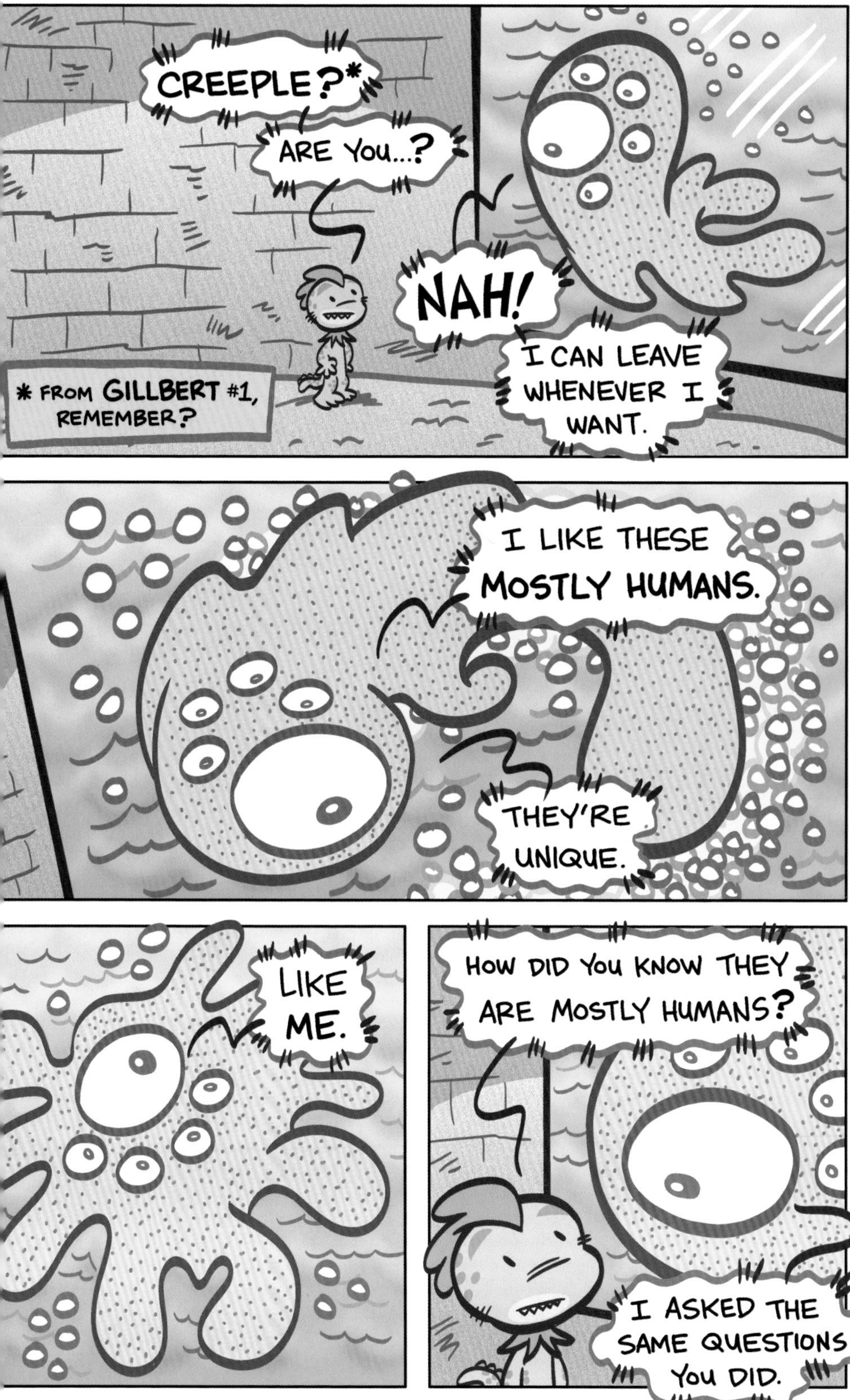
CREEPLE?*
ARE YOU...?
NAH!
I CAN LEAVE WHENEVER I WANT.
* FROM GILLBERT #1, REMEMBER?
I LIKE THESE MOSTLY HUMANS.
THEY'RE UNIQUE.
LIKE ME.
HOW DID YOU KNOW THEY ARE MOSTLY HUMANS?
I ASKED THE SAME QUESTIONS YOU DID.

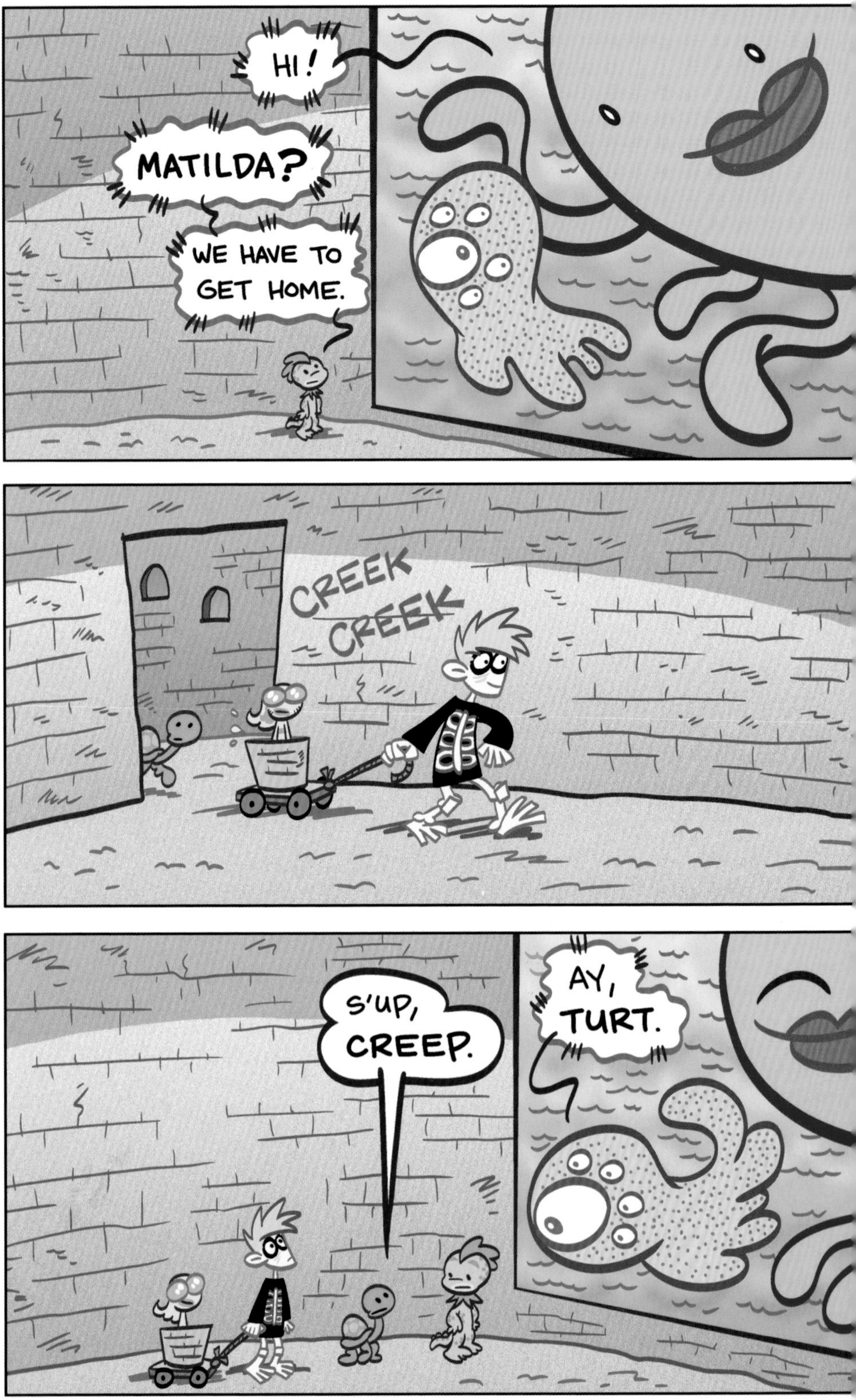
HI!
MATILDA?
WE HAVE TO GET HOME.
CREEK
CREEK
S'UP, CREEP.
AY, TURT.

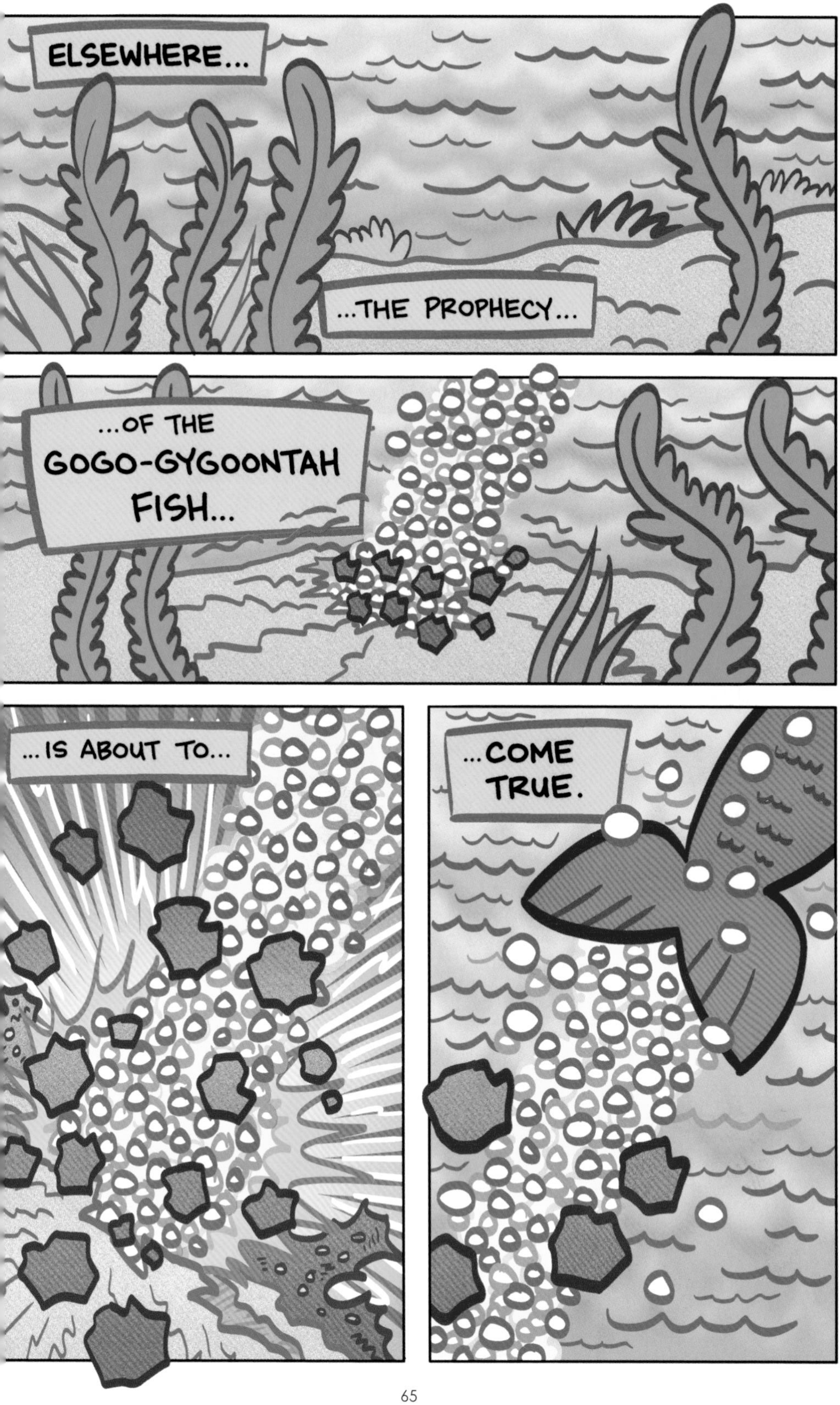
ELSEWHERE...
...THE PROPHECY...
...OF THE GOGO-GYGOONTAH FISH...
...IS ABOUT TO...
...COME TRUE.

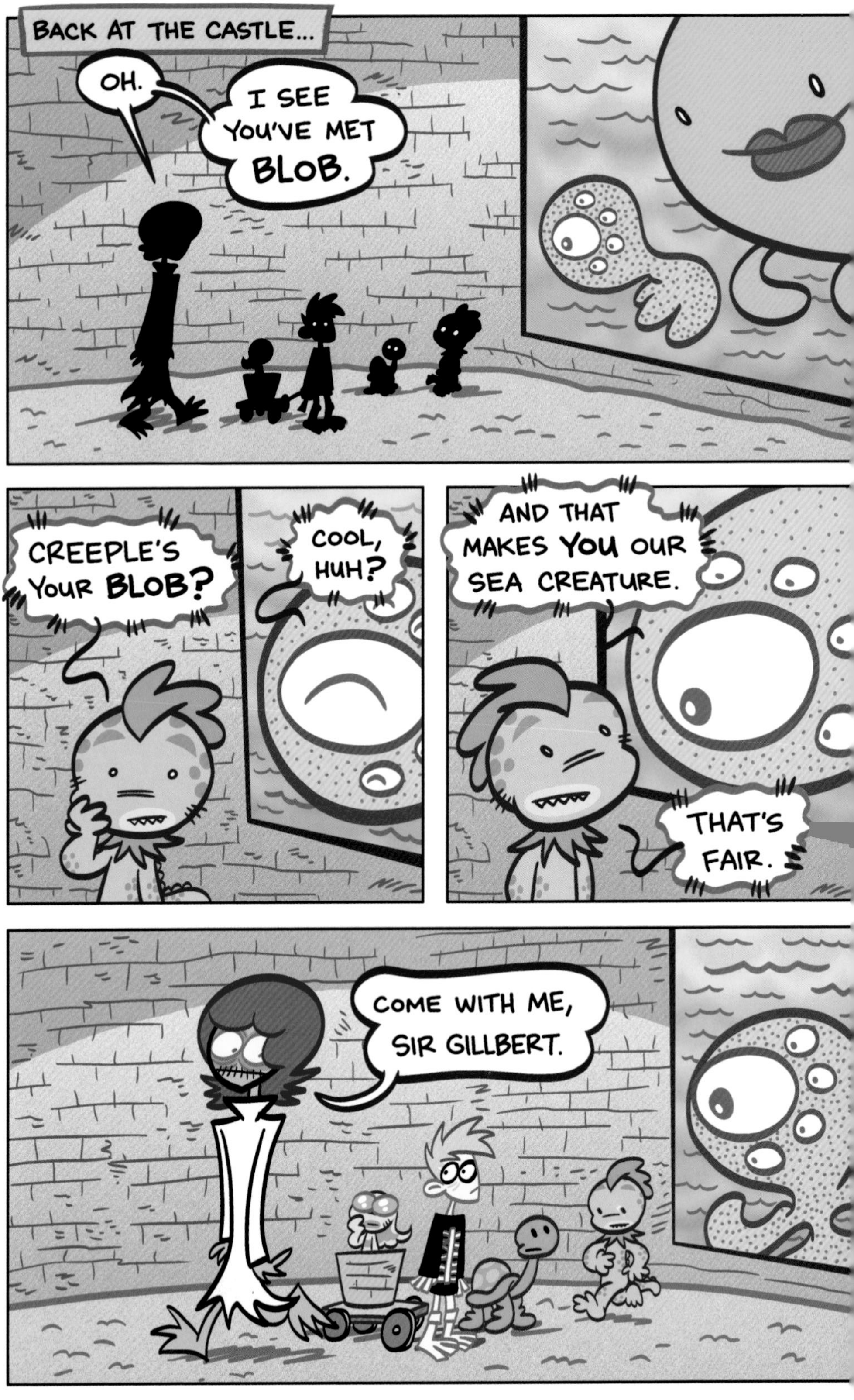
BACK AT THE CASTLE...
OH.
I SEE YOU'VE MET BLOB.
CREEPLE'S YOUR BLOB?
COOL, HUH?
AND THAT MAKES YOU OUR SEA CREATURE.
THAT'S FAIR.
COME WITH ME, SIR GILLBERT.

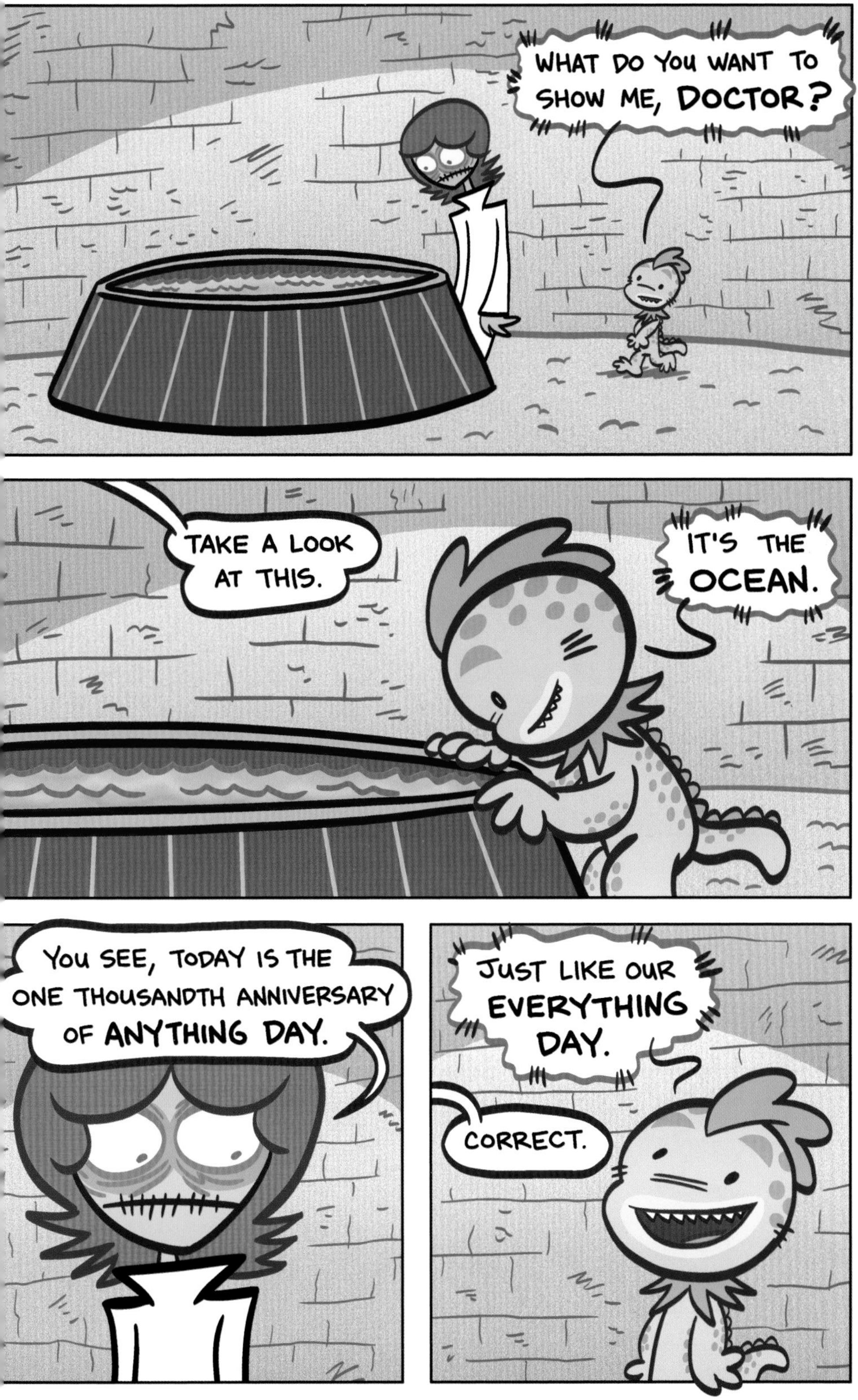
WHAT DO YOU WANT TO SHOW ME, DOCTOR?
TAKE A LOOK AT THIS.
IT'S THE OCEAN.
YOU SEE, TODAY IS THE ONE THOUSANDTH ANNIVERSARY OF ANYTHING DAY.
JUST LIKE OUR EVERYTHING DAY.
CORRECT.

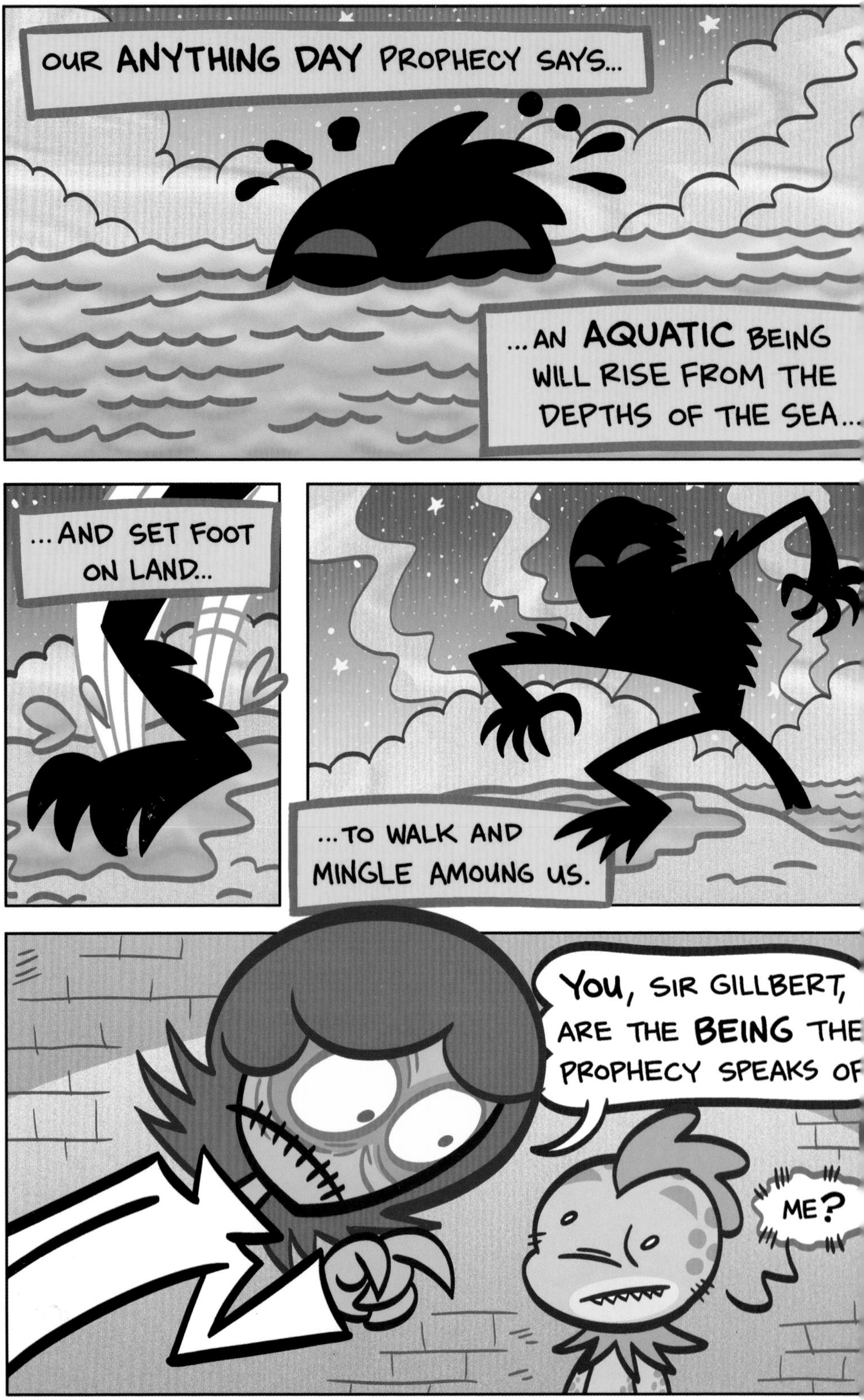

OUR ANYTHING DAY PROPHECY SAYS...
...AN AQUATIC BEING WILL RISE FROM THE DEPTHS OF THE SEA...
...AND SET FOOT ON LAND...
...TO WALK AND MINGLE AMOUNG US.
YOU, SIR GILLBERT, ARE THE BEING THE PROPHECY SPEAKS OF
ME?

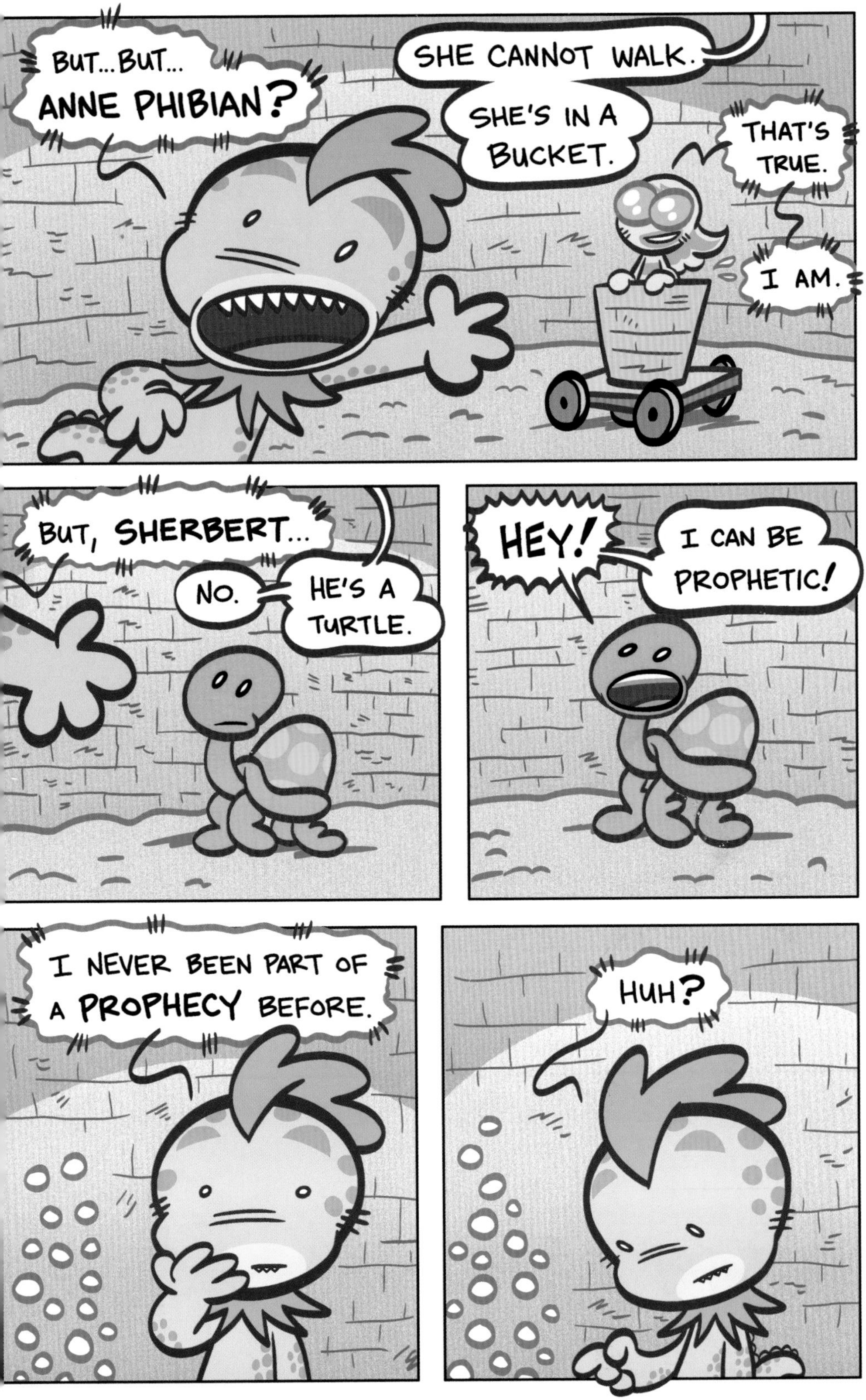
BUT...BUT... ANNE PHIBIAN?
SHE CANNOT WALK.
SHE'S IN A BUCKET.
THAT'S TRUE.
I AM.
BUT, SHERBERT...
NO.
HE'S A TURTLE.
HEY!
I CAN BE PROPHETIC!
I NEVER BEEN PART OF A PROPHECY BEFORE.
HUH?

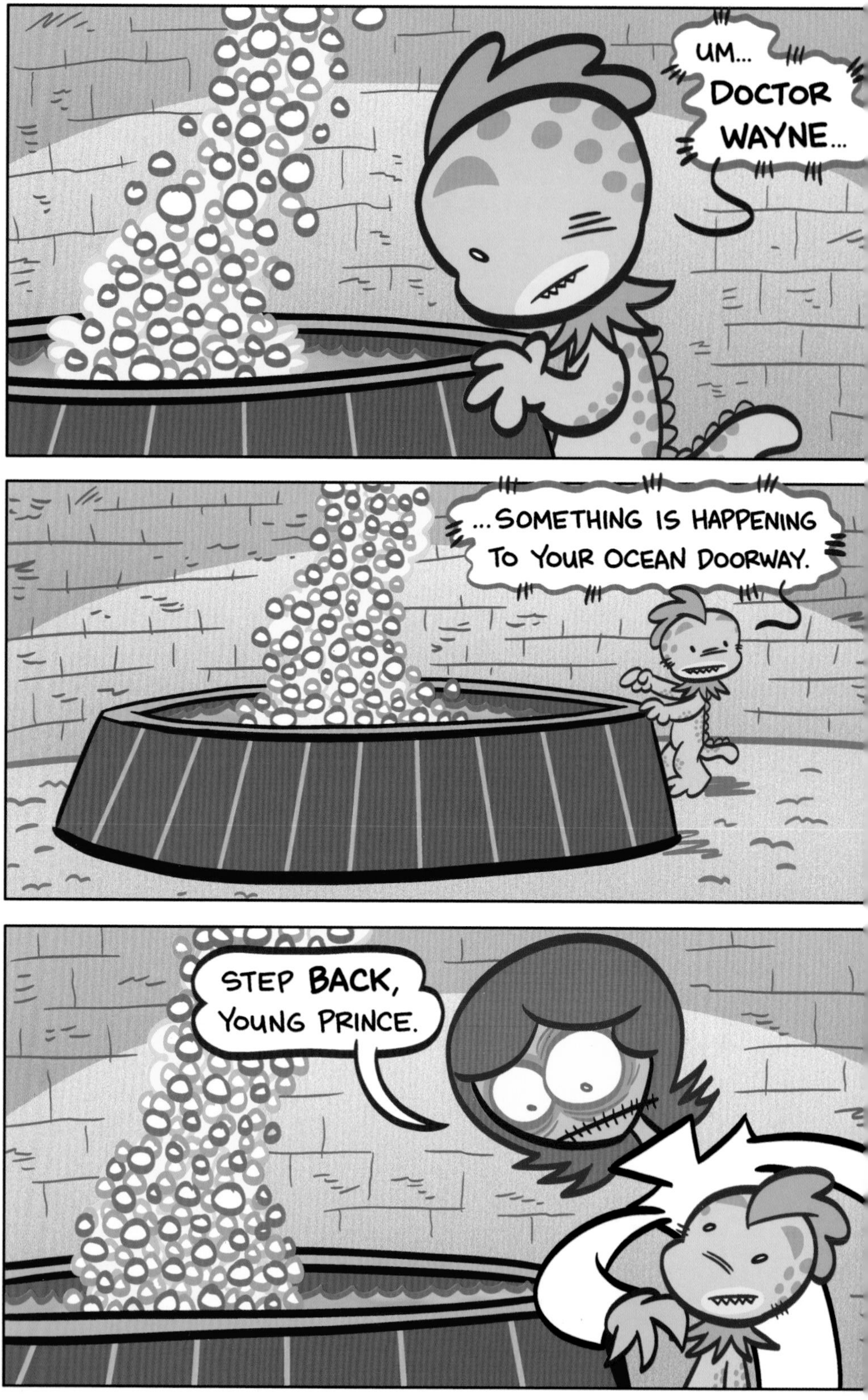
UM... DOCTOR WAYNE...
...SOMETHING IS HAPPENING TO YOUR OCEAN DOORWAY.
STEP BACK, YOUNG PRINCE.

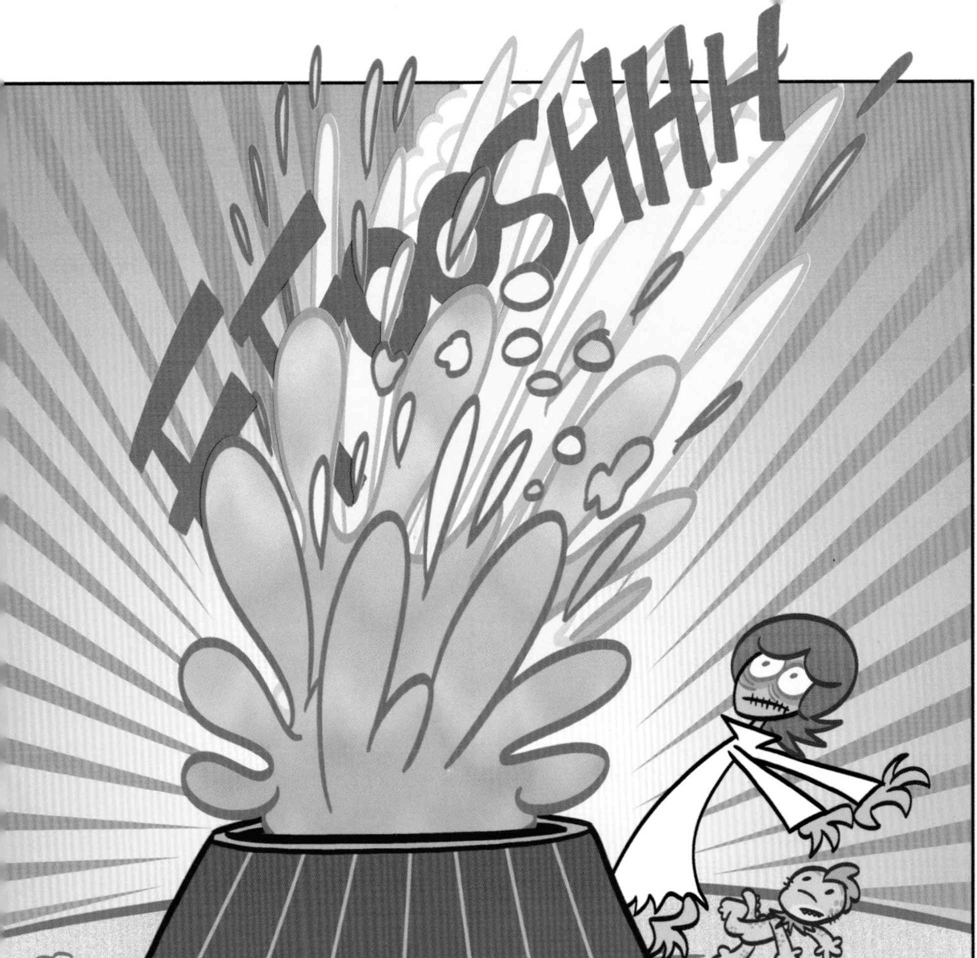

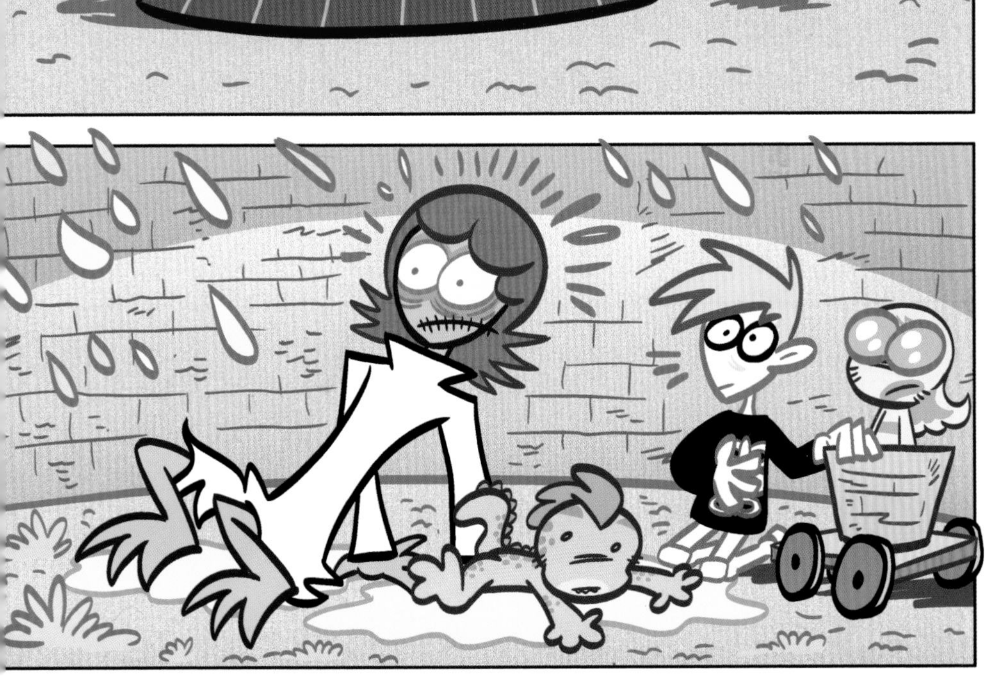

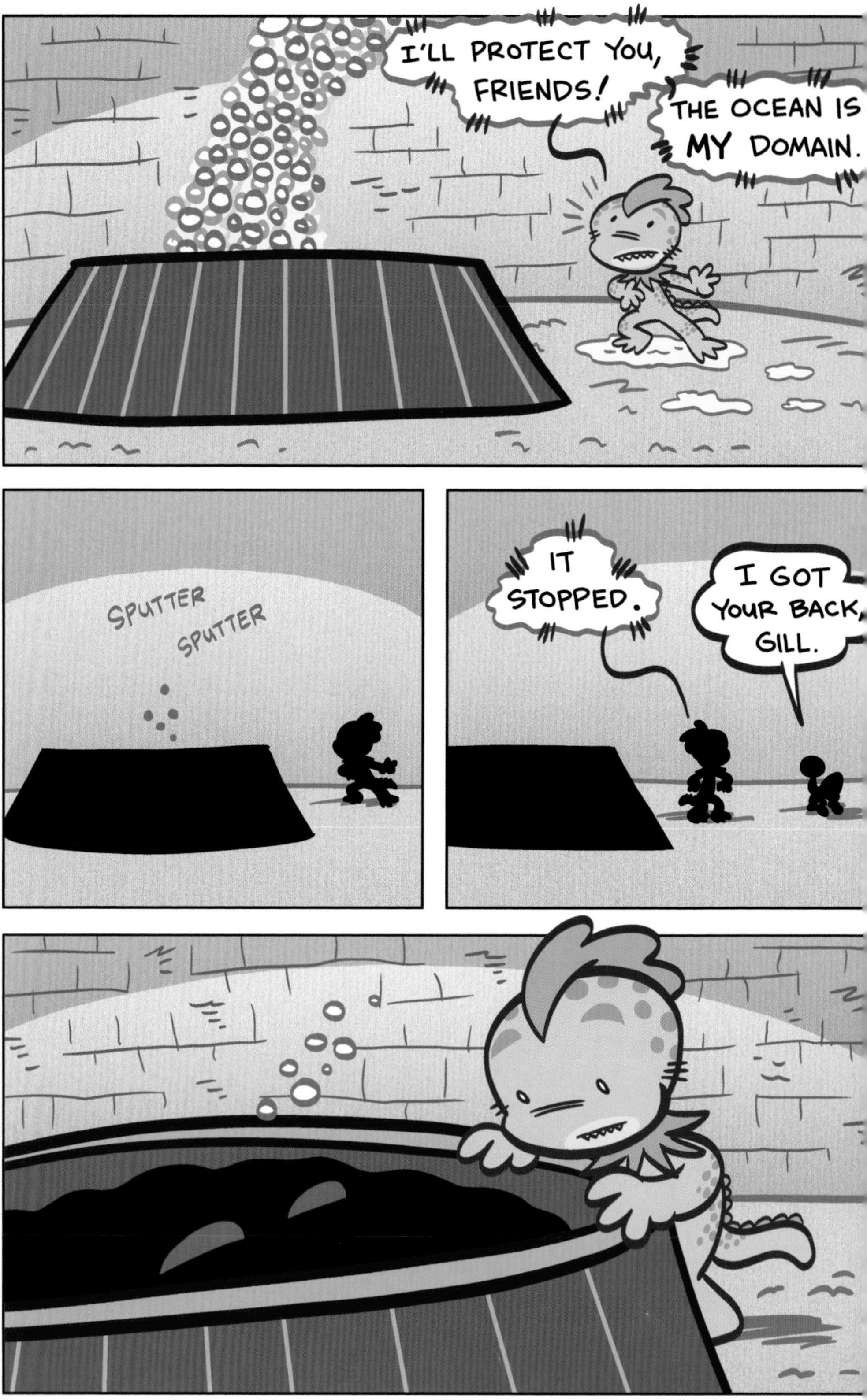
I'LL PROTECT YOU, FRIENDS!
THE OCEAN IS MY DOMAIN.
SPUTTER SPUTTER
IT STOPPED.
I GOT YOUR BACK, GILL.

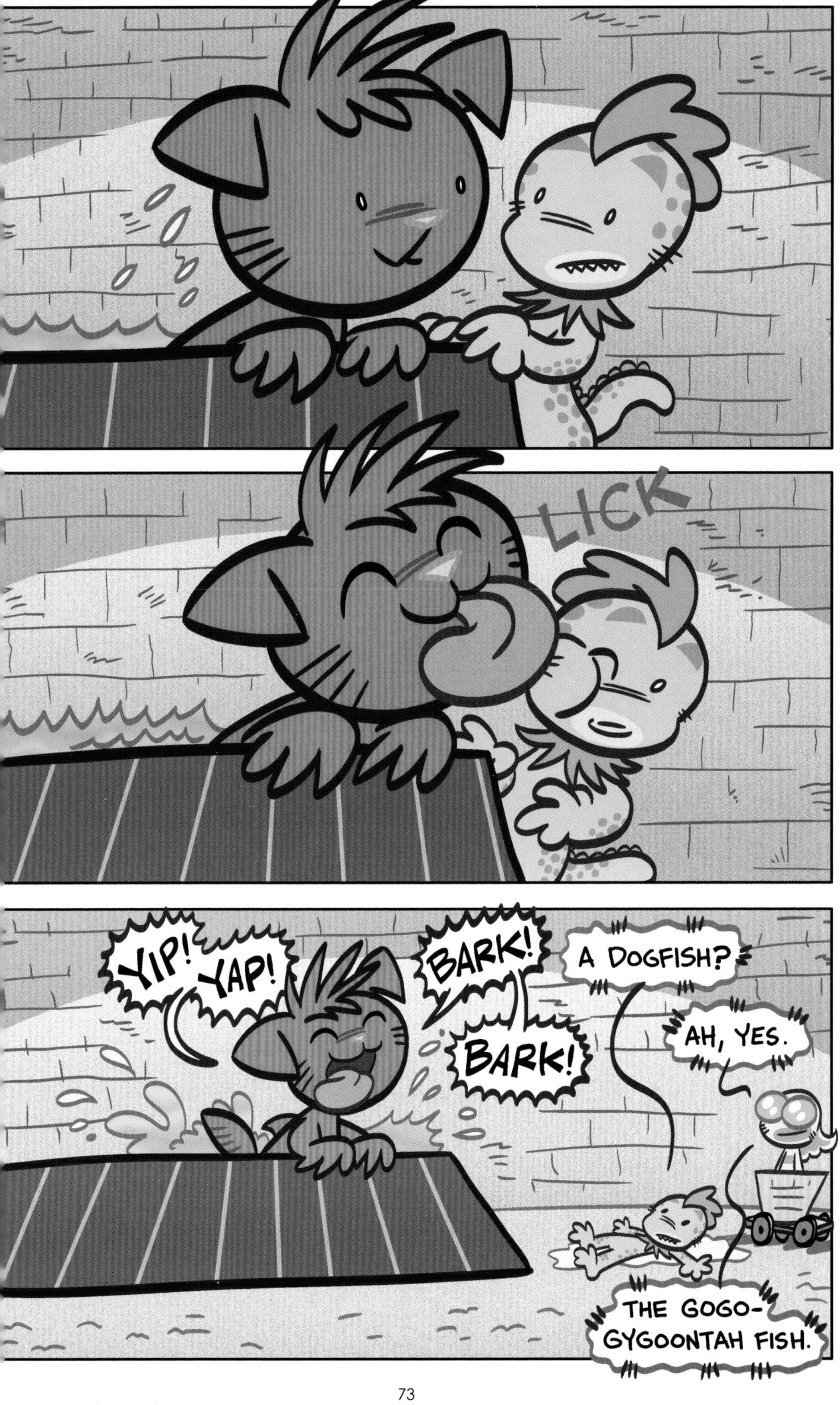
LICK
YIP!
YAP!
BARK!
BARK!
A DOGFISH?
AH, YES.
THE GOGO-
GYGOONTAH FISH.

WHILE OUTSIDE...

SWEEP
SWEEP

LOOK.

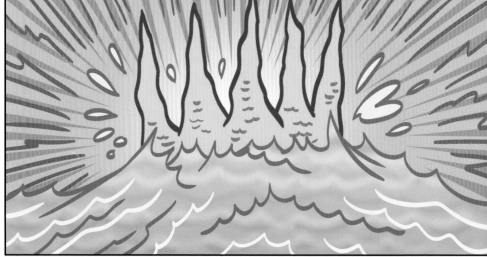

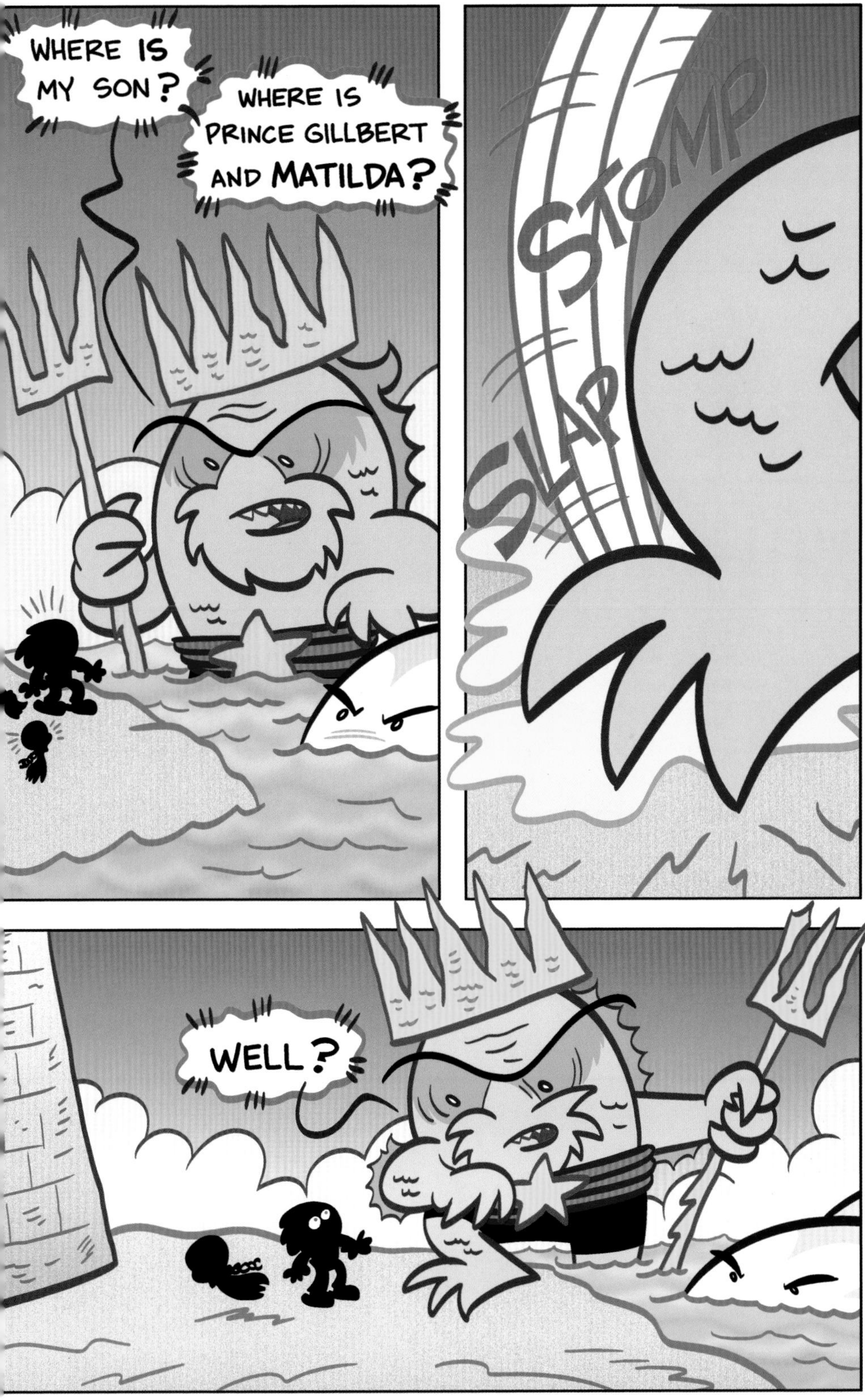
WHERE IS MY SON?
WHERE IS PRINCE GILLBERT AND MATILDA?
STOMP
SLAP
WELL?

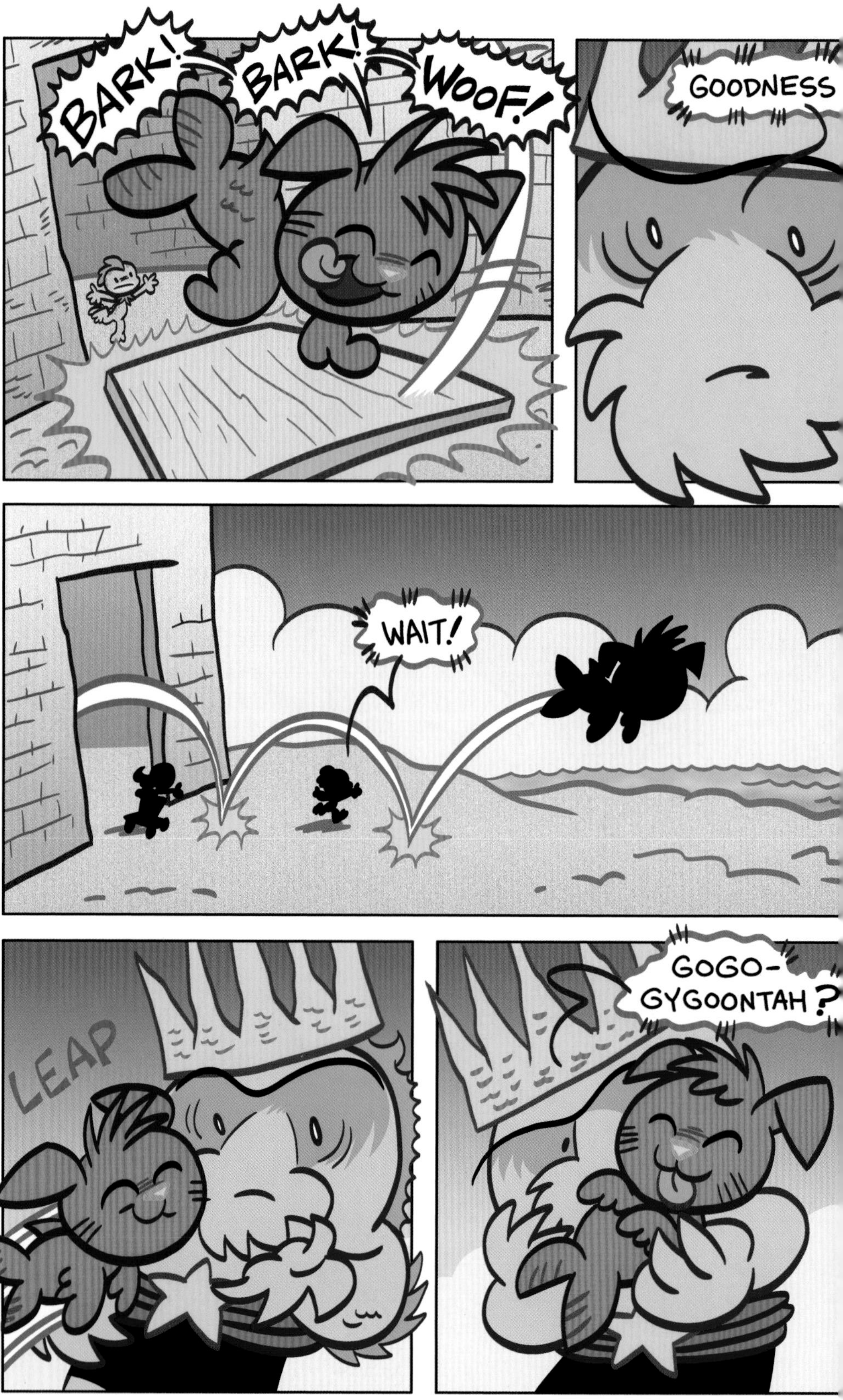
BARK!
BARK!
WOOF!
GOODNESS
WAIT!
LEAP
GOGO-
GYGOONTAH?

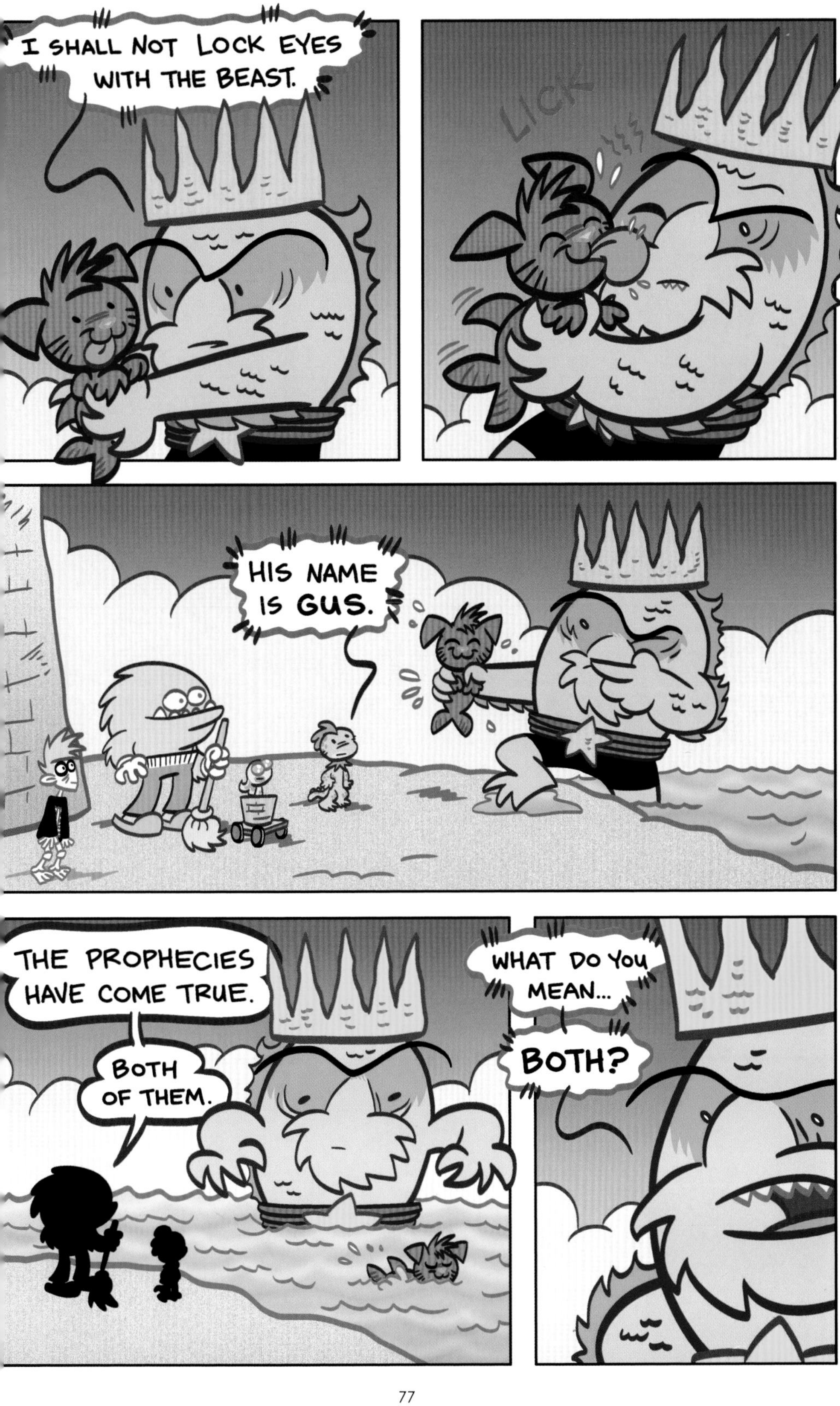
I SHALL NOT LOCK EYES WITH THE BEAST.
LICK
HIS NAME IS GUS.
THE PROPHECIES HAVE COME TRUE.
BOTH OF THEM.
WHAT DO YOU MEAN...
BOTH?

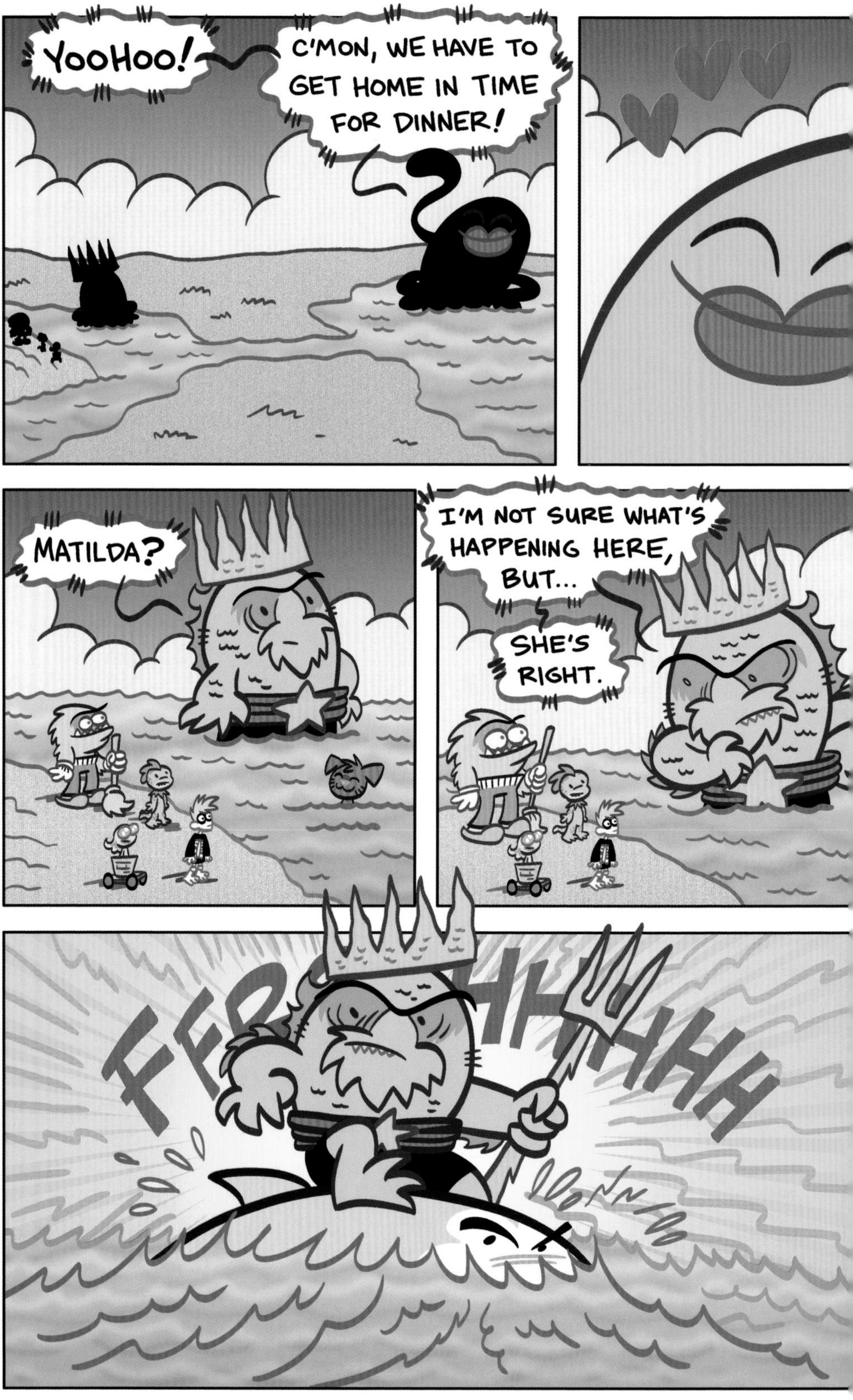
YOOHOO!
C'MON, WE HAVE TO GET HOME IN TIME FOR DINNER!
MATILDA?
I'M NOT SURE WHAT'S HAPPENING HERE, BUT...
SHE'S RIGHT.
FFRSHHHHHHA

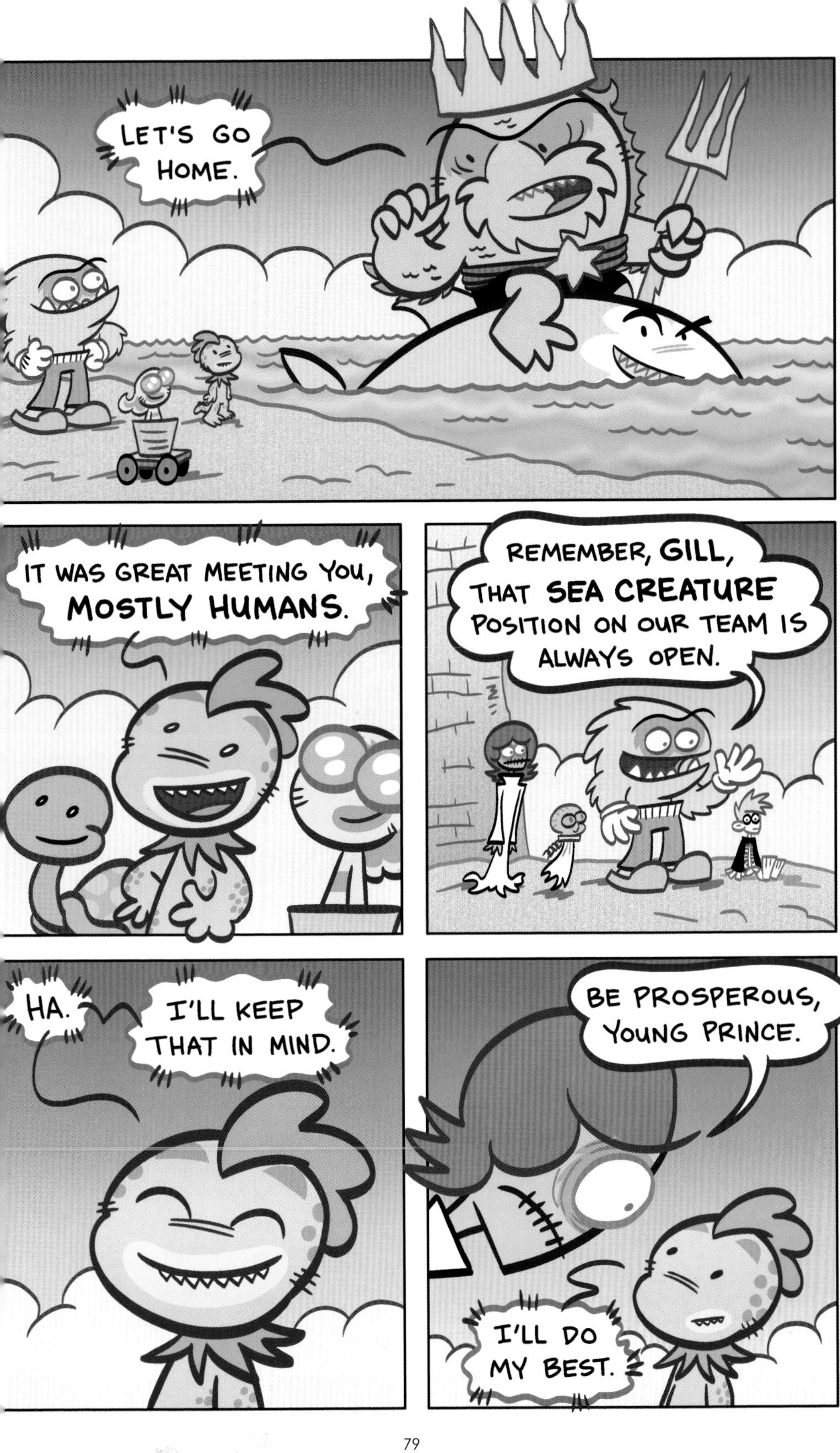
LET'S GO HOME.
IT WAS GREAT MEETING YOU, MOSTLY HUMANS.
REMEMBER, GILL, THAT SEA CREATURE POSITION ON OUR TEAM IS ALWAYS OPEN.
HA.
I'LL KEEP THAT IN MIND.
BE PROSPEROUS, YOUNG PRINCE.
I'LL DO MY BEST.

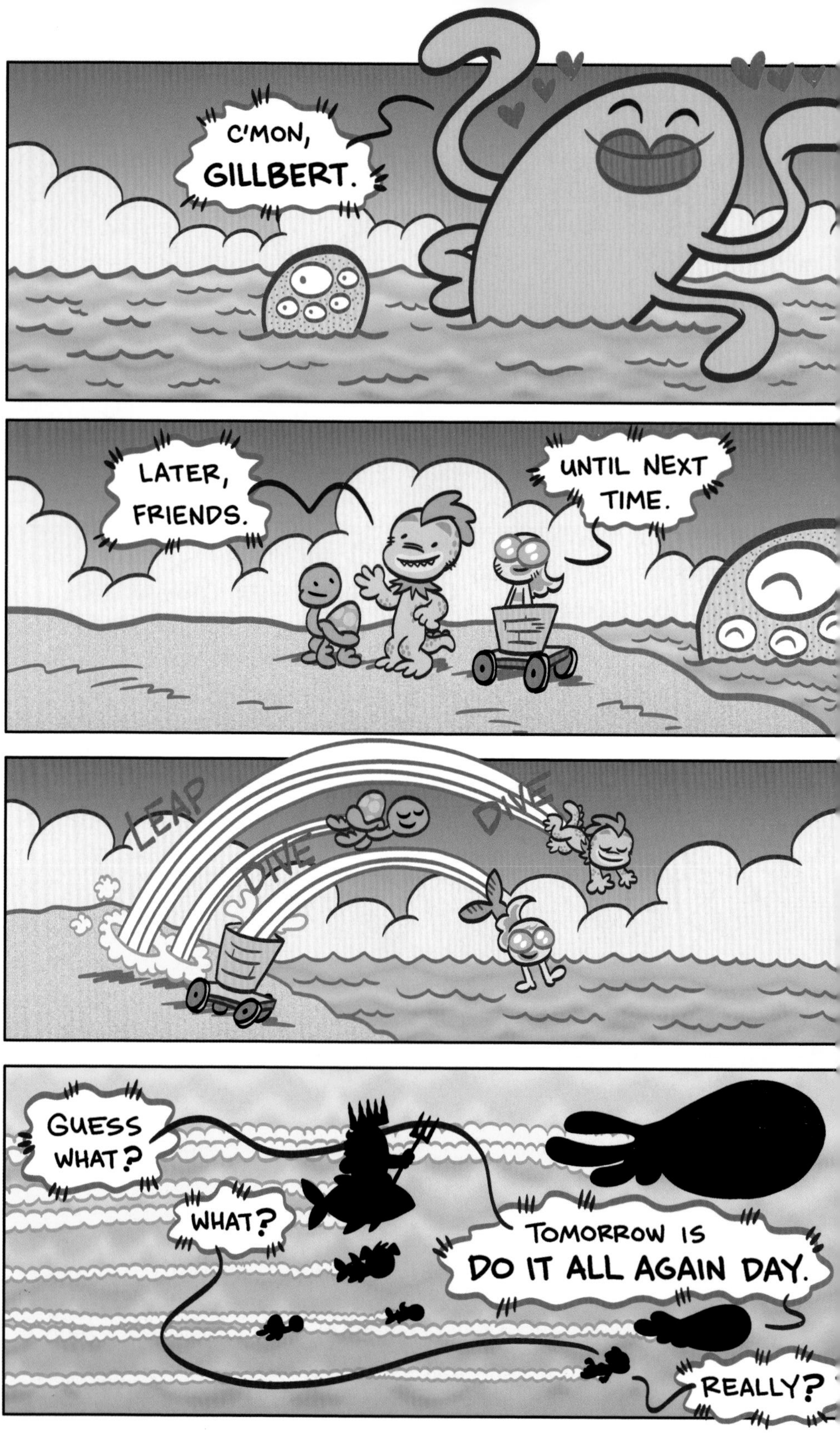
C'MON, GILLBERT.
LATER, FRIENDS.
UNTIL NEXT TIME.
LEAP
DIVE
DIVE
GUESS WHAT?
WHAT?
TOMORROW IS DO IT ALL AGAIN DAY.
REALLY?

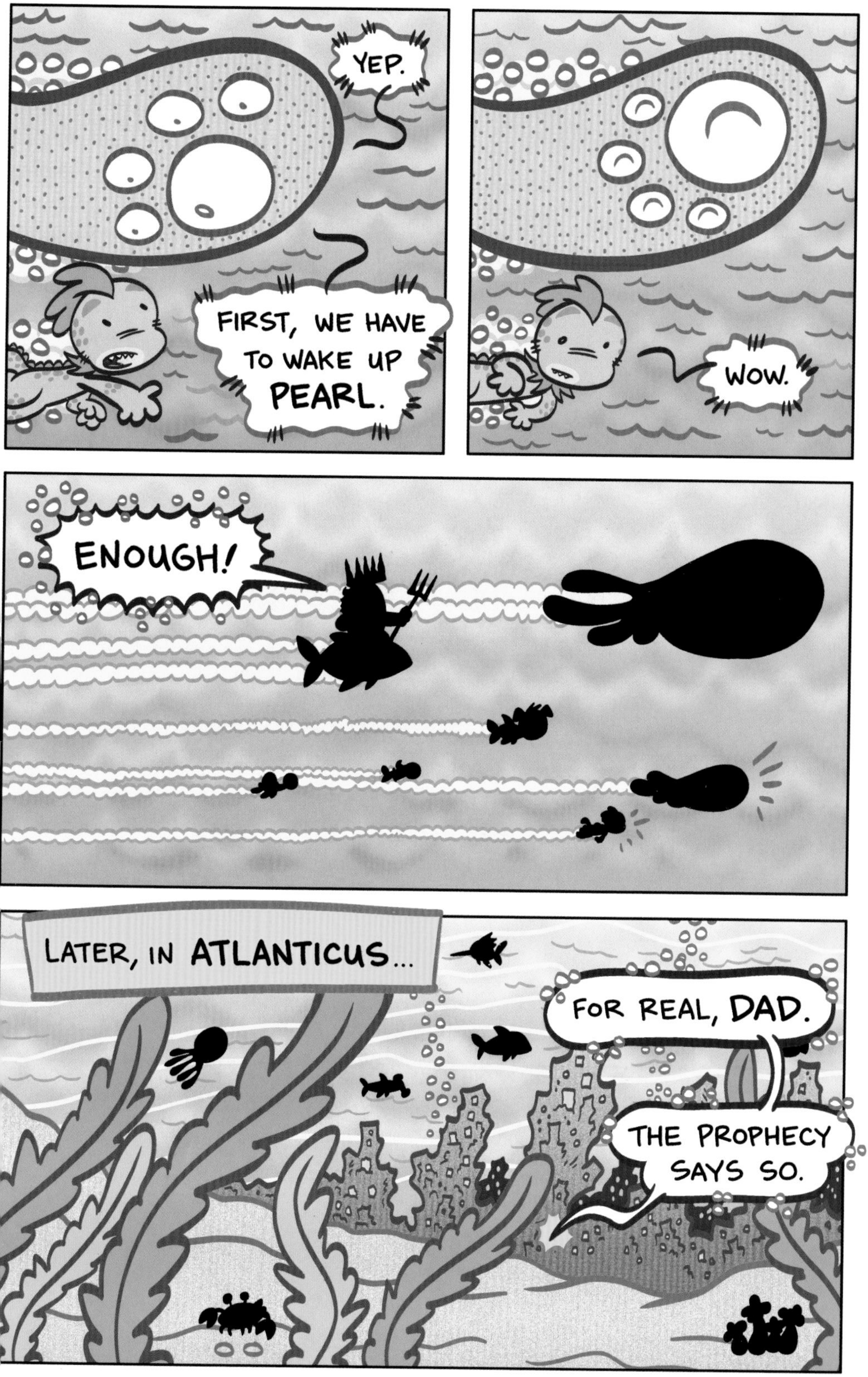
YEP.
FIRST, WE HAVE TO WAKE UP PEARL.
WOW.
ENOUGH!
LATER, IN ATLANTICUS...
FOR REAL, DAD.
THE PROPHECY SAYS SO.

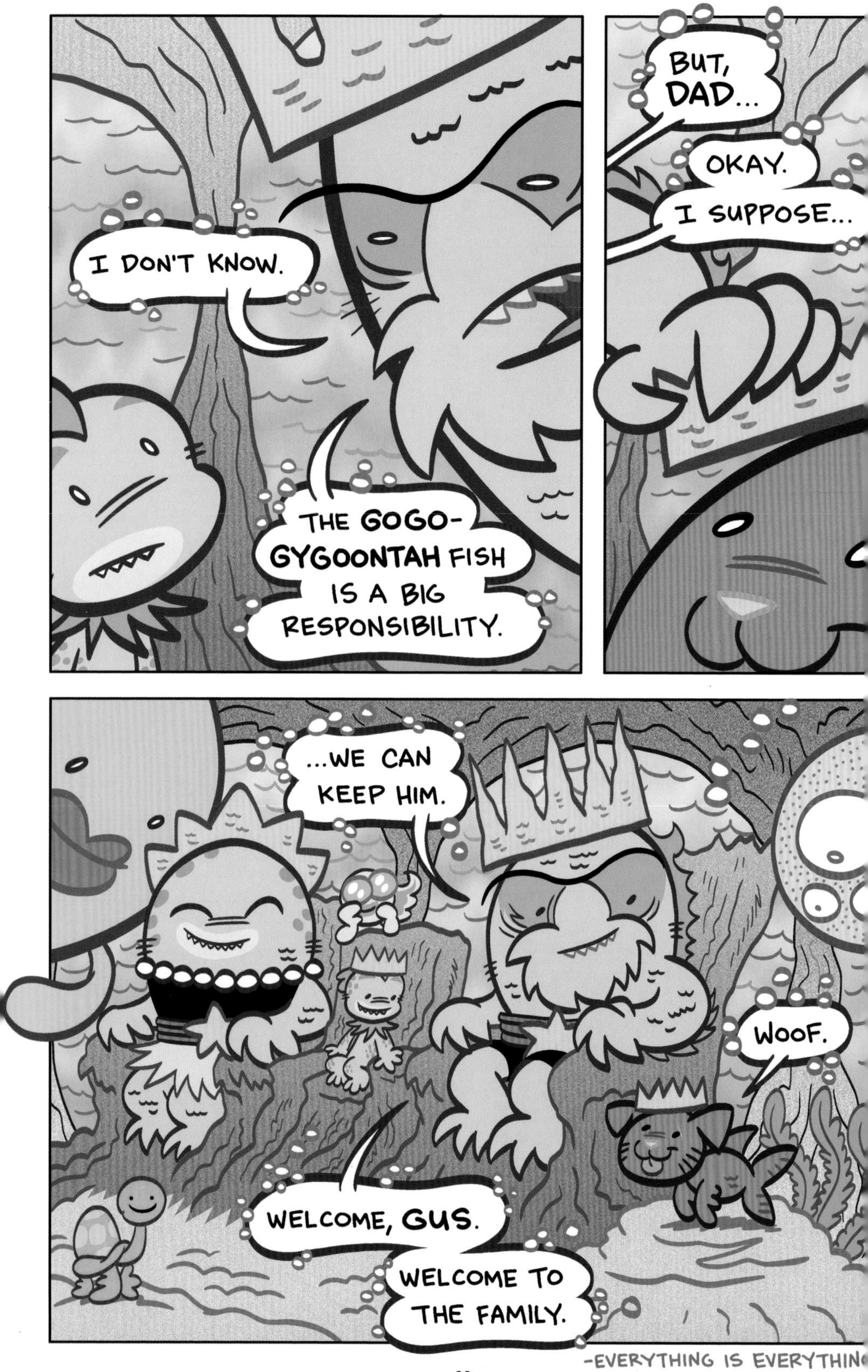
I DON'T KNOW.
THE GOGO-GYGOONTAH FISH IS A BIG RESPONSIBILITY.
BUT, DAD...
OKAY.
I SUPPOSE...
...WE CAN KEEP HIM.
WOOF.
WELCOME, GUS.
WELCOME TO THE FAMILY.

-EVERYTHING IS EVERYTHIN

WATCH OUT FOR PAPERCUTZ

Welcome to the second scaly and slippery volume of GILLBERT as we delve into "The Curious Mysterious" and put on our party hats to celebrate Everything Day AND Anything Day. I'm Jim Salicrup, Editor-in-Chief and captain of the ship here at Papercutz. We at Papercutz are big fans of all things underwater. In GILLBERT #1 we did mention Metaphrog's THE LITTLE MERMAID and David Gallaher and Steve Ellis's THE ONLY LIVING BOY. We have a confession to make, I am allergic to shellfish and our Managing Editor won't eat anything with fish in it except New England Clam Chowder. How curious and mysterious! Nevertheless, Papercutz has you covered for all your underwater book needs.

What's that? You enjoyed the Mostly Humans and their fun brand of horror? Well, Papercutz again has you covered! Join vampire Mavis, her husband Johnny, and her dad Dracula. THAT Dracula. The owner of HOTEL TRANSYLVANIA! Straight from the hit animated movies and Disney Channel series comes all-new adventures of the hotel and its ghoulish guests! Grab the three spooktacular volumes today before they disappear!

If you want your horror fun with a mix of romance, check out STITCHED from our Charmz imprint. Crimson Volania Mulch is piecing together her past as she wakes up in a cemetery uncertain of who she is or where she came from. While she is working on herself, she meets some great friends in a vampire, a werewolf, a not so mad scientist, and a sea creature! Volumes one and two are available wherever books are sold.

Lastly, also from Charmz, comes GFFs: GHOST FRIENDS FOREVER. Between high school, dealing with her stubborn twin brother, Felix, and her ex-boyfriend Jake, and the family business of ghost hunting, Sophia Green-Campos knows ghosts. But nothing can prepare her for meeting Whitney, a ghost who died in high school. This heartwarming tale of romance and family is available in two volumes.

Not creepy and not all-wet is GILLBERT's creator, Art Baltazar! Art Baltazar has been creating comics since 1994. Art calls his Art Studio (get it?) Electric Milk Creations. Among his hundreds of character creations and worlds, Art has been work-shopping GILLBERT and his dad, King Nauticus, since 2001! Turn the page for a special feature on the creation process for GILLBERT and the Mostly Humans! And watch the seas later this year for GILLBERT #3 "The Flaming Carats Evolution" but you might not want to get your books wet! Now, if you will excuse us, we have a Do It All Again Day to prepare for. It's tomorrow, you know!

Thanks,
Jim

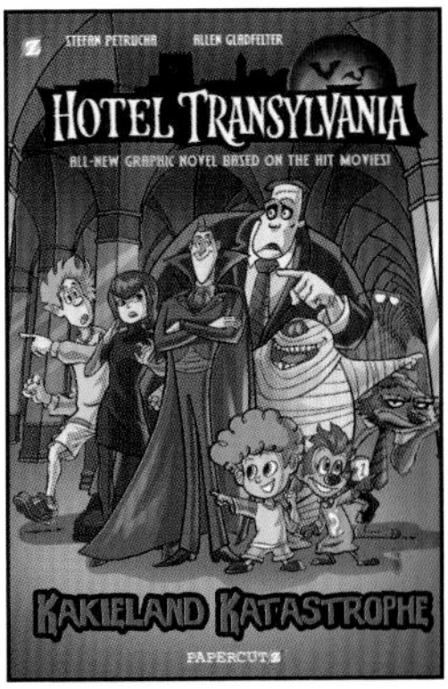

STEFAN PETRUCHA ALLEN GLADFELTER
HOTEL TRANSYLVANIA
ALL-NEW GRAPHIC NOVEL BASED ON THE HIT MOVIES!
KAKIELAND KATASTROPHE
PAPERCUTZ

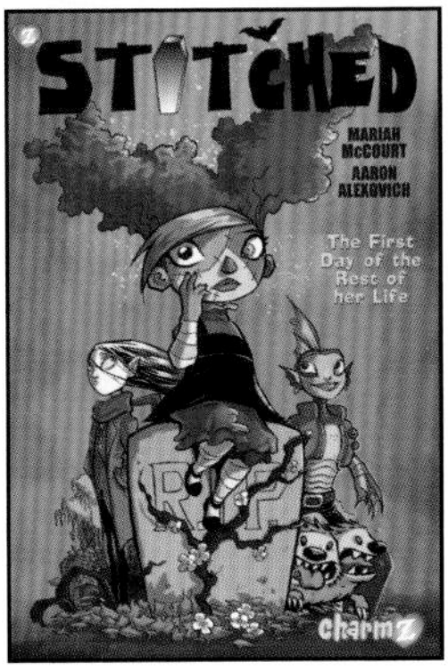

STITCHED
MARIAH McCOURT
AARON ALEXOVICH
The First Day of the Rest of her Life
charmz

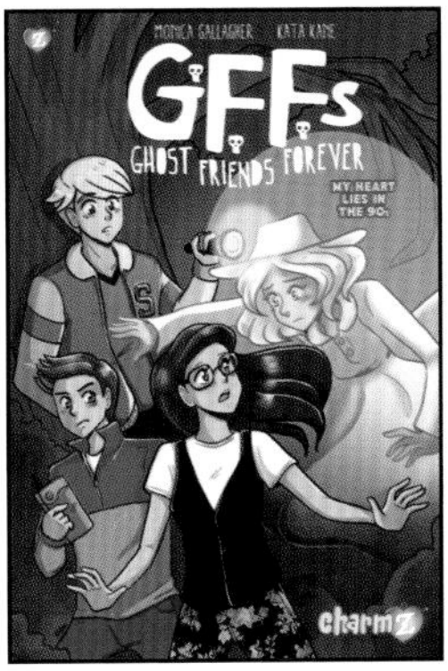

MONICA GALLAGHER KATA KANE
GFFs
GHOST FRIENDS FOREVER
MY HEART LIES IN THE 90s
charmz

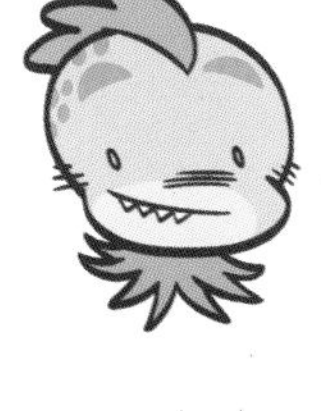

STAY IN TOUCH!

EMAIL:	salicrup@papercutz.com
WEB:	papercutz.com
TWITTER:	@papercutzgn
INSTAGRAM:	@papercutzgn
FACEBOOK:	PAPERCUTZGRAPHICNOVELS
FAN MAIL:	Papercutz, 160 Broadway, Suite 700, East Wing, New York, NY 10038

Gillbert's first comic pitch!

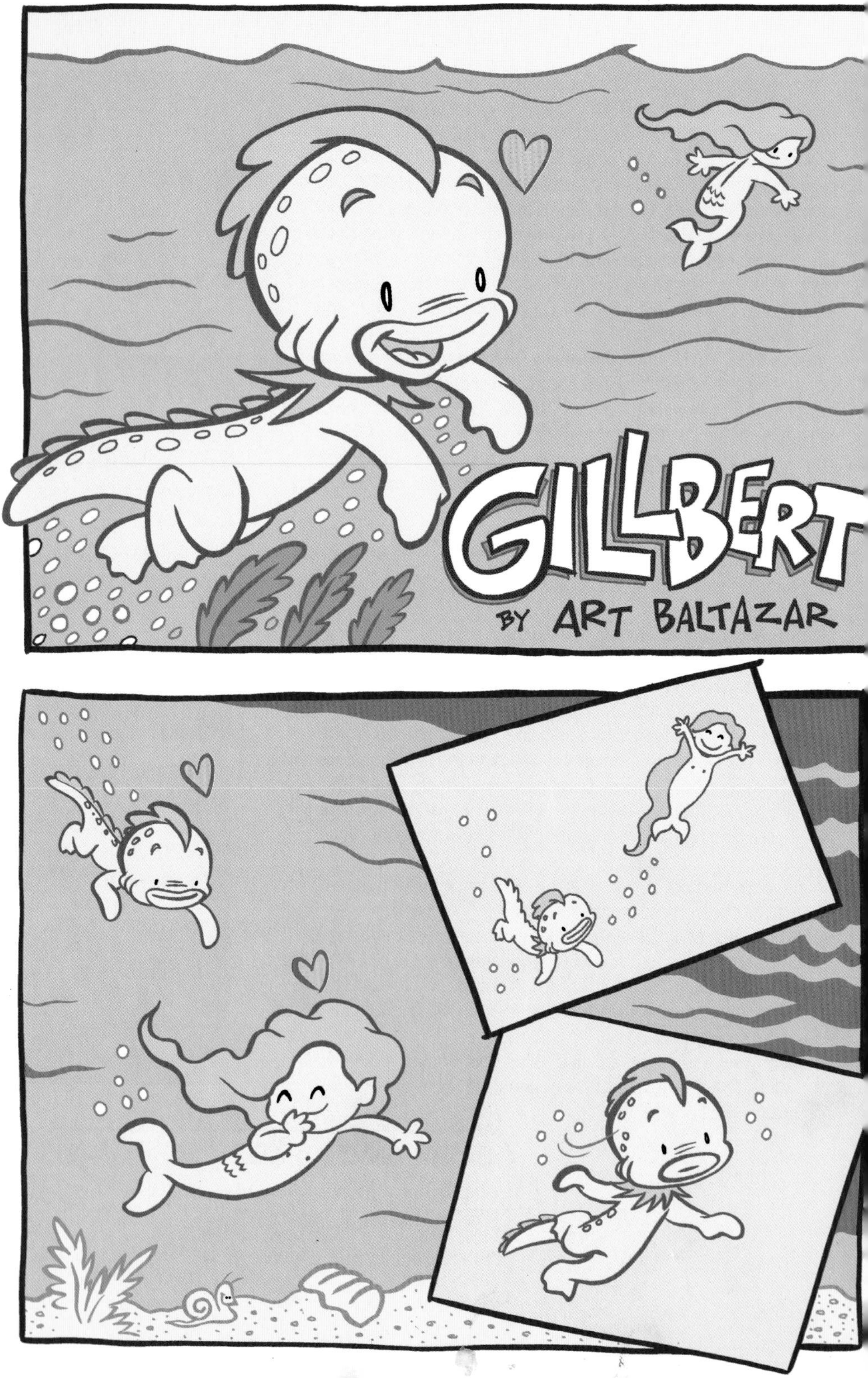
GILLBERT
BY ART BALTAZAR

'amous cartoonist Art Baltazar has created hundreds of characters and given ı Eisner Award-winning spin on classic comicbook properties like HELLBOY, EEN TITANS, and the gang at ARCHIE. Art always keeps a sketchbook with m to be ready when inspiration hits. In 2001, he had an idea for a cute sea onster boy...

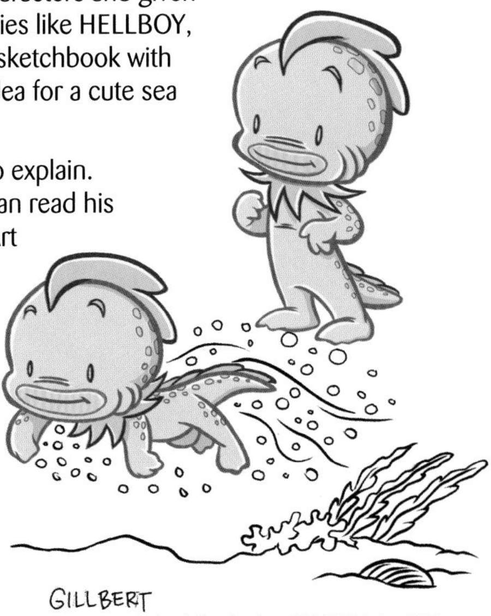

GILLBERT

Art Batlazar's first sketches of GILLBERT, circa 2001

But Gillbert was not always destined for royalty. Allow us to explain. rt first created a creepy tragic tale of Doctor Wayne. You can read his eepy silent Wayne comic story at artbaltazar.com. Then, Art eated a special school summer camp for Doctor Wayne teach at, or to conduct experiments at. Art filled the :hool with some mostly human characters....

Art describes it this way: "While other kids go to ımmer camp, 'Gifted' kids attend Ms. Wayne's 'special' :hool. Come and visit the school where monsters are :sidents and Mad-Scientist experiments are a must. ears ago, Ms. Wayne lost her husband in a freak acci- ent. Being a scientist, she tried and tried to bring her usband back from the dead."

Art named the group "LABCOAT JUNCTION." Look miliar? At Labcoat Junction, the students are trained the ways of a mad scientist and also how to care for, train, and live nongst monsters. What monsters you ask? Here they are:

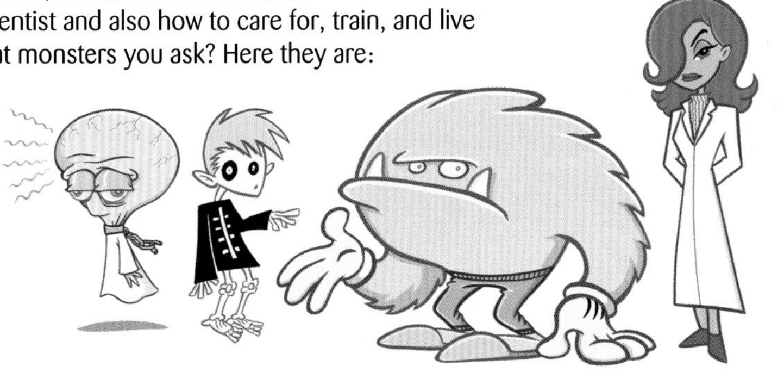
The Mostly Human(s) who Gillbert befriends in this volume. L to R: Wallace, Sonny Bone, LooEes the Beast , and Doctor Wayne,

So, that is the circle of eation. GILLBERT 1 "The Little lerman" premiered 2018, 17 years ter Art first created illbert! Now, the lostly Humans have ıade their graphic ovel debuts with ILLBERT #2 "The Curious Mysterious"! What surprises does Art Baltazar have in his sketchbook for olume 3? Only time will tell!

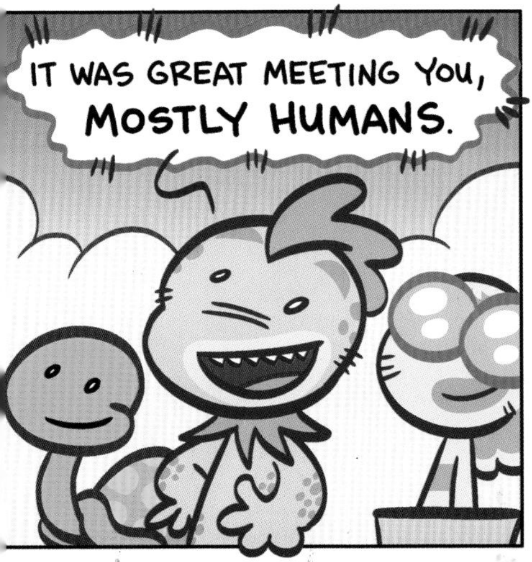

IT WAS GREAT MEETING YOU, MOSTLY HUMANS.

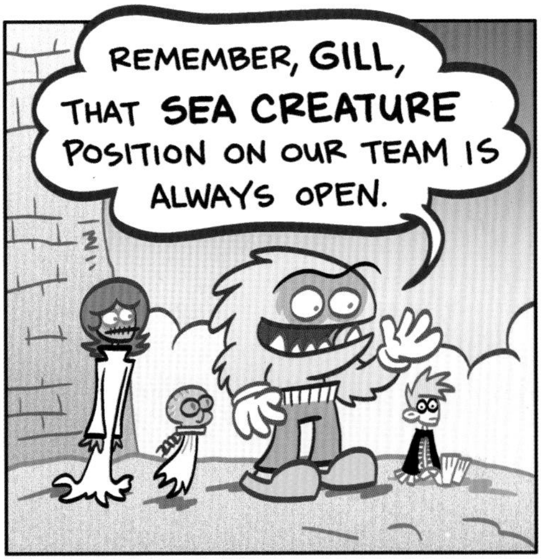

REMEMBER, GILL, THAT SEA CREATURE POSITION ON OUR TEAM IS ALWAYS OPEN.

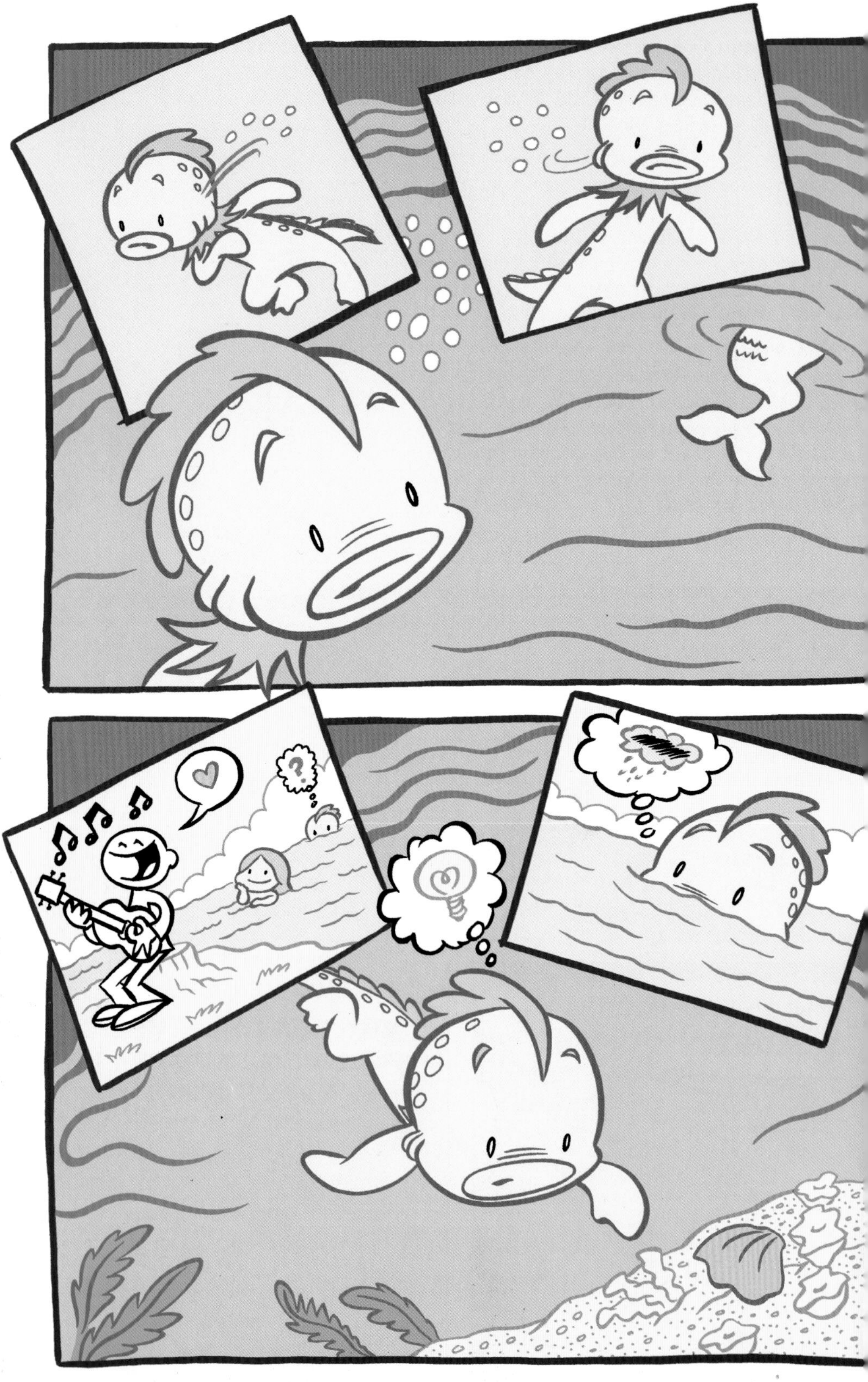

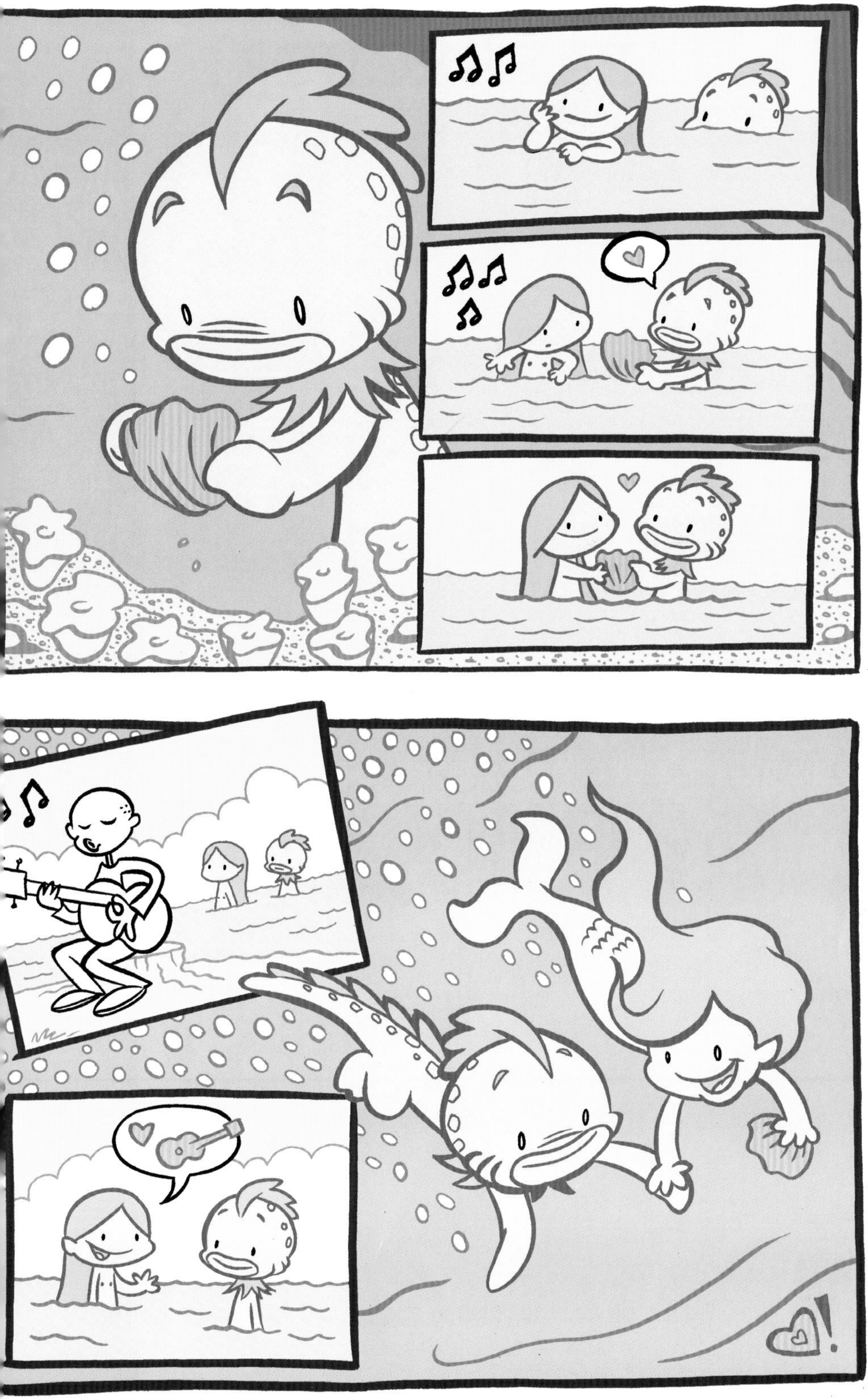

MORE GREAT GRAPHIC NOVEL SERIES AVAILABLE FROM PAPERCUTZ™

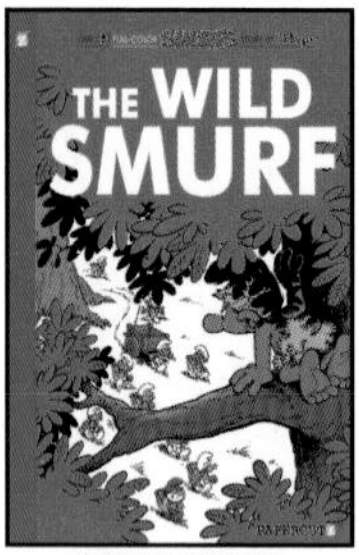
THE WILD SMURF
PAPERCUTZ
THE SMURFS

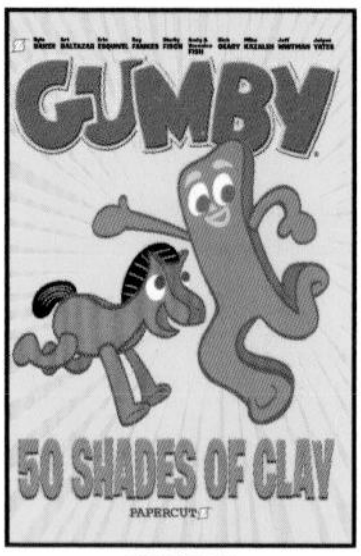
GUMBY
50 SHADES OF CLAY
PAPERCUTZ
GUMBY

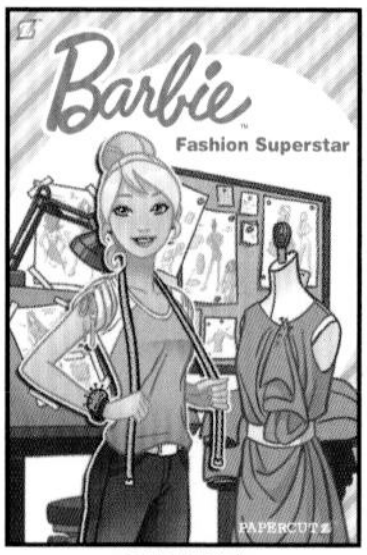
Barbie
Fashion Superstar
PAPERCUTZ
BARBIE

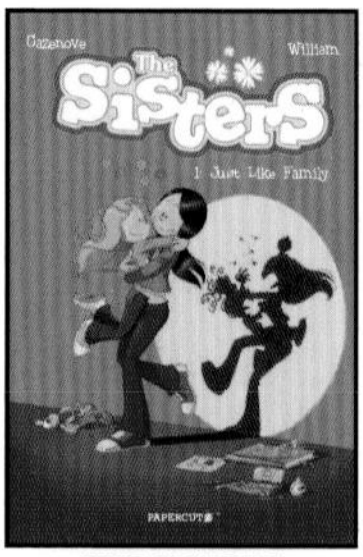
Cazenove
William
The Sisters
I Just Like Family
PAPERCUTZ
THE SISTERS

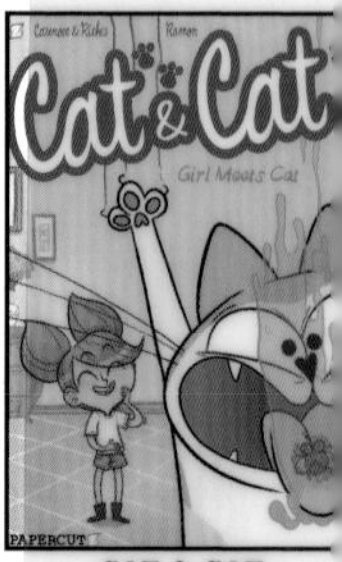
Cat & Cat
Girl Meets Cat
PAPERCUT
CAT & CAT

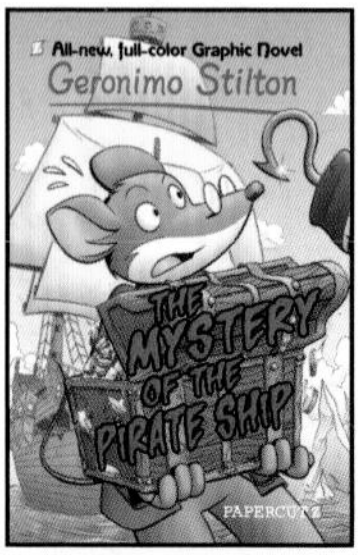
All-new, full-color Graphic Novel
Geronimo Stilton
THE MYSTERY OF THE PIRATE SHIP
PAPERCUTZ
GERONIMO STILTON

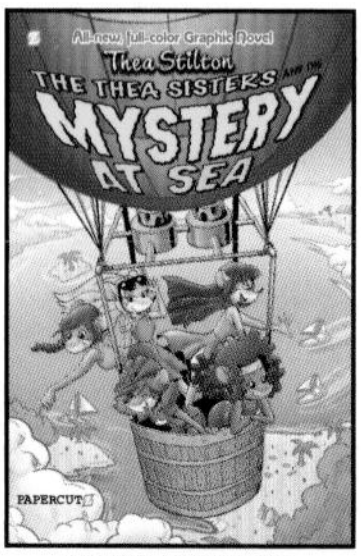
All-new, full-color Graphic Novel
Thea Stilton
THE THEA SISTERS
MYSTERY AT SEA
PAPERCUTZ
THEA STILTON

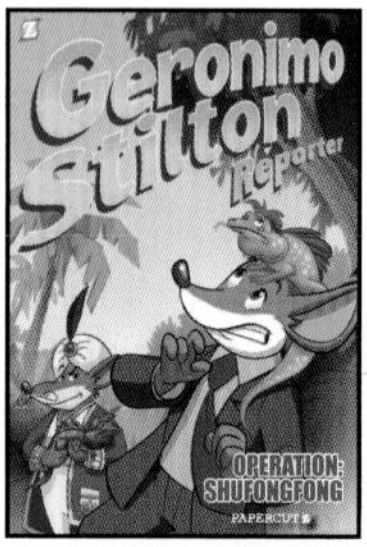
Geronimo Stilton
Reporter
OPERATION: SHUFONGFONG
PAPERCUTZ
GERONIMO STILTON REPORTER

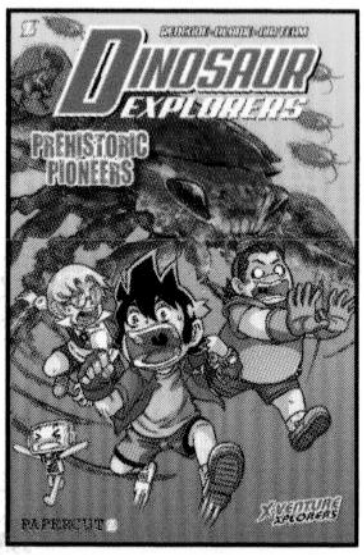
DINOSAUR EXPLORERS
PREHISTORIC PIONEERS
PAPERCUTZ
DINOSAUR EXPLORERS

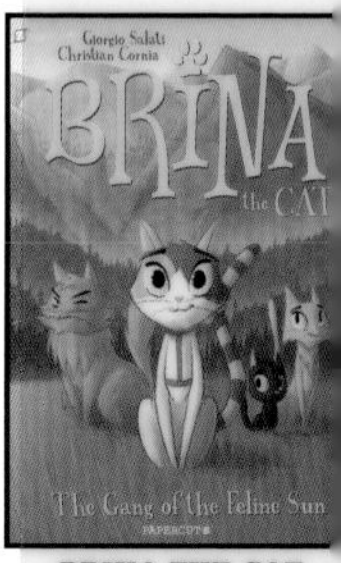
Giorgio Salati
Christian Cornia
BRINA the CAT
The Gang of the Feline Sun
PAPERCUTZ
BRINA THE CAT

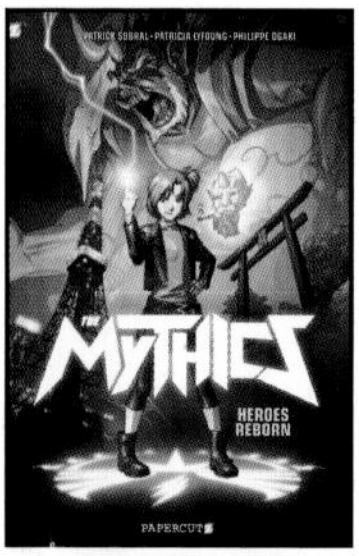
MYTHICS
HEROES REBORN
PAPERCUTZ
THE MYTHICS

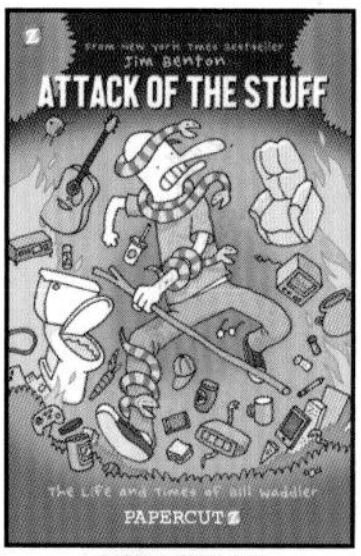
Jim Benton
ATTACK OF THE STUFF
PAPERCUTZ
ATTACK OF THE STUFF

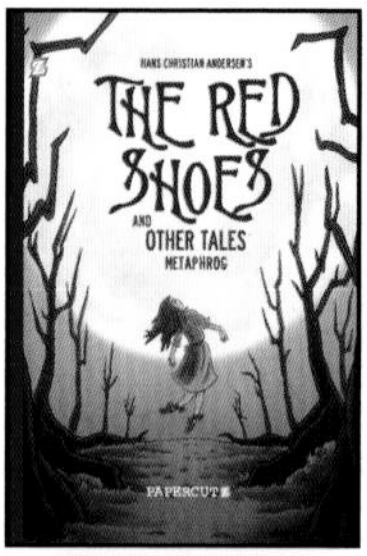
HANS CHRISTIAN ANDERSEN'S
THE RED SHOES
AND OTHER TALES
METAPHROG
PAPERCUTZ
THE RED SHOES

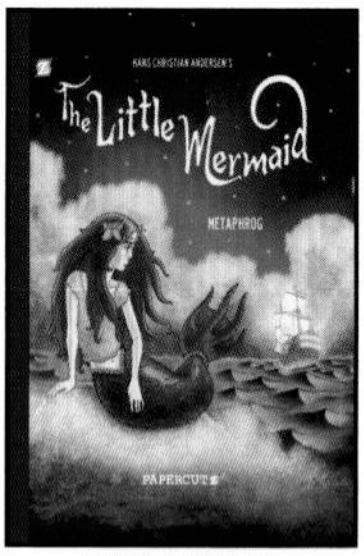
HANS CHRISTIAN ANDERSEN'S
The Little Mermaid
METAPHROG
PAPERCUTZ
THE LITTLE MERMAID

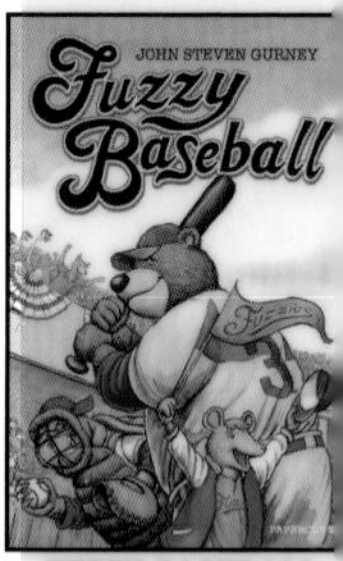
JOHN STEVEN GURNEY
Fuzzy Baseball
FUZZY BASEBALL

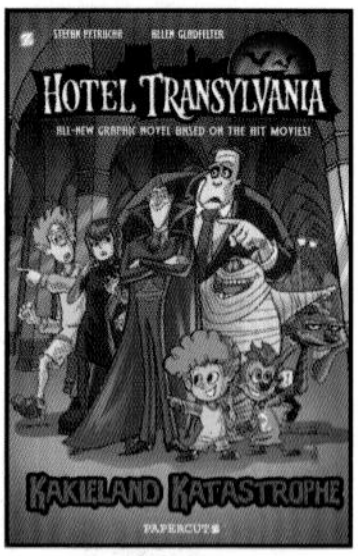
STEFAN PETRUCHA
HOTEL TRANSYLVANIA
KAKIELAND KATASTROPHE
PAPERCUTZ
HOTEL TRANSYLVANIA

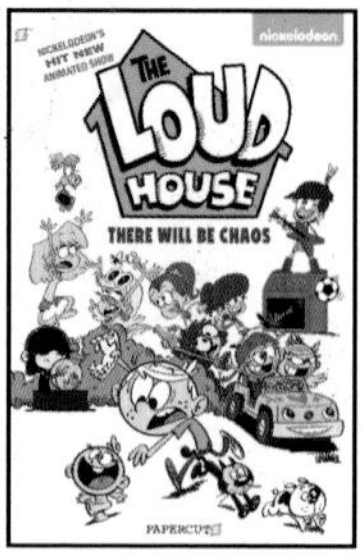
nickelodeon
THE LOUD HOUSE
THERE WILL BE CHAOS
PAPERCUTZ
THE LOUD HOUSE

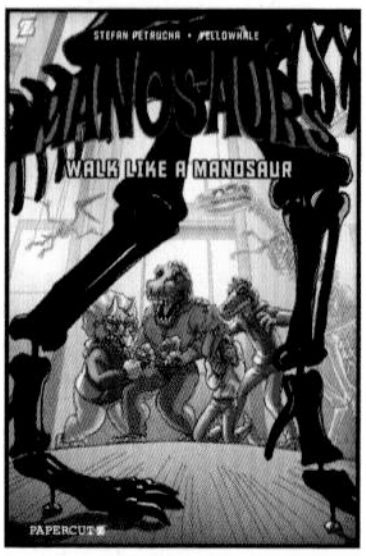
STEFAN PETRUCHA
MANOSAURS
WALK LIKE A MANOSAUR
PAPERCUTZ
MANOSAURS

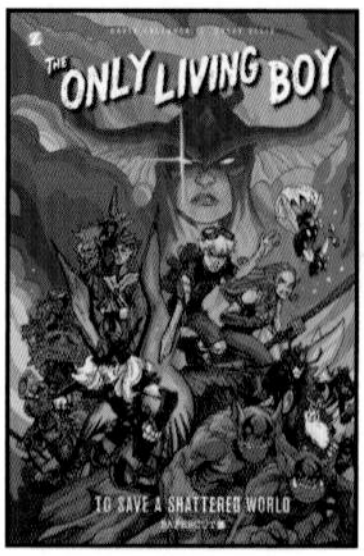
THE ONLY LIVING BOY
TO SAVE A SHATTERED WORLD
PAPERCUTZ
THE ONLY LIVING BOY

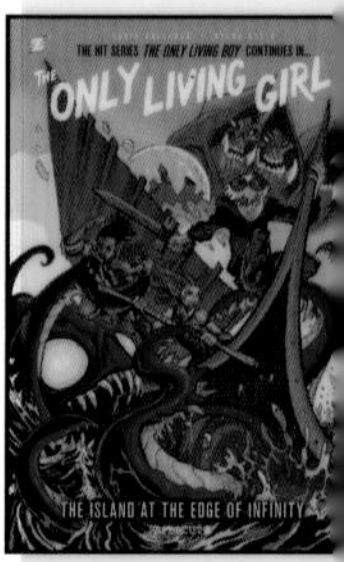
THE ONLY LIVING GIRL
THE ISLAND AT THE EDGE OF INFINITY
PAPERCUTZ
THE ONLY LIVING GI

Go to papercutz.com for more information

All available where ebooks are sold.